For the fangirls ...
keep speaking u ...

Halfway round the world
She can't remember if it's
Samhain or Beltane
Winter or spring

But she's
Walking walking
Walking to Babylon
Walking the spiral path
Walking on home

And she's
Walking to the city that touches the sky
And the questions and dancers
Questions and dancers
Walking the spiral path
Walking on home

'Walking to Babylon' by Comes The Trickster
From the HvLP: *All the Way From Heaven* (2465)

Author's Note

Much of this story is taken from Bernice Summerfield's *Memoirs*, currently in progress. I have added other scenes based on her diary entries, notes and interviews. She has in turn added numerous footnotes.

The language of the People contains three consonants unfamiliar to English speakers: !x, !q and !c are all clicks produced with the tongue. For more information, see 'Notes on the Pronunciation of Proper Names' at the beginning of *The Also People* by Ben Aaronovitch.

WALKING TO BABYLON

'You realize, of course,' I said, in an oddly high-pitched voice, 'that you would be changing history.'

'Yes.'

'WiRgo!xu and !Ci!ci-tel haven't chosen any old backwater. They've chosen a pivotal time in human history. A population centre that can shelter a quarter of a million people. I know that might not sound like much to you, but it's the largest city in its era on Earth.'

God said, 'If we blow the Path away, we can claim it was a natural phenomenon. And the other parties to the Treaty can pretend they believe us.'

'Plausible deniability,' I said flatly. 'You don't care about collateral, as long as your meta-arse is covered.'

THE NEW
ADVENTURES

WALKING TO BABYLON

Kate Orman

First published in Great Britain in 1998 by
Virgin Publishing Ltd
332 Ladbroke Grove
London W10 5AH

Bernice Summerfield originally created by Paul Cornell

Cover illustration by Mark Salwowski

ISBN 0 426 20521 9

Typeset by Galleon Typesetting, Ipswich
Printed and bound in Great Britain by
Mackays of Chatham PLC

The progress of the war will be easy to track. You simply take a radio telescope, point it at the patch of sky that contains the Worldsphere, and check to see if the People's homeworld is still there.

Sometimes it is, sometimes it isn't. Very occasionally you might see its ruins – the sudden appearance of the star like the yolk inside a broken egg, chunks of its shell larger than gas giants floating loose, obscuring the yellow disc. Sometimes it will be half finished and abandoned, a skeleton of crisscrossing ringworlds like a cage around the star.

But most of the time, it simply won't be there at all. Far easier than raising an army, or building great battle Ships: stop the People's history before the Sphere can be built, their power in the galaxy consolidated. Reach out through history with a time loop, and trap their original homeworlds before space travel can be invented, or before they can develop stellar engineering, or before they can develop the technology needed to create the Worldsphere.

This won't be a crude war, like the cat-and-mouse game with the Insects. Ships chasing one another, comparing the size of their guns, antimatter bombs, remote forced quantum singularities, none of it. This will be a much simpler, more elegant war. You stop us from having existed, we stop you from stopping us. Free agents, allies and spies protected by temporal bubbles will survive each disappearance of the Worldsphere, find the time-loop generator responsible, and destroy it – after learning how to build their own.

Of course, the People's opponents won't dare give away their own location by operating from their own planet. They'll establish bases in the People's own galaxy. From time to time, an X-ray source will suddenly move and then vanish, as a black hole is captured as a natural well of energy for their weapons. One or two fat, ripe stars will conveniently collapse, adding to the stockpile.

More stars will abruptly flare or burst as the People turn to brute force. Any star exhibiting certain characteristic behaviour, suggesting enemy activity, will become a target.

Of course, both sides will avoid destroying the suns that shine on innocent bystanders. At first. As the double bluff becomes a tactical advantage, both sides will hide their bases on or near inhabited worlds. Daring their opponents to genocide.

Those worlds, and the living worlds cooked in the radiation from the numerous novae and supernovae, will be counted as collateral damage, to be dealt with after the war's conclusion.

As the war presses on, the People's forces will find ways to reach their enemy's home galaxy, the same spiral which contains the Earth. The pattern of the war will remain unchanged as the People search for and strike towards the homeworld of their opponents.

Meanwhile, their enemies will attack again and again at the People's most vulnerable point, their most important asset. God will die, and never have existed, and exist once more, and be lobotomized, and live, and die, over and over.

Seen from a great enough distance, over a long enough period of time, both galaxies will flare like a box of fire-crackers. Some impossibly distant, alien astronomers may even realize that they are seeing a war, a war that took place millions of years ago. Perhaps they will wonder if and when the war will reach their own galaxy – if ten million years, a thousand million years, a million million years is long enough for the conflict to jump across the void and infect them.

All of which assumes that the cumulative damage to space–time doesn't cause the entire cosmos to collapse in on itself in a premature Big Crunch.

Both sides would agree that that was the ultimate technical achievement.

o

AN INVITATION FROM GOD

Medical advice: never stick anything in your ear smaller than your elbow; never stick anything larger in your skull than, say, a continent.

– Kate Orman

Professor Bernice S. Summerfield lay on her stomach on the bed, staring into the screen of her puter, a pencil clenched between her teeth.

The bed was a circle of silks and cushions, red and orange, vibrating in the whiteness of the cabin. The room was three times the size of her lodgings at St Oscar's University. There was a vast bath shaped like a shell, an ambulatory table that served snacks and drinks on voice command.

Gossamer screens of light hung in the air, displaying animated works of art, while miniature robots like jewelled insects traced lazy curves of song through the air. Or they would have done if Benny hadn't switched them all off so she could concentrate.

She stared at the title of the article, her teeth leaving impressions in the pencil. 'Devil Gate Drive: The Influence of *The Descent of Inanna* on Twentieth-Century Popular Culture'. All she had so far was the title and a few scribbled notes on the pad next to her, and a woody taste in her mouth.

She was only messing around with the essay to avoid the real work. The Book. The BOOK. The long-awaited, especially by her publishers, sequel to the bestselling *Down Among The Dead Men*.

Well, actually, the BOOK would have to wait, just a little longer. Her portable computer was crammed with her notes and research, file after file of alien poetry, all of it waiting for her to somehow pull it together into *Repetitive Poems of the Early Ikkaban Period*.

Such was the exciting life of the academic. You could spend only so much time mucking about on field trips, rummaging in muddy ruins and collecting data, before you had to sit down and actually do something with what you'd found.

In between journeying to distant, exotic Dyson Spheres for drinkies with the stupendously advanced locals, of course.

'We'll be arriving in thirty of your Earth minutes,' said the Ship. 'How's the book going?'

'Argh!' said Benny, almost knocking over her hickory daiquiri. The pencil shot out of her mouth and bounced off the puter screen. 'Don't you ever knock?'

'Sorry,' said the S-Stone. 'I just thought I'd look in on you.'

Benny drained her cocktail before the Ship could do anything else startling. 'I'm glad you didn't decide to look in while I was in the bath.'

'Well, you *were* in there for three hours.'

'What!'

'Water-usage records,' said the S-Stone. 'Anyway, I'm *not* looking. I'm on audio only.'

'Oh?' said Benny. 'So you haven't been trying to read over my shoulder?'

'Why?' said the Ship innocently. 'What have you been writing?'

'Nothing,' admitted Benny. 'I'm having trouble getting started. Anyway, it's not anything that interesting. Just a lot of very old poetry.'

'If it's not that interesting, why are you writing about it?'

'*I'm* interested in it,' said Benny.

But *you* wouldn't be, she thought – it wouldn't tell you anything you want to know about the Milky Way. Nothing

2

tactically important. Which is why it was safe for me to bring it along, especially since I'll bet you've got sensors that could read my hard drive from a hundred light years away.

The People weren't allowed to archive information about anything in the Milky Way. Of course, you couldn't *stop* folks who juggled stars for entertainment from doing whatever they pleased. But they'd signed a treaty, after all. They'd *promised*.

When you were that powerful, when you could do anything at all, you had to keep your word, if you wanted to maintain any kind of civilization. Most of the time. S-Stone was probably taking notes on her speech, her behaviour, what she ate for breakfast, but the Ship wouldn't raid her puter or try to scan her head. She hoped.

'Anyway,' the S-Stone was saying, 'if you want to pop down to an observation lounge, we'll be making Spherefall in half an hour.'

She shut down the puter. 'I'll be down there in twenty minutes,' she said.

Benny walked into the nearest observation lounge twenty minutes later. She had put on her travelling clothes, having unrolled them from her satchel. A tough brown shirt and industrial-strength jeans, leather jacket, laced-up boots, a white hat in her hand and the banged-up leather satchel slung over her shoulder. Plus a low-maintenance haircut, her dark hair cropped short. All-purpose, any-planet gear.

Though it was harder to play the rugged archaeologist aboard a luxury starliner giving you a free lift to a party.

The observation lounge was a wide, dark space, a few long steps leading down to a floor. They were dotted all over the Ship, so you could always get a good view of whatever was worth looking at. Here, the lights were turned right down. A few dozen People were watching Spherefall. Mostly passengers, Benny guessed – the crew, if you could call them that on a Ship that ran itself, would have seen this many times.

The organic People were sitting on floating 'chairs' made of yielding force fields, or standing at a bar, drinks and munchies appearing from the plastic heralded by a miniature 'pop'. The artificial People, the drones, bobbed about like friendly balloons come to life.

Organic and artificial, the People came in a variety of colours and shapes. Benny could see extra fingers, silver irises, a headful of livid green hair. The drones were round or ovoid, sometimes covered in designs like circuit tracings, sometimes covered in little bumps and hatches and decals, sometimes unmarked except for their face ikons.

The ship had a crew of a quarter of a million. Most of them were part of an exploratory team, members of the Obscure and Unlikely Civilizations Interest Group. They wandered the People's home galaxy, ferreting out isolated species and cultures, quietly taking some notes, and moving on.

The rest of the People on board were a mixture. The obligatory representatives of the Shipboard Lifestyle Interest Group, some astronomers and other scientists, and thousands of passengers. The S-Stone moved constantly back and forth between the planets it was investigating and the World-sphere, the People's home. As far as Benny knew, she was the only non-Person aboard.

That was a slightly unnerving way of putting it.

She went to the bar and leant on it. A few People glanced at her, and one drone turned its oval body to stare at her outright, its face ikon a cartoon of a curious human face done in a few holographic lines.

She knew what was on their minds. They were wondering about the barbarian's reaction to the extraordinary sight through the observation window, a clear rectangle the size of a wall.

'Shirley Temple,' she told the bar, 'and a packet of crisps.'

'What's a Shirley Temple?' asked the bar.

'Lemonade and grenadine,' said Benny. 'No straw.'

'You're sure you don't want something a bit stronger?' said the bar. 'I've got a vast range of drinks, soft, alcoholic and other –'

'That's fine, thanks,' said Benny. 'Cheese-and-onion flavoured crisps, please.'

'Whatever you say,' said the bar. A moment later, the drink and a basket of crisp analogues rose up out of the dark plastic like a sword from a lake. Droplets of moisture formed on the chilled glass. Benny took a mouthful of the drink and looked out of the observation window.

They were hurtling towards the Dyson Sphere like a bat out of hell. Benny didn't know how the S-Stone's drive worked, but there were no weird hyperspace or supralight effects – it just looked as though they were travelling through normal space at an obscene velocity.

The Worldsphere was a globe of darkness, a black circle widening to blot out the stars, growing by the second. She wondered just how fast they were moving; there was no sensation of movement at all, not even the pretend one your brain creates when you watch a film of a roller coaster. The sheer size of the Worldsphere made it impossible to deal with the scale.

A globe big enough to hold a sun. A globe as wide as the Earth's orbit, tame star at the centre.

And two trillion People walking (or floating) around on the inside, enjoying the sunshine.

For a moment, Benny wished for a tour guide. She wanted to know how the thing had been made. There were no other planets in the solar system – had they been towed away for safety's sake, or dismantled for building material? How did they keep their world from falling apart or drifting into its sun? How much did the gravity of the thing distort local space? How many different kinds of plants grew there? And what was its principal export?

The ship braked. The Dyson Sphere was suddenly a vast wall rushing towards them, swelling and swelling, structures and patterns of light unfolding incessantly on its surface like the details of a fractal. At the centre of the window, a point of light swelling to become a line, a slit, a rectangle of light, a hexagonal gap in the Sphere.

You could see into the interior through the gap, opened wide while Ships dozens of kilometres long moved in and out, and thousands of smaller vehicles and large drones buzzed around like a cloud of insects. You could see past them, see an infinity of blue sky stretched across the inner surface. See the captive star glittering in its cage, the yolk in the egg.

5

For a moment, you could grasp the sheer mind-crunching obscene *size* of the thing, the largest artificial structure in this galaxy. You could cram thousands of planet Earths inside like gumballs in a machine. Maybe millions of Earths – she didn't want to think about the maths.

Everyone was pretending they weren't watching her. Benny deliberately put down her Shirley Temple and took a handful of crisps. She crunched on them, thoughtfully.

'Big,' she said, after a moment. The other passengers turned away, impressed or disgusted or mildly amused.

Not bad for a barbarian, she thought to herself. And she hadn't even needed alcohol to survive the experience.

Benny's internal clock told her that it was Saturday night. On Friday night, she had been returning from a late meeting with Dr Follett, only to find an angel in her stairwell.

'Hello, Clarence,' she said, breaking into a grin.

The angel had smiled back at her. Just like the first time they'd met, he was sitting on the stairs to her rooms. Just like the first time they'd met, he was stark-naked. He was stretched out on the stairs, showing off a perfectly muscled and softly glowing body, his great swan wings stretched out behind him. The dark of his hair, aesthetically rumpled, contrasted with their pure white.

'Hello, Beni,' he said. 'How would you like to come to a party?'

She sat down on the step below him. 'As it happens,' she said, 'I'm free.'

'Great!' Clarence sat up. 'Grab your things. We can leave as soon as you're ready.'

'Wait a minute!' said Benny. 'Just where is this party? What am I letting myself in for here?'

'On the Worldsphere, of course,' said Clarence. 'It's just a party. But God wants you to be the guest of honour.'

'And why is that?'

Clarence reached out and touched her shoulder with the tip of a wing. 'We miss you,' he said. 'And we need your insight on certain things. God will tell you all about it when we get there.'

They wanted her to go to another *galaxy*, and all just for a bash. That was the People through and through. But how can you resist an invitation like that? Benny got up. 'How long is this going to take? I'll need to arrange leave –'

'I can have you back by early Sunday night,' said the angel. 'You can get an early night and be bright and fresh for Monday tutorials.'

'You've been talking to my porter,' she said suddenly.

'He gave me a lecture,' said Clarence. 'He wants you back by nine p.m. on Sunday.'

Benny couldn't help laughing. 'Let me get my toothbrush.'

Clarence had carried her in his arms. He had once been a Ship, not unlike the S-Stone. That had been before the accident. God had built him a new body, force-grown from a few donated human cells. The People's rivals would never be able to detect that he was one of them, so it was safe to send him on errands to the Milky Way.

But he didn't breathe, and he could fly like a bird. Benny knew he'd need to have a two-metre breastbone to support those wings. There was far more to him than a human body with a couple of decorative wings and the remnants of a Ship's colossal intelligence squeezed into the brain.

For one thing, he could travel through hyperspace.

When Benny emerged, wearing her travel clothes and with a well-stuffed bag slung over one shoulder, he'd simply picked her up and leapt into the sky.

She wondered how many students and professors caught a glimpse of the angel as he soared into the sky, defying every law of anatomy and aviation.

They had broken through the clouds before she got her breath back. 'Clarence!' she shouted. 'I'm not going to be able to breathe!'

'Don't worry,' he said, his voice quiet but strangely audible over the rushing of the wind. His arms tightened around her.

As the air thinned, she felt the warmth of his body, a sensation of heat drifting through her as the sky became colder and colder. She had begun to drift off. For a moment, she felt panic, convinced she was passing out from oxygen deprivation. Then she fell into a gentle slumber, cradled against his smooth chest.

She had woken up aboard the S-Stone, in the palatial room. Clarence had had an errand to run, the Ship told her, but he'd wanted to make sure she had a chance to see Spherefall. It would be a couple of days before they arrived, but he could still get her back by Sunday night. They were old friends, said the S-Stone, though of course Clarence couldn't remember because of the accident and all. But he'd see her right.

She had shrugged, feeling oddly abandoned.

The Ship was crammed with People and with every kind of recreation facility, but she'd spent most of her time in the cabin, working on the book, tapping out the odd paragraph about the Ikkaba and their poetry in between games of Tetris.

As she stood on the surface of the S-Stone, the starry hexagonal gap of the Spaceport behind her, those long dull hours seemed like a million years ago.

No, they seemed like a hundred years ago. The human brain wasn't built to think in millions of years. It certainly wasn't built to think in millions of kilometres. Human eyes weren't designed to look down at the forests and lakes and cities of every size below, to move across the landscape, across a seeming infinity of trees and water and buildings, tracing the slow curl of the Worldsphere until the details of the inside surface were lost in a distant haze of atmosphere.

Standing on the surface of the Ship, in a protective bubble of air and warmth, Benny took her eyes off the immense floor far below them and looked up.

The distant opposite crust of the Worldsphere, blurred into deep blue by the distance, the furthermost side obscured by the tamed sun. The miniature world of Whynot, orbiting within the Sphere. It looked a lot like the Earth seen from the moon.

Benny had visited the Sphere once before. But she hadn't had a view of it like this. She'd stayed in a village, her primate brain insisting she was on flat ground, that there was a horizon somewhere out at sea. A tiny, snug bit of the Sphere, just the right size to cope with.

This was the real reason to travel. Not because of the places you knew you wanted to visit, the views you set out to see. Because of the ones you *didn't* know about.

She must remember to get Dr Follett a souvenir.

'God,' she said, after a while.

'You called?'

She looked down, rubbing the crick in her neck. A remote drone had been patiently waiting for her, bobbing out of the corner of her eye. It was a few feet across, a floating yellow ball, its face ikon set in a sketch of a smile.

'Hi, God,' said Benny. 'Is that you in there?'

'The one and only,' said God, floating up to her. 'S-Stone said you'd asked to be left alone. I hope I'm not intruding.'

'No,' said Benny, hefting her satchel. 'I'm finished with the awe-struck gawping tourist bit. I just wanted to wait until there wasn't an audience gawping at *me*.'

God was the computer that ran the Worldsphere. More accurately, God was the colossal artificial meta-intelligence that managed the Sphere, monitoring every square inch and keeping everything from the weather to the public transport running smoothly. The remote drone was just a representative, like a terminal – the real God was partly on Whynot, partly all over the Sphere in hidden nodes, and mostly in another dimension big enough to pack in all those bytes.

For a being that was such a good approximation of all-seeing, all-knowing and all-powerful, thought Benny, God was remarkably chatty. Almost as though it needed a little attention and approval from mere mortals.

'You're a celebrity,' God was saying, floating after Benny as she walked across the hull. The bubble force field moved with her, and the air and heat with it. Around them, hundreds of ships buzzed about the green and white Christmas ornament of Spaceport Facility, from the kilometres-long Travelling Space Habitats to shuttles and travel capsules. One was waiting to take her the hundreds of thousands of kilometres to her quarters.

Benny groaned. 'Oh no. I hope I haven't travelled unimaginable distances across space and time, just so you could persuade more people to come to your party.'

The corner of God's mouth ikon turned up slightly. 'I didn't tell anyone you were coming. But the crew of the S-Stone have been telling all their friends. Expect to be popular.'

'As long as they don't print my face on any T-shirts,' said Benny.

God's remote drone got into the shuttle with her. It was a small vehicle, designed to hold six passengers. Benny took one of the long couch seats while God came to rest on the seat opposite.

There was a yellow, metallic circle on the seat. Benny picked it up, curiously. 'Translation device,' said God. Benny realized it was an earring, and clipped it into place. 'S-Stone translated for you while you were aboard, but from now on this will do the job.'

Benny closed her eyes as the shuttle moved away from the S-Stone. It felt good to be in a small space after all that Big. She didn't want to let on to God, though.

'But seriously,' said God, 'I wanted a word with you before the party.' Benny opened her eyes. The drone's face ikon had formed a serious, neutral expression.

She waited. God went on, 'As you know, the War ended thirty years ago, but we're still feeling the effects.'

'I remember,' said Benny. 'Ships and drones with psychological damage.' Thirty years wasn't a long time, not in People terms. And the War had been a bit of a surprise. When you're that powerful, you don't expect anyone to be stupid enough to attack you. But that hadn't stopped the All of Us.[1]

God bobbed, as though nodding. 'Most of the machines have been sorted out in one way or another. It's the organic People who are the problem now.'

'Ah,' said Benny.

'The damage took longer to show up, and in more subtle ways. Members of the Abnormal Psychology Interest Group

---

[1] That's a rough translation of the name used by the natives of C-Mita-C-Rho, now a part of the People. The People often just call them the Insects.

have been working with the veterans who need help, but a lot of them have been keeping their problems to themselves. Even fairly major problems.'

'They didn't want to be ostracized,' realized Benny. 'Am I right? What's the People's attitude to mental illness?'

God's face ikon managed to look slightly embarrassed. 'Attitudes vary. But People with psychological problems do tend to be left to their own devices.'

'As though they were being punished,' said Benny. The People didn't send their criminals to prison: they sent them to Coventry. Permanently. 'That can only make it so much worse for them. And so you've invited a lot of them to your party – to show that God is on their side?'

'I'm hoping it will become fashionable,' said God. 'Besides, it's not just the actual veterans who were damaged in the War. It affected all of the People, in one way or another – soldiers, agents, pacifists, People who didn't care either way. But what better therapy than food, drink, dancing, and far too much sex?'

Benny laughed. 'You're a deity after my own heart, God.'

'Anyway,' said the remote drone, 'I just wanted to let you know what you're in for here. No one at the party will be dangerous, or completely out of their heads. There have only been a handful like that.'

'What do you do with them?' Benny wanted to know.

'There's an island continent put aside for the Truly Crazed. For the most part, we keep an eye on them and let them get better under their own steam. In some ways, they're better off – it's the ones who're only partly broken who are the problem. Some of them will be fragile and lonely. Be prepared to smile and nod a lot.'

'No problem,' said Benny. 'I've been through extensive training for that at faculty parties. Oh, we're here.'

The shuttle had touched down, silently, in a cleared field on an island. The door hissed open, and Benny hopped out. There was a small house twenty metres away, oddly like a child's drawing – rectangular front door, flanked by windows with wooden frames, pointed roof, smoking chimney. There was even the obligatory tree growing next to it.

The house stood at the top of a gentle slope, leading down to the sea. A fresh, salty breeze was blowing inland.

'I had it built for you this morning,' said God. 'If you want company, there's a largish village about half an hour's walk away through the forest. Or send for a travel capsule, go anywhere you like. Otherwise, put your feet up, and I'll see you this evening.' God's face ikon formed a cartoon smile on the front of the bright yellow drone.

'Have a nice day,' said Benny.

During their long phase of space travel, the Ikkaba inspired the pyramid-builders of dozens of worlds. But how often did the natives of those worlds understand the pyramid or ziggurat in the same way as the Ikkaba themselves? For the Sumerians and Babylonians, the ziggurat was a connection with heaven: the great ziggurat of Marduk inspired the story of the Tower of Babel, arrogantly built to reach heaven itself. But the ancient Yemayans may have been closer to the Ikkaba in their own symbolic construction of the construction.

Benny frowned at the last sentence. 'Gibberish,' she declared.

Oh well, if she stuck in enough pictures they could still sell the thing as a coffee-table book, and just use the good paragraphs as captions.

She pushed the puter away and laid her head on her arms for a moment, eyes closed. She was lying on the floor in the lounge, ignoring the baggy furniture scattered about the huge room.

Surprisingly, the house smelt faintly of recent construction, a mix of sawdust, concrete, fresh paint. God could have synthesized the building, she supposed, but somewhere in the two trillion People there was probably a Very Rapid House Construction Interest Group.

She ought to be out and about, taking photographs and investigating the ways in which the locals got drunk. Not cooped up in what was essentially a hotel room, fiddling about with work, like a businessperson stuck in an unfamiliar city. 'You're being boring,' she told herself. 'Go out and do something at once.'

Maybe it was the thought of going out under that daunting sky again . . . Maybe it was the thought of those two trillion People, their myriad little interests and little projects and little eccentricities, the strange sameness despite all that room, all that freedom . . .

Maybe it was just that she didn't like being under the microscope, the way she had aboard the S-Stone. On her last visit, she hadn't been the only barbarian visitor, the only one to bear the weight of all that attention.

All this time, she'd been assuming God had invited her just because the People were such incredibly social animals. But did that really make sense? Wasn't it obvious that God had brought her all this distance for a reason – something to do with its party? Was she a curiosity to take the veteran's minds off their troubles?

The puter made a noise as its screensaver activated. 'Maybe I'm just jet-lagged,' said Benny.

The house asked, 'Do you want a glass of *catchup*?'

'Aaargh!' said Benny.

'Are you all right?' asked the dwelling politely.

'Are you sentient?' demanded Benny.

'No.'

'Good,' she said. 'I'm going to take a bath.'

The Spherequake struck two hours later. Benny was awake in seconds, the cooling bathwater splashing insanely as she grabbed at the sides of the tub.

'House!' she yelled helplessly. 'What's happening?'

'It's all right,' said the structure. 'It's just the island moving into position for the party.'

The sloshing was losing its chaotic intensity, settling down into a steady rhythm from her toes to her chest. 'Did you know that was going to happen?' said Benny, clinging to the side of the bath.

'No,' said the house. 'The island has a mind of its own.'

Benny wondered if it meant that literally. If so, she was going to have a chat with the island about the concept of seasickness. 'How long is this going to take?'

'Another ten minutes,' said the house. 'Would you like to discuss clothing for the party while you wait?'

It was a basic principle of packing that, beyond certain essentials, you avoided bringing things you could buy cheaply at your destination. Here, Benny could obtain whatever she wanted from central stores just by asking for it. Anything. If she asked for another house, a small nuclear device, or a unicycle, they'd just wrap it up and send it on over. Though if she wanted to do some *real* shopping, as the house reminded her, she'd have to do it in person.

'That would mean getting out of the bath,' she protested. The house gave in and projected a series of catalogues into the air around her, gossamer pages hovering above the miniature waves.

Benny was half tempted to just wear her travelling gear – they wanted primitive alien? She ignored the catalogues, the steadily changing images, frowning at the water swirling around her toes.

When you could do anything, why do anything? What kept the People going? After absolute luxury and security lost their novelty, then what?

She sank under the warm water for a moment, listening to the sound of her heartbeat.

It seemed ridiculous to compare her own life, as battered and worn as her satchel, her bills and bruises and hassles and decisions, to life in this utopia – and to still feel a strange urge to ask God to send her right home. She didn't have to go to his party. The People didn't have rules, not as such. She didn't *have* to do anything.

Benny glared at the mirror, towelling her short hair vigorously so it stuck out in all directions. The quake had finally quietened enough to allow her to haul her red and shrivelled body out of the bath.

She had brought the outfit, rolled and crammed into her satchel. The house had obligingly ironed it for her. It was based on a twentieth-century film design, one of her

14

favourites: black trousers, a white shirt and off-white jacket. The house ordered a red blossom so she could have a buttonhole.

She turned back and forth, checking herself in the mirror. Eat barbarian chic, you feckless Eloi, she thought, and grinned evilly.

If only her hair would behave.

'House,' she said, 'you said the island was moving into place for the party. Does that mean it's happening here?'

'Not here,' said the house, 'I'm far too small. In the village in the centre of the island. It's a forty-minute walk – would you like me to organize transportation?'

'Yes please,' said Benny. 'Yes. Something flashy. Preferably capable of VTOL.' She thought it over. 'Nothing that looks even slightly military, though.'

'Coming right up,' said the house. 'Er.'

'Er?'

'Forgive me if this shows ignorance of your culture's etiquette or your species' biology,' said the house, 'but would you care for a small glass of *prevention* before you join the other partygoers?'

Benny laughed. 'The outfit doesn't look *that* good.'

Ten minutes later, she heard something landing outside. 'All right, Fairy Godmother,' she said, 'take me to the ball.'

She pushed open the house's front door, and felt her breath catch in her throat. There was a giant butterfly waiting for her on the front lawn.

It was lit up like a carnival display, all soft oranges and yellows – thousands of tiny lights, like glowing beads, covered every inch of it. The body was thick and metallic. She could see through a window to a single seat. The six triangular wings were wide and diaphanous, folded back. There were even antennae, a complex array of slender silver wires that bristled from the machine's narrow head.

For some reason, the metal butterfly made her realize how far she was from Dellah. From her own *galaxy*. Ye gods and little fishes.

She stepped up to the creature and put a hand on its side.

15

Smooth beads of light under her fingers. It shifted, as though reacting to her touch. 'You're beautiful,' she said.

The door in the side opened, with the sound of gears and teeth smoothly meshing. Benny couldn't help laughing, a schoolgirl giggle of delight. The star engineers had sent her a helicopter that ran on clockwork.

She climbed inside, and the door wound itself shut again with a pocket-watch sound. The butterfly flapped its great, fragile wings, and they were suddenly in the air, diving upward towards the other side of the sphere.

The machine continued upward for hundreds of feet. Benny pressed her nose and hands to the window, looking down at the island. The sky was slowly darkening as God turned down the sun to create the required party conditions: a warm evening, cooled by the breeze from the sea.

The island was a long oval, the ocean stretching out in all directions. Benny thought she could see distant land masses, but she wasn't sure. There were five stubby projections from the island, like small peninsulas, or perhaps enormous jetties. Or . . . no, it couldn't be.

As if in response to her surprised thought, the butterfly swooped, heading for the projection at the point of the oval island. The forests and the savannas rushed by beneath them, tiny patches of light glowing here and there in the dark. Other houses?

And then they were swinging out over the black ocean, turning sharply as they passed the promontory, and Benny caught a glimpse of a vast orange eye and a mouth yawning as the sea water drained from its sides, and then they were back over the land, heading towards the collection of coloured lights at the flattened top of the island's back.

There was a miniature landing strip at one end of the – party? It was more like a full-blown Mardi Gras. Benny guessed there were three or four hundred People, chatting, dancing, eating. Lamps had been hung in the trees, illuminating small crowds and long tables. There were probably even more of them in the warm darkness of the surrounding forest.

The landing strip was a double row of lamps marking a

length of cleared ground. Benny's butterfly settled behind a triplane and a shuttle. As she climbed out, she realized that the two vehicles were talking voice to each other, clicking and popping away in the People's language. Their low engine murmurs hid the words from her translator badge.

She looked around. The party seemed to stretch off into the distance, the darkness. Crowds of aliens she didn't know. She felt a familiar nervous scrunching inside. Now what?

'Hi,' said the plane. 'You must be that barbarian woman.'

'That's me,' she muttered. 'Have either of you seen God around?'

'I'll give him a yell,' said the shuttle. 'Nice duds.'

'Thanks.'

A moment later, a familiar smiling drone floated up. 'Hello, Beni,' said God. 'Come on over to the hors d'oeuvres – there are some People I want you to meet.'

Benny followed the drifting ball through a flock of barefoot dancers and past a tight knot of drones chattering in binary. She was wearing her boots, although the house had assured her the island was free of spiky plants and small, sharp stones.

Was the yellow remote the same drone she'd encountered before? Or did God have hundreds of thousands of the things, floating about the Sphere like talking bubbles?

God bumped up against a table covered in nibbly things of every kind. 'Here we are,' he said. 'Allow me to introduce WiRgo!xu. This is Beni.'

A tall Person turned from the drone he was talking to and looked down at her. He looked quite human, at first glance: light-brown skin, large, utterly dark eyes, wavy dark hair.

He gave her a smile. 'You arrived in the butterfly,' he said.

'That's right,' said Benny. God and the other drone had already hovered off, firing machine code at each other.

'I built it,' said WiRgo!xu.

'You did? It's marvellous!' Beni picked up something purple and spiky from the table. 'You must be in the Weird Aviation Interest Group.'

WiRgo!xu's pupils widened. 'You already know something about us,' he said.

Benny nodded, trying to work out how to eat the purple

thing. It gave her an excuse to avoid WiRgo!xu's unnerving black stare. Don't mention the war, she thought. 'Just a tiny bit. I visited once before.'

'And what did you think?'

'Big,' said Benny, after a moment.

WiRgo!xu laughed. 'You know, I was born outside the Sphere. On an actual planet. My parents were on a geological survey. I spent the first five years of my life there.'

'Really?' said Benny. She glanced up, but the other side of the Sphere was hidden by distance and darkness. Whynot was a glistening ball, an oversized moon hanging overhead. 'Everything must have seemed upside down when you moved here.'

'Not really.' WiRgo!xu smiled again. 'I could have moved to Whynot, but by then I knew that it was normal to live on the inside of the ball, not the outside. Much safer.'

Rabbits in a warren, thought Benny, turning the purple thing round and round in her hands. 'Many civilizations live underground,' she said, 'often because of severe changes in surface conditions. At least, in my galaxy, which I'm sure I'm not supposed to be telling you anything about.' I've travelled light years to eat this hors d'oeuvre, and I will not be defeated!

'Pull the spikes,' said WiRgo!xu. 'The edible part is the fruit inside.'

He obligingly reached down and plucked one of the long spikes out. There was a small berry on the end, covered in tiny seeds, like a strawberry. She opened her mouth to say something, and he popped it in, grasping the spike so the fruit slid easily off.

'Sweet,' she said, after a moment.

'The gossip has it you're an *archaeologist*,' said WiRgo!xu, careful with the English word. 'What is that, exactly?'

'I study ancient civilizations,' said Benny.

'You can time-travel?'

She shook her head, grinning. 'No, I usually study their remains.' He peered at her. 'Old buildings. Graveyards. Bits of pottery. Whatever clues they've left behind.'

'Right!' WiRgo!xu nodded enthusiastically. 'I'm a sort of

archaeologist myself. Weird Aviation is just my hobby – I spend most of my time with the Seriously Primitive Societies Interest Group.'

Benny plucked loose another of the fruits. 'Almost everyone must seem Seriously Primitive to you,' she said.

'We study mostly pre-, post- and non-industrial societies,' said WiRgo!xu. 'I'm especially interested in civilizations which develop machinery without real power sources. The butterfly is based on a design from a world with no fossil fuels.'

Benny glanced back at the landing strip, but the butterfly was hidden behind the crowds. 'How does it work?'

'You have to wind it with a huge key,' he said. 'I cheated and put in a solar power pack to keep it wound. Hi, !Ci!ci-tel.'

'Hello,' said another of the People, wandering up with a couple of friends. 'Has she broken the Treaty yet?'

'We narrowly avoided it,' said WiRgo!xu.

'Benu, right?' said the newcomer. He took Benny's free hand and shook it, almost making her drop the fruit. 'Great to meet you.' !Ci!ci-tel was a head shorter than WiRgo!xu, with yellow-white skin and squiggly hair the colour of an orange skin. 'I'll bet he hasn't said a word about the War yet.'

WiRgo!xu managed to look embarrassed. His friend said, 'You know it's healthier to talk about it. That's why she's here, after all. That's why we're all here.' !Ci!ci-tel smiled at Benny. 'He's terribly shy. An awful lot of them are terribly shy. I can't seem to get a conversation going.'

'Maybe we'd rather dance than talk about ordnance,' sighed WiRgo!xu.

'That's half the problem. No one wants to talk about it. But everybody knows what this party is all about.' !Ci!ci-tel looked at Benny. 'You must know an awful lot about war, after all.'

'What?' said Benny.

'Barbarians are always fighting one another. I'll bet you've gunned down a sizable number of individuals in your time.'

'!Ci!ci-tel,' said WiRgo!xu, 'shut up.'

'Actually,' said Benny, putting down the fruit, 'I was forced to join the military at one point. I hated it. It's a colossal waste of resources and a personality-warping authority structure which ought to be dismantled as soon as practically possible.'

The People both blinked at her.

'Of course, it's probably very different here,' she sighed.

'What's a *military*?' said !Ci!ci-tel.

'You don't go digging those civilizations up,' said Benny. 'The Seriously Primitive ones you study. You go around your galaxy until you find one at the right stage of development. Like going to the supermarket. We have a special this week on the Bronze Age.'

She was sprawled atop a comfy-field, while someone whose name she couldn't remember gave her a back massage. Her jacket was folded under her head. Half the People at the party had taken off their clothes, enjoying a warm sea breeze provided by God. She didn't feel quite up to that standard of casualness.

'More drinks, anyone?' asked the house cheerfully.

'I'll have another *surprisingly sober*,' said Benny. 'I'm right, aren't I?'

WiRgo!xu was sitting on the floor, eating munchies from a big paper bag and playing a computer game with his toes. 'Of course,' he said. 'With much more limited travel opportunities, you're obliged to study whatever civilizations you can, including long-dead ones.'

'You can learn as much from a long-dead civilization as from a living one,' said Benny. A tray hovered down with her drink, a goblet of clear liquid that smelt of oranges. There was a long curly straw in it so she wouldn't have to get up to drink it. 'Especially if they're your ancestors, physically or culturally.'

She had expected Clarence to come to the party, but he was obviously still off running whatever errand he'd come up with to avoid the veterans. It would have been nice to see a familiar face. God was floating about, but other than that she was on her own.

WiRgo!xu's toes were long and flexible, disturbingly like fingers. He had been wearing thick, complicated shoes at the party, like . . . like gloves. Now they lay in the corner, while he moved a joystick around with one foot and tapped buttons with the other.

He pushed the game away from himself and picked up her puter in his toes. 'Is that what you're working on now?' he said. 'A study of some extinct Milky Way species?'

'Yes,' said Bernice. The *surprisingly sober* was starting to work, making her feel as though the inside of her head was too large. 'They spent thousands of years travelling our galaxy, leaving behind bits of their culture. Big influence on lots of civilizations.'

'We're more cautious,' said WiRgo!xu. 'We go in disguise. The Serious Primitives don't ever know we've been.'

'Ah,' said Benny. 'You don't want to interfere in their natural development.'

'No,' he said. 'We don't want them turning into a threat one day.'

'One day? But it would take hundreds of thousands of years . . .'

'We'll still be here.' He tapped keys on the puter, experimentally, and called up a translation window. It hung in the air like a thin sheet of stained glass.

'I don't think you should be doing that,' said Benny.

'You're right, of course,' said WiRgo!xu. He shut the puter down. 'Where's !Ci!ci-tel got himself to?'

'I think he's upstairs having sex with someone,' said Benny. 'Or he might be one of the ones dancing in the kitchen.'

'I can check if you like,' murmured the house.

'No, don't disturb him,' said WiRgo!xu.

'So what do you learn?' said Benny. 'From these Serious Primitives? Is it an idle curiosity?'

'The Apathy Interest Group are always asking that,' he said. 'The theory is that we can learn more about ourselves from those civilizations that are the least like us. Crisp?' He held one out in his toes.

'No thanks,' said Benny. 'I wonder if you could learn more by revealing yourselves and seeing how they react.' She put a hand on her face. 'I hope that got translated right.'

'I suppose that's why you're here,' said WiRgo!xu, looking at her with his dark eyes.

'So,' said Benny. Her massager got up and wandered off in search of food. 'Daddy, what did you do in the War?'

'I was a tactician,' said WiRgo!xu. 'I stayed in a Ship and ran simulations. !Ci!ci-tel was a front-line soldier. Went on a lot of missions, blew a lot of All of Us away. Face to face on at least two occasions.'

'How many is a lot?' said Benny.

WiRgo!xu counted on his toes. 'Seven,' he said.

'Seven million?' said Benny. 'Seven billion?'

'Seven people is a lot of *people*,' he said.

'Actually seven.' Benny let out a breath. 'You do everything on such a large scale . . .'

'You barbarians have it easy,' said WiRgo!xu.

'We do?'

'You fight your wars on such small scales,' he said. 'A few million people, a biosphere or two. Not like us. We're *big*. The War against the Great Hive Mind was a joke, a game for XR(N)IG. The All of Us never got anywhere near the Sphere. Any Very Aggressive Ship could have wiped out every solar system they inhabited and done sculptures with the rubble.'

'That's nightmarish,' Benny said.

'You're telling me,' said WiRgo!xu. She wished she could read his night-sky eyes. '!Ci!ci-tel obsesses over his head count, just seven people out of the twenty-six billion who died. But I imagine fingers of brilliance and darkness stretching through the galaxy in the wakes of angry Ships . . .'

Benny held up a hand as though to hold back the image. 'If seven people is a lot,' she said, 'then we don't have it any easier, believe me.'

'You said you were forced to join the military.'

'My dad was in the navy, in a war with some aliens, and disappeared. My mum was killed in the war. I was packed off to a military school for orphans, but I managed to escape.'

'I begin to see the source of your dislike,' said WiRgo!xu drily. 'You know, it's such a difficult concept.'

'Being forced to join?'

'I'll try to comprehend *forced* when I comprehend *joined*.'

'Mmmf. Your Interest Groups are more like disorganizations than organizations.' Benny ruffled her own hair. Her drink was empty again. 'OK, here's my official amateur diagnosis: you're worried about the future. What if it happens again?' Her eyes widened. 'That's just it. Your safe, static world changed. Far more than when you were brought here as a child. The War turned everything inside out.' She looked at WiRgo!xu. 'You're not *certain* any more.'

'Is that what it's like being a barbarian?' he said.

Morning.

God had turned the sun back on. The light was streaming through the house's wide windows, dust motes dancing in fat yellow beams. A fresh, salty breeze was blowing in through an open door, and delicious breakfasty cooking smells wafted into the lounge from the kitchen.

Benny threw her arms over her head and moaned.

'Good morning,' whispered the house. 'Can I help?'

'Why isn't that drink called *surprisingly hung over*?' Benny whimpered. She was sprawled on one of the comfy-fields, one of a pile of bodies crashed out in the lounge. WiRgo!xu had fallen asleep on the stairs.

'That's the point of it,' said the house softly, so as not to wake anyone else up. 'It leaves you able to really savour the aftereffects the next morning.'

'Could you please,' whispered Benny, 'either give me a glass of *purge* and a huge pitcher of orange juice, or arrange to have my remains cremated? Thank you.'

Her drinks arrived a few moments later, borne on a floating tray. 'Would you like anything to eat?' murmured the tray.

'God no,' said Benny. 'Speaking of whom, is it anywhere about?'

Benny tiptoed over the sleeping bodies and across the front lawn. The yellow drone was waiting for her in the tree, like a round and garish owl.

'You're all packed,' said God.

'Ready to go,' said Benny, patting her leather satchel. The *purge* was already working, her whole body feeling like a window that someone was cleaning. 'I'm just waiting for central stores to deliver something.'

'So,' said God, 'how did everything go?'

Benny sat down at the base of the tree, and the drone floated down to face her. 'Pretty well,' she said. 'I talked to maybe a dozen People, including two drones. I don't know if I did them any good. I hope I did.' She poked at the drone with a finger. 'That is, after all, why you invited me.'

God settled on to one of her knees. 'I wanted to say hello, catch up, all of that.'

'You needed a barbarian, but not one from your own galaxy. You don't want them finding out that even the People have their problems. Because one day they might be a threat.' Benny nodded as God's neutral expression became even more neutral, its 'mouth' flattening out into a line. 'And nobody wants another war.'

'That's the problem,' said God. 'With a population of two thousand billion, there'll always be at least a few People crazy enough to want anything.'

Clarence took her home again. He made some excuse as to why he hadn't been at the party, something to do with a mission in the Andromeda spiral.

Waiting for him on the beach, she took out Dr Follett's souvenir and turned it over in her hands. She'd spent ten minutes describing it, to make sure central stores got it just right. It was a glass model of the Worldsphere, big enough to fill her palm. There was the sun in the centre, there was Whynot, the crazy planet where God lived. The outlines of the largest continents were traced on the inside of the glass.

When Benny turned it over, a snowstorm rushed through the glass bubble, tiny white flakes suspended in thin, clear oil.

It was strange how People didn't mind her taking away a detailed model of their homeworld, but didn't want the local savages finding out how the War had affected them. There was no treatment for losing your sense of certainty. And God was right – there was no way to be certain there wouldn't be another war.

What made it worse was that the People could be pretty certain they wouldn't start the war. And quite certain of who would win it.

Clarence dropped her off in the quad in the middle of the night. 'Oops,' he said. 'It is Sunday, but only just.'

'Don't worry, I'll just tell Joseph the porter that we were up late shagging madly.'

They did a complex thing of looking at each other without looking at each other. There had been some serious tonsil-hockey involved the last time they had encountered each other.

'Um,' said Clarence. 'Bye, then.'

Not even a goodbye kiss? 'See you next time God needs help.'

Clarence touched her with his wing again. Then he was gone, a white blur rising into the sky.

Benny had gone inside and overslept, missing her 9 a.m. tutorial. Other than that, everything was routine. In fact, even that was fairly routine. The whole thing might as well not have happened, she thought, during one particularly dull staff meeting when she wasn't paying attention. You can touch utopia, but then you come home to the washing up. Back to normal.

It wasn't until God came looking for her that she realized there was a problem.

1

IN TOO DEEP

How many miles to Babylon?
Three score miles and ten, sir.
Can I get there by candlelight?
Oh yes, and back again, sir.
If your heels are nimble and light,
You may get there by candlelight.

– Children's skipping rhyme

THE RUINS OF BABYLON, DECEMBER 1901

In the dream John Lafayette was travelling down a river. A broad mass of water, cool and glassy, sweeping him along. He was never sure exactly how he was making the journey – was he lying in some sort of canoe, or was he submerged to the neck, bobbing along like a buoy?

This part of the dream was always pleasant enough. The English countryside idled by as the water carried him, smooth and rapid. He saw square fields in different shades of green, cattle and sheep, thick forests, occasionally a house or the spire of a nearby church. A landscape conjured from childhood memories.

Perhaps he had taken on the role of one of his own paper boats, and a dream version of his younger self had launched him into the river, watched him bobbing and meandering, wondering about his eventual destination.

Knowing it was impossible to know.

But, as always, the river began to move more quickly. He felt the depth and the power of the water tugging at his body, pushing him forward. Sometimes he tried to break free of the current, make his way to the shore; but it seemed as impossible to swim in dreams as it was to run. The water carried him on.

The conclusion was always the same. The river opened on to a mighty ocean. His body rose and fell among waves ten, twenty feet high, until he lost his mysterious buoyancy and was dragged under, pulled inexorably deeper and deeper into the sea.

There he would remain suspended, surrounded by lightless water, warmed and comforted as he drifted in its grasp. But after a short while his mind would begin to protest that it should be cold, not warm, that there should be a terrible pressure on his eyes and chest, and, what was more, that he ought not to be able to breathe.

He would then wake up gasping like a dying fish, his entire chest heaving. This morning was no different.

Lafayette lay still in his cot, allowing his breathing to right itself. He rolled down his blankets; the warmth of the day was already gathering after another freezing night.

After a little while he got up and opened the flap of his tent. The sun was rising over the desert. He watched for a little while as the colour of the plain lightened, grey, reddish, yellow-brown. Stones were sharp-edged black shadows on the empty landscape, palm trees tall, bare trunks with a single spray of sharp leaves at the top.

Work had already started. He could hear the singing.

ST OSCAR'S UNIVERSITY, DELLAH, 2594

Extract from the Memoirs of Bernice Summerfield

When I got back home, it was, of course, raining. I started to experience that strange state where you've been away, and come back, and nothing has changed, making the trip seem as though it was an illusion, a dream. Life went on at St Oscar's, and you might never have known I'd just been over the rainbow.

It would have been nice to feel a bit more smug about the People's problems. In stories, utopias usually have some terrible flaw, just as immortality is always a curse. Sour grapes – no surprise when the writers aren't living in a perfect world, and aren't immortal. Sitting there among my unpaid bills and the general detritus of my rooms – over which Joseph the Porter[1] is fussing – it was hard to feel superior.

The People's blissful world was essentially intact. They weren't innocents before the War, they certainly weren't innocents during the War. There had been changes, but their vast population and flexible culture would absorb this problem. There'd be an Interest Group about it soon enough.

There's a thesis in all this, if anyone would believe it.

God only knows what it was thinking when it chose *me* to try to counsel ex-soldiers. Was it one of those odd jokes you have to be a machine to understand? Did it expect me to end up in a shouting match with the veterans, prompt some kind of healing anger, forcing them to justify themselves?

The navy got me so dirty. I spent so much of my childhood, my adolescence, in the mud, instead of in libraries, where I belonged. First grovelling around in a uniform, trying to learn how to crawl and shoot at the same time. And later, AWOL in the woods, hiding from my own teachers.

I hated mud back then. Especially in the forest, it was so difficult to ever get really *clean*. Now I don't mind it so much. I decide to go on digs – I'm not sent by some general who can get a hot shower whenever they like.

But that's true of the People too. You went to war if you wanted to. You could chuck it in any time.

Maybe they just wanted someone else to see how sorry they are. After all, the All of Us are People now, too. Maybe I was just there, the ultimate outsider, to assuage their collective guilty conscience.

Extract ends

---

[1] Joseph reminds me of a miniature People drone, actually, though he's smaller and doesn't have a face. He looks like a white billiard ball.

As usual, Lafayette ate breakfast by himself. Once or twice he heard laughter coming from the other tents, caught snatches of conversation in German or Arabic. He could understand them perfectly, but he was here to work, not to meet people.

After breakfast he shaved, boiling a panful of dirty Euphrates water before he rinsed the razor and started scraping at his ginger stubble. The mirror balanced against the fabric of the tent, forcing him to hold his head at an odd angle.

Pale eyes peered back at him out of a narrow, pink face. He'd tried to cut his own hair last week, with imperfect results. His red hair sat on his forehead in a sideways wave, already damp with sweat.

Lafayette planned to spend the day in the shade of his tent, nursing a painful sunburn. He'd earned it yesterday, painstakingly transcribing a clay tablet they'd recovered from one of the mounds. Sometimes, despite the best of care, the tablets would be damaged when they were moved; he didn't want to miss a glyph.

He didn't really need to be here. He could have waited back in the comfort of Cambridge, had transcriptions sent to him and translated them at his leisure in between cups of tea, instead of in between picking scorpions out of his bedclothes.

But Herr Koldewey needed epigraphic experts on site, translating inscriptions on walls and bricks and tablets. Lafayette hadn't expected his application to be accepted, but, now he was here with the heat and the flies, he suspected he hadn't had as much competition as he'd thought.

This brief stint in the desert should be greatly beneficial for his career. To be right on the spot as each inscription was unearthed, as the ancient words saw the light of day once more . . .

Besides, he *needed* to be here.

Among the old things, the ancient things. Not paper copies, but real stone, heavy with the weight of thousands of years. He would brush his fingers across the words, over and over, while the Arab workers watched and remarked on the effect of the desert heat on their foreign employers' minds.

Lafayette towelled his face and combed his hair, trying to straighten it up.

He remembered visiting Avebury, a child with one small hand in his father's hand and the other in his mother's. They had told him not to touch the stones, because they were very old, and dangerous, and might fall.

He had nodded, already serious and silent at the age of seven. He waited until they were picnicking and he could get away before he went up to one of the stones. Rough moss and fine cracks beneath his fingers. And a warm feeling in his chest, as safe and comfortable as falling asleep in his mother's lap.

THE WORLDSPHERE

'All packed,' said WiRgo!xu.

He sat down on the sand next to !Ci!ci-tel. For a while they both watched the water, the edge of a nearby continent hazy with distance. The island was moving very slightly, noticed WiRgo!xu; the waves were hitting the beach at an odd angle.

!Ci!ci-tel turned to look at him. There was sand in his orange hair; he'd slept on the beach again. WiRgo!xu preferred the comforts of the house.

It had been two weeks since the party. The rest of the partygoers had hung around for a while, but a steady trickle of departures over the last week had ended this morning, leaving them alone on the back of the turtle.

!Ci!ci-tel said, 'I like the feet.'

WiRgo!xu wriggled his new toes. They didn't want to move much. Ten stubby, vestigial lumps of flesh, incapable of anything except being stood on. He'd had the soles thickened to compensate. 'They look like an industrial accident,' he said.

'You can walk all right, though?'

'Well enough.' WiRgo!xu pushed his toes into the edge of the surf, letting the foaming water ripple across them. 'But I'll never play the violin again. How's your packing going?'

'Everything's been organized for this afternoon,' said !Ci!ci-tel. 'Mostly cosmetic changes, skin and hair colour. I think I'll have my heart moved up and to the left.'

WiRgo!xu made a face. 'Is that really necessary?'

!Ci!ci-tel shrugged. 'This is our last chance,' he said. 'Should I expect any awkward questions?'

'All the old drone wanted to talk about was skin fashions.' WiRgo!xu smiled bleakly. 'He tried three times to sell me a scale job. Anyway, I told it that it was just a barbarian fashion going around. Everyone's using those barbarian words and wearing those T-shirts.' Beni had spoken with dozens of People at the party. Some of them had even recorded her conversations; they were a popular favourite on the central entertainment network. All over the Worldsphere, it had become fashionable to drop incomprehensible barbarian concepts into conversation. 'It didn't think twice about it.'

!Ci!ci-tel stood up. 'You have a think, make sure there's nothing you've missed. I'm going to have a talk with our friend the island.'

'I'll come,' said WiRgo!xu.

'You don't need to.' !Ci!ci-tel watched as his friend pushed himself to his new feet. 'Are you sure you're all right on those things?'

'You are.'

'Yeah, but I've always been this way.'

'I'd better be all right, hadn't I?' said WiRgo!xu. 'Come on.'

Lafayette glanced at his pocket watch. Ten a.m. Normally Smith would have stopped in by this time for his daily chat. Happily, the man seldom stayed for more than a few minutes, merely in search of a few words' conversation with a fellow Briton. There was always something more for him to fetch and carry.

In fact, recalled Lafayette as he rubbed at a stiff shoulder, the man had been sent to Baghdad yesterday afternoon for supplies. It was usual for him to stay overnight – no doubt enjoying himself in the wicked city.

The table in Lafayette's tent was covered with yesterday's transcriptions. The morning's work had been slow. Sometimes recovering the meaning was as simple as translating Greek or Latin. Sometimes it was like squeezing blood from the proverbial stone. If only they had more vocabulary!

But he already knew what this tablet was – a fragment of

31

the creation epic named *When On High* for its initial words. Much of the story had been found on various expeditions, but parts were still missing. Lafayette would not know if he had something new to add until he had completed his translation.

The transcription that had cost him the sunburn concerned Ti'amat, the demon who represented the primal watery chaos. Lafayette carefully took a Hebrew Bible from his little treasure chest of reference works.

There, in Genesis, was one of the similarities that had sparked such interest in the Mesopotamian creation story. *Tehom*, 'the deep'. From the same root as *Ti'amat*, a word meaning 'ocean'. The parallels between this story and the creation of Genesis had long been recognized – without them, this expedition might have been far less likely. Now, what if –

Someone was standing at the door of his tent. One of the German handlers, he'd forgotten the man's name.

'Herr Lafayette,' he said, 'could you please at once come? Herr Smith has returned. He is injured. We need you to understand the English for us.'

Lafayette pushed the papers away. 'Injured?' he said. 'What's happened?'

'He's seen a ghost,' said the handler. 'We don't understand him, please come at once.'

'If I didn't know for a fact your psychological profiles checked out,' said the island, 'I'd say you were both a few ganglia short of a central nervous system.'

!Ci!ci-tel was sitting cross-legged on the turtle's head. Her scales were larger than his hands. 'As you know only too well,' he said, 'the War made many of us do strange things.'

'Hmmf,' said the island. She had lowered her roaring boom of a voice to a polite conversational level. 'Strange perhaps, but not *criminal*.'

'What does that mean?' said WiRgo!xu.

'It's a word I picked up from the barbarian,' said the island.

'You're so trendy,' said !Ci!ci-tel.

'It means violating a formal legal system,' huffed the turtle.

'You mean the Treaty.' !Ci!ci-tel drew shapes on the turtle's vast head with a finger, tracing between the scales. 'If the Treaty is violated,' he said, 'and there are no consequences, no one even knows about it, has the Treaty really been violated?'

'I don't want to hear this,' said the island. 'As long as no one's going to get hurt, I'm officially uninterested.'

'No problem,' said !Ci!ci-tel. 'You know you can trust us.'

'Of course I do,' said the island. 'You've kept my secret all these years – now it's my turn to help keep yours.'

'Hey, this isn't blackmail,' insisted WiRgo!xu. 'If you said no, we'd find some other way to do it.'

'A few people know who I used to be,' said the island. 'God knows, but then it arranged my . . . conversion.' She breathed a mighty sigh into the waves. 'It doesn't matter – I owe you one anyway. I just wish I knew what the pair of you were *really* looking for.'

'Same thing you were before you got yourself turned into a giant reptile,' said !Ci!ci-tel. 'A little peace of mind.'

'You two have always been looking for something. Cruising around with SLIG before the War. Even the War was just a chance to see some really exotic places and people.'

!Ci!ci-tel said, 'This time we've really hit on it. This isn't a small step –'

'You can say that again!' said WiRgo!xu, massaging the aching balls of his feet.

'I just hope this really *is* what you need,' said the island. 'There aren't any EXIT signs where you're going.'

Lafayette followed the handler through the camp, waving away the flies. Here and there, the archaeologists were poring over their maps. In the distance, he could see the top of a hat poking up from one of the excavation pits. And further away, one of the wall gangs hard at work: Arab labourers, become skilled in tracing the remains of a wall of unbaked bricks. Men broke the ground with pickaxes, carried away great baskets of dirt. A field railway carried the soil away, the carts creaking and rattling along the metal tracks.

Previous expeditions had not been able to tell sun-dried mud bricks from simple sun-dried mud, missing much of the city's surviving structure. It was remarkable to Lafayette that there was so much still to find. Time and the elements had been kind to Babylon, but far less so the human race. From the moment it was abandoned, the mighty city had been quarried for its high-quality bricks – some of the hundreds of Arab workers were converted brick thieves. And no doubt much had been carried off during the last century's scramble for oriental treasures.

With the new century had come a new approach. Robert Koldewey's was the first expedition to study the site scientifically, bringing his skills as an architect and not just a lust for precious items. Oh, those would be sent back to Germany without a doubt, but careful notes were being made of where everything was found. As much could be learnt from where things were found as from the things themselves – tiny bits of pottery and flint, discarded bones, all kinds of rubbish. The buildings were slowly emerging from the rounded, shapeless mounds of dirt, palaces and temples protruding like broken teeth.

Lafayette was not interested in any of it unless it had writing on it. But then, it seemed as though every brick in Babylon boasted the name of the king who had paid for it.

Sometimes he wished he was one of the Arabs, turning the bricks around in his hands, finding out the lines of the streets and buildings. Touching the ancient clay from dawn to dusk.

With an effort, he brought his thoughts back to his injured countryman. Given Smith's smoking and drinking habits, he would not be surprised at all if the handler had seen a ghost, or indeed anything else at all.

Smith was lying on the cot in his tent. He was ruddy and rounded, his high forehead and broad cheekbones peeling with sunburn. 'Lafayette, my good friend! Thank goodness you're here!' His right sleeve had been cut open, and his arm was bandaged. There was blood on the cloth of his shirt.

There was no one else in the tent. 'They said they wanted me to translate,' said Lafayette.

'They don't believe a word I say!' Smith had a bottle of

something strong-smelling. He took a mouthful from it. 'I can't say I blame them. You won't believe it either, Lafayette. If I get enough of this down me, I hope I'll stop believing it myself.'

'Calm down,' said Lafayette, pulling up a chair. He sat down, just outside the radius of Smith's cloud of fumes.

'I'm working on it,' said Smith, taking another drink. 'I was on my way back with the supplies, I swear I was. I'm lucky I got back with my life, I tell you.'

'You were attacked by bandits,' Lafayette suddenly realized.

Smith nodded vigorously. 'But what bandits, my friend! What bandits!' Lafayette shifted on the chair, already longing to return to his translations. 'I was leading that wretched camel along by the nose,' Smith was saying. 'You know the one. Wretched beast. It was all loaded up with the things I'd bought in Baghdad – there was no room for me on board. There were six of us in the caravan, and the Arabs were getting further and further in front of me. They're used to all this sand and rock, and my feet were hurting.'

'You became separated from them,' prompted Lafayette.

'Why, in the end, that's just what happened,' said Smith. 'I found myself in one of those twisting ravines, goodness knows how far behind the rest of the party. I must have come up in the wrong stretch of desert, because when I got out of that narrow gully, there was no sign of any of them. Let me tell you, I was more than a little terrified.'

'And then the bandits attacked you,' said Lafayette.

'Not yet. This, my friend, is the most extraordinary part of the story.' Smith turned the bottle around in his hands. 'It was then I saw the Path.'

Lafayette didn't say anything, marshalling his patience.

'The *Path*,' Smith said. 'At first I thought I saw a wire, or perhaps a narrow piece of metal, but so long . . . As I drew closer, I saw it was some kind of road. Straight as a ruler, stretching from one horizon to the other. It . . .' He waved his hands, trying to describe it. 'It *appeared*, like some creature breaking the surface of the ocean. There was a great ripple, and a sound like coins falling on to metal. And then it was simply there, right in front of me.'

'In the middle of the desert?' said Lafayette.

'At first I thought I had been lucky, and found some track that would lead me back here, or at least to a village,' said Smith. 'But as I approached, the camel began to become even more uncooperative. Until finally the animal dug its heels in and refused to come any closer. Heaven help me, I wish I'd had as much sense.'

'You went up to the Path,' Lafayette said, scratching his stubble.

'Stood right on it, heaven help me.' Smith wiped sweat from his rough forehead. 'I think it was made from some kind of metal – steel, perhaps, polished, shining like silver. None of the dust of the desert had blown on to it – it was as pristine as though someone had just swept it clean. I reached down and touched it, and do you know, it was cool to the touch? Even in the afternoon heat. It was so cool I thought it was wet, but my fingers came away dry. Well, what do you think I did then?'

'Then you were attacked by the bandits.'

Smith shook his head. 'I decided to take a little walk along this mysterious Path,' he said. 'I don't know what possessed me, but heaven help me, I ended up trudging along it for an hour. It was smooth, easy on the feet, so much easier to travel than the rocks and sliding sand . . . It must have been an hour, maybe more . . .'

A mirage, thought Lafayette – one of the illusions he had been warned about. The shimmering heat of the desert reflected the colour of the sky, creating a vision of water.

That was Smith's Path, luring the old drunkard on to the horizon. He was lucky to have escaped that trap with his life.

'It was then I saw the city,' Smith was saying.

And the bandits – local ruffians who preyed on desert travellers. Once Smith had finally wound down, Lafayette could make a brief report to Herr Koldewey, and then get back to work.

'Oh, a great city,' Smith burbled on. 'With great walls. In the distance I could see the entrance, surrounded by crowds. A huge gate, projecting forth from the wall. I looked at it through my binoculars. It was covered with blue tiles, and decorated with tremendous creatures. Bulls, and snakes with legs.'

Lafayette looked at him.

'I kept walking towards the city. There were people all around, crowds entering and leaving the city by that great gate, with their donkeys and camels. I was so astonished that I didn't even realize I'd walked right off the end of the Path. Well, that was when the bandits spotted me.'

'The creatures on the gate,' said Lafayette. 'Were they coloured?'

Smith thought for a second. 'They were covered in red and white tiles. Anyway, the bandits were friendly at first, four or five of them all chattering away at me in some babble or other. It wasn't Arabic – I know enough of that by now to get by. I tried telling them who I was and where I was supposed to be, but they just kept jabbering away.'

'What were they wearing?'

'Long linen tunics, and some kind of armour. Each of them had a sword. Let me tell you, by this time, I was more frightened than I can say. I tried backing away, apologizing all the time in English and Arabic, but one of them grabbed me. Well, I hit him and ran for it, stumbling over the desert stones, trying to find that Path again. They were all coming after me, shouting, and I knew I was done for – they would skewer me with those blades. And then I saw it. Glittering, a little distance away. My salvation – the Path!'

'Go on, go on,' said Lafayette.

'The bandits were almost upon me. I held my ground, took out my pistol, and let off a shot, but I don't mind telling you that my hand wasn't as steady as I'd have liked. It frightened the ruffians, but one of them kept coming. It was his weapon that did this to me.' Smith ran a finger along the edge of the bandage on his arm. 'You won't believe how this itches – even the pain isn't as bad as the itch. At any rate, I ran on to the Path and kept running, as fast as I could. When I looked back, none of the bandits were following me. I ran all the way back until I found that camel, patiently waiting for me, and I never thought I'd be so pleased to see the brute!'

Smith stopped, taking a long drink from his bottle. 'I

looked and looked for the Path, but I couldn't find it again. Even though I was certain I remembered just where it was. In the end I had to give up, exhausted and thirsty. The camel rescued me, in the end. It found its way back to camp. It must be smarter than it looks.'

Lafayette pushed his damp hair out of his face. 'All right,' he said. 'You're right, it's a difficult story to believe – no wonder you couldn't convince the Germans.'

'Do you imagine I did this to myself?' Smith said, pointing at his arm. He eased a finger under the edge of the bandage, in search of the elusive itch.

No, thought Lafayette, but any thug or cutthroat might have given you that wound. But the details – the tunics, the enamelled bricks!

This was surely some bizarre prank that one of the archaeologists was playing on their taciturn English visitor. They'd tutored Smith, read him Herodotus's description, even worked his injury into the fantastic story.

And yet –

Lafayette looked at Smith, who was watching him think. The man was exhausted, ready to put his head down and sleep off three-quarters of a bottle of whisky.

The drunkenness, the sunburn, the dull eyes, all of it was the same, but something had changed. There was something *different* about him, and Lafayette couldn't give it a name.

Perhaps fear and loss of blood had made some difference to him, made him more serious. Or perhaps he had had some kind of vision, some moment of peering through the centuries.

Whatever it was, it troubled Lafayette profoundly. In fact, he had the feeling people described as someone walking over their grave.

'I want to see this Path for myself,' he said. 'Can you take me there?'

'I told you, it vanished away.' Smith clutched at his arm, sagging on the cot. 'Heaven help me, I couldn't move if those bandits were after me again.'

'Then you'll have to describe the place for me as best you can. Wait here while I get a map.'

*   *   *

For the last part of their journey, WiRgo!xu and !Ci!ci-tel flew a glider, a clear plastic bulb between two broad red wings. The solar collectors and the rest of the machinery were hidden inside the wings. WiRgo!xu had designed the plane to give the impression that nothing was powering or steering the craft at all.

WiRgo!xu watched the landscape rushing up beneath him as the glider brought them down. They'd taken a travel capsule from the island, then a travel capsule around the coast to a small city.

WiRgo!xu had left the glider there a few weeks ago as part of a WAIG display. This morning he'd picked it up, telling the aviators that he planned to fly it home with a friend.

!Ci!ci-tel had told him off afterwards for trying to make it sound as though he had a good explanation. 'You wouldn't normally give a reason for everything you do, would you?' he'd said, as the glider had powered up and lifted them above the city. The bulb was so clear it looked as though they were flying inside nothing.

Now they were over a hundred kilometres away, rushing down over one of the Sphere's wilderness areas. It had been seeded when the Sphere was first created, and then left to itself – with occasional attention from God or the Wilderness Gardening Interest Group.

WiRgo!xu could see occasional trees, a creek here and there, but most of it was savanna. Long grass, short bushes, stretches of hardy purple flowers. He wondered if there were any animals about – maybe even dangerous ones – but he didn't see anything.

The glider braked gently, only a few tens of metres above the ground now. WiRgo!xu had taken it on a single test flight. It had worked perfectly that time, but that had been on a landing strip with plenty of drones standing by in case anything went wrong.

!Ci!ci-tel was silent, watching the ground come up, that distant look on his face. Thinking. !Ci!ci-tel was always going over his plans, again and again, as though perpetually convinced that he'd forgotten something.

Ten metres. Any second now.

!Ci!ci-tel yelled as the wings detached themselves, leaping away from the bulb. Then they were rolling, no faster than a child rolling down a grassy hillside. He had calibrated the deceleration curve perfectly. The bulb jumped into the air as it ran over a bush, landed with a bump, and came to a sudden stop against a tree trunk.

'Perfect!' shouted WiRgo!xu.

'It was supposed to do that?' said !Ci!ci-tel, who was lying against the wall of the sphere, upside down. 'You didn't say it was supposed to do that!'

'This was my last chance.'

'Last chance?'

'To impress someone.' WiRgo!xu ran his fingers down the side of the bulb, and the plastic separated neatly at the seam. They climbed out, booted feet crunching in the long, dry grass. 'There's no aviation, weird or otherwise, where we're going.'

!Ci!ci-tel tried to smooth his newly dark and curly hair, but succeeded only in making himself look even more astonished. 'This can only be a good thing,' he said. 'Let's go over our packing while we wait for I!qu-!qu-tala.' He looked at his chronometer.

Extract from the Memoirs of Bernice Summerfield

I spent a few days trying to edit some of the rougher passages in *An Eye for Wisdom*. It was nearing completion, which was good, because I could really have used the delivery advance. It's not the pop-archaeology sequel my publishers were nervously waiting for, but it is a solid piece of academic work. It ought to keep them happy for a bit.

I did the bulk of the translations myself – Dellah has the galaxy's largest database on Ikkaban and related languages. The real work was cooking up the commentary. Since nobody knows anything about the Ikkaba, that's not hard – you just come up with a bunch of educated guesses, like everybody else. Some of the poems have common authors, while some, like 'In The Queen's Temple', are firmly anonymous.

There are a few pieces I wasn't able to fully translate. Part of the problem is that we don't have a complete vocabulary; no one's ever found a schoolbook or a dictionary, just scattered lines of poetry. So you have to guess at English equivalents for a lot of the words, substituting *rose* for *flower pain pleasure*, human mythological figures for unknown Ikkaban ones.

So much of what I do involves trying to understand aliens. At least my nonhuman students can just explain what they mean – unlike a bunch of centuries-old chisellings. Even human cultures can be difficult to grasp,[2] unless you can dive right into them, try to see the world from their point of view. The Aztecs seem almost insanely violent until you begin to grasp their economics. It becomes even more difficult if you've only got access to the culture through a narrow channel – like the records of the winning side, for example.

When the All of Us attacked the People, it must have been like having monkeys throw nuts at you. After ignoring them the first few times, you'd start to feel that it was time to teach them a lesson.

I don't think there was anything more to the war than that. Surely the People couldn't have felt threatened when they had such superior fire power. A lot of them must have treated the war like a huge game, played with real spaceships and maps and everything – come out of it without ever being hurt, ever doing anything terrible.

A lot of the People must get through their entire, extended life spans without ever being hurt or doing anything terrible.

Now, *that's* difficult to get your head around.

Extract ends

'God!' said the island.

'God here.'

'I need help, fast! My security sensors have just detected an explosive device hidden somewhere on me!'

---

[2] I've done some notes for a paper on the recurring use of the samurai as models for alien races in pre-first-contact twentieth-century fiction. *Alien Honour: from the Klingons to the Minbari.* I must see if the *Journal of Atomic Literature* is interested.

'A bomb-disposal drone is on its way,' said God. 'Stay calm. What details do you have?'

'I need a shuttle right away,' said the turtle. 'I've got three People here, snorkelling.'

'Already en route,' said God. 'Those details.'

'The security scan has narrowed the location down to somewhere in Beni's house. Oh shit, it's a big bomb – it could blow a hole right in my shell.'

'Stay calm. The shuttle is there and loading right now.'

'Where's that drone?'

'Arriving right now. I'm sending it into the house. OK, I've found the bomb.'

'Can you defuse it?'

Pause. 'It's less risky to let it detonate above the atmospheric envelope. Stand by.'

The remote drone, a matt-black cylinder with a dozen mechanical arms extruded from its fat body, burst through the roof of Beni's house. It had located the bomb in a kitchen cupboard, analysed it, then carefully lifted it out with its forward fields and wrapped several layers of containment shielding around it.

The drone calculated it had forty-seven seconds before the bomb exploded, but it wasn't taking any chances.

'The shuttle is away,' God told the island.

'How about the bomb?'

'Already above the cloud layer.'

'What about fallout?'

'It's a standard *popper*.'

'Hell's teeth! A singularity bomb?'

'The drone's shielding it, so there won't be any radiation, but expect your communications to be down for a few seconds. There might also be some peculiar sensory side effects, given that you're directly under the thing.'

'I'm swimming as fast as I can.'

'I'd dive as well, if I were you. Ten seconds to go,' said God. 'A *popper* is a very serious bit of ordnance. Any idea of who'd want to blow you so thoroughly away?'

'Dozens of People,' said the Turtle. 'If any of them found out who I used to be.'

'Here it goes,' said God.

Seventy kilometres above the Worldsphere's inner surface, the *popper* popped.

It was designed to tidily eliminate annoying enemy bases and small ships by exposing them to a miniature black hole for a tiny fraction of a second. A puff of radiation marked the detonation, and then the black hole would neatly consume itself, taking a spherical area of matter with it.

The area of destruction could be precisely calculated – say, a turtle the size of an island, plus a quantity of sea water and a small chunk of atmosphere – so it was categorized as a *surgical* weapon.

The remote drone's containment shields absorbed the initial burst of hard radiation from the device. The bomb then swallowed the drone and all the dust particles and stray gas molecules it could eat in a radius of two kilometres. Sucking on vacuum.

God tried to monitor the explosion, in case of any nasty little surprises, but as far as its detectors could detect it all went by the *popper* manual.

Then the secondary shock wave hit, and communications and scanning went down in a hundred-thousand-kilometre radius for almost four seconds. For a moment, even God was blind.

At that instant, thousands of kilometres away, a compact and dangerous machine punctured a hole in space-time.

In the first nanosecond, the puncture was a single point, with no volume and no mass. In the second nanosecond, it began to expand, widening through two dimensions until it was a metre across. It had no thickness; if you approached it from the other side, you could put your arm right through it.

From the top, it was a flat silver ribbon, cold and reflective. It suggested a frozen river, stabbing away from you and towards the horizon. But – except at those mathematically defined points at which it intersected the universe – it had no real existence. It would penetrate an endless series of times and places without leaving a mark.

You might catch a glimpse of it as it passed you, in your spaceship or your kitchen, the barest flicker for the briefest moment out of the corner of your eye.

To those walking the Path, it was a continuous, steady track, soft on the feet and straight as a die.

The Temporal Interest Group had long since theorized such a Path. If a singularity or an incompetent time traveller could tear space-time a new wormhole, reasoned TIG, surely it could be done in an intentional and controlled manner.

The Treaty banned all research and development into time-travel technology. Observing was one thing, building was another. TIG, for the most part, kept their speculations to themselves. Probably because they knew that if they accidentally managed to start a war, both sides would be gunning for them.

Doing the research, building a time machine, and activating it – hidden in the shadow of a singularity bomb – was without question the worst treaty violation in the People's history.

Even with the help of the map, Smith's descriptions had been terribly vague. Lafayette ended up consulting one of the Arab labourers who had accompanied the man to Baghdad. The Arab laid the map down on the ground and traced the ravine they'd travelled along with a finger. There were four or five likely places where Smith might have emerged, once he'd become separated from the group. They'd searched for him when they realized he was lost, said the labourer, but they hadn't seen any sign of this strange road he was talking about.

That meant that – assuming Smith was telling the truth – his Path couldn't have been anywhere on the northern side of the ravine. That left just two places to check.

Lafayette waited until the late afternoon to make the trip. The ravine wasn't more than an hour's walk from the camp. Even so, thought Lafayette, as he trudged across the baked plain, he really ought to have brought a handler or two. Armed, in case

Smith's bandits were more than the inhabitants of a mystical vision.

He wasn't entirely sure why he was doing this.

He hadn't been entirely sure that he wanted to join Koldewey's expedition, even for a few months. He had been half convinced he would catch some dreadful exotic illness and perish long before he reached Turkish Arabia, or be sunburnt to death before he made it to the ruins.

He only knew, in a vague way he couldn't have put into words, that he ought to be there. Among the old things.

He paused in the shade of a palm tree, drinking from his canteen. If what he really wanted in life was to handle ancient stones and bits of pottery, he wondered, why had he become a linguist? But his talent was for translation, not for exploring and digging and map-making. As a boy he had spent his time in libraries, not adventuring in the mud.

His father had hoped young John would take some well-paid government position as a translator. Young John had still vaguely clung to a hope of travelling to distant lands, discovering treasures. They'd come to a compromise in the end. Lafayette would study languages, but ancient ones as well as modern.

He put away the canteen and went on.

He supposed he would spend the rest of his life translating ancient inscriptions, rather than the conversations of ambassadors. There was plenty of work to do, entire peoples whose writings were only just coming to light. There would be occasional opportunities for travel, to see and handle the actual inscriptions and documents. To stand among the stones themselves.

Lafayette had come to the ravine. He double-checked the map, and turned west, keeping well away from the precarious edge. He imagined Smith tottering about in a state of drunken revelation, a few steps away from plummeting to the stones below. The man was more lucky than he deserved to be.

There was a rough wooden bridge across the ravine, strong enough for a man or two but far too weak for a caravan. Lafayette stepped on to it, nervously listening to the ropes and planks creaking.

The bridge swayed as he made his way out on to it, holding on to the waist-high ropes at either side.

Halfway across, he felt a peculiar pressure in his head, almost a rippling sensation. He looked around, with the sudden and intense feeling that he was being watched. His eyes ran over the cliffs, looking for human shapes. If there were bandits, he would be at their mercy; he had a pistol, but he was no sharpshooter.

No bandits emerged. He turned and turned again, but, if someone was secretly observing him, they were well hidden.

The sensible thing to do would be to head back to the camp, keeping the weapon handy, just in case. He wasn't entirely sure why he kept going.

He breathed a sigh of relief as he stepped off the bridge and back on to solid land.

It was ten minutes later that he saw the Path.

The initial investigation was carried out by the Interpersonal Dynamics Interest Group, once its members had stopped arguing about whose turn it was.

IDIG spent most of its time turning out reports and fictional series about life and love in the Worldsphere – fashions, parties, anecdotes about affairs and practical jokes. It was a cover for their real interest: those rare incidents of violence between members of the People. Or it would have been a cover, if everyone didn't already know what IDIG was really interested in.

IDIG's representatives interviewed the island and several other individuals, and then cross-checked with the Weapons Development Interest Group, who had been poring over God's record of the explosion.

Their initial, confidential report stated that it was unlikely that someone had tried to kill the turtle; any enemies it had would be a lot more likely to try to expose it, have it ostracized. IDIG's guess was that someone had been trying to kill the barbarian Beni – not realizing that her stay on the Worldsphere had been so brief.

God seemed oddly distracted when IDIG's representatives made their report. They took this as a sign that God disliked their theory, particularly as it assumed incompetence on the part of the would-be murderers, and possibly that there was some fact or facts about the matter that God wasn't sharing.

They were wrong. Something else entirely had got God worried.

Lafayette had the intense sensation of the hairs on the back of his neck standing up. It was what people meant when they described their hackles rising, he was sure – the same physical reaction you saw in a frightened dog.

He ran forward, then stopped, measuring his steps. It was just as Smith had described it: a perfectly straight, metallic ribbon, an idealized road. He stepped up to it, his entire scalp tightening, and reached down cautious fingers to touch the surface.

It felt *old*. It felt older than the clay tablets, older than the stone at Avebury. He had the strangest impression that he had been separated from it, somehow, that he had come home. Like the peculiar sensation of visiting a childhood haunt you have consciously forgotten, only to have the cupboards of memory come tumbling open.

Lafayette made himself concentrate on the physical. The Path felt cold and smooth, almost wet. In this heat, metal should have been unbearably hot. There was no dust on it – the other peculiarity that Smith had described.

There was no doubt left in Lafayette's mind: Smith had been entirely truthful. He knew – with the same clarity he experienced when a row of cuneiform suddenly made sense – he knew that if he walked along this Path, he would see Babylon.

Lafayette sat down in the dust, beside the miraculous Path. What should he do? Return for the others, for cameras and notebooks? What if the Path was a temporary phenomenon, and was gone when he returned? What if he walked along it, and it vanished once more, stranding him? Where would he find himself?

Still trying to decide, Lafayette stepped on to the Path.

A shock ran through his whole body, like a blow to the spine. Lafayette gasped, imagining for a moment that he was being electrocuted. But the feeling passed, travelling out through the top of his head.

He peered down the length of the mysterious silver road. Its end was lost in the haze of distance.

For the first time in his life, there was something that he really *wanted* to do.

Lafayette started walking.

The first report came from a remote drone God had sent to do a brute-force scan of the area. God decided the drone must be malfunctioning, recalled it, and sent out another in its place. When the second drone sent back the same report, God dispatched a third to do a close-up scan.

When it had read the third drone's report, God wiped the memories of all three remotes and sat back to have a little think and a very restrained panic.

Extract from the Memoirs of Bernice Summerfield

'Wake up!'

My eyes popped open. I'd fallen asleep on the sofa in my study, after drinking one more bottle of Crimson Star Lager than I ideally ought to have. My mouth tasted like carpet in need of a good vacuuming.

My screensaver is a clock. It was 11.10 p.m., said the figures floating about on the darkened terminal. I must have only been asleep for an hour, after nodding off in the middle of *Danger on the Frontier: the Next Generation*. The 3D was still on, muttering away to itself; it must have been what woke me up. I fumbled for the remote, snapped the screen off, considered heading for bed, and decided to stay where I was.

Something moved across the floor. 'Argh!' it said.

'Argh!' I said. I jumped up on to the sofa, like a woman in a cartoon confronted by a mouse, dropping the remote on to the floor.

The thing moved again. I'd thought it was possibly a rodent, maybe a really large bug, but the movement was more like . . . like *rolling*.

'Joseph?' I squeaked, coughed embarrassedly, and said in my normal voice, 'Joseph? Is that you?'

The thing on the floor uttered a peculiar series of noises, rolled another inch towards me, and lay still. In the near-blackness with the 3D off, I could barely see it.

I crouched down on the sofa, wondering if I could get to the remote before whatever it was rolled up and bit me. I started reaching down, keeping my eyes on the almost invisible shape.

Then my cat jumped on it.

'Wolsey, no!' I yelled, as he batted the thing. It flew across the rug and fetched up against the wall. Wolsey bounced after it. I reached down, grabbed the remote, and snapped the lights on.

It *was* Joseph. I picked up Wolsey before he could knock my Porter behind the desk. 'Were you trying to save me from the nasty robot?' I said, smoothing the fur on his head. 'Or did you think he was a cat toy?'

Wolsey wriggled free and jumped on to the sofa. He looked genuinely spooked. 'Joseph?' I said, keeping my distance from the little robot in case it exploded or something. 'Can you talk? What's the matter with you?'

The small white sphere rolled from side to side, as though shaking its head. 'You must have blown a valve, or something,' I said. 'Don't worry, I'll give Maintenance a call, and we'll get you fixed up in time to bring me my breakfast.' I reached for the terminal.

'It's me,' said Joseph, indistinctly.

Wolsey hissed, his fur exploding outwards. He scrambled over the back of the sofa and ran out of the study.

'I'm God,' said my Porter.

'Joseph,' I said, 'I know your ego circuits have always needed a bit of adjusting, but really . . .'

'Beni, this isn't a joke!' said the white ball. Its voice was tinny, as though coming from a great distance. 'We have to talk!'

It sank in. I picked up my possessed Porter and put him on the desk. 'You don't normally make house calls. What's up?'

'It's an emergency,' said God, 'or I wouldn't be here, even

in these reduced circumstances. Good grief, it's cramped in this thing! It's like trying to park a truck in a taco shell.'

'Try not to break him,' I said. I sat cross-legged on the floor, looking up at the ball. 'Joseph's a pain, but I'd never remember any of my appointments without him.'

'Relax,' said God, 'I don't plan to leave behind any sign that I've been here.'

'How can you be here?' I asked.

God then said something complicated about hyperdimensional extrusions and personality miniaturization, which I had trouble following. Suffice it to say that God had pushed a tiny part of its vast machine intelligence through some kind of relay system, and anchored the other end of its mental pseudopod in my Porter. 'I was aiming for your terminal,' said God, 'but the Porter is a self-contained unit. Less chance of leaving fingerprints this way.'

Panic was prickling in my toes by this point. 'Why didn't you just send one of your agents to see me?' I said. 'What's the emergency?'

'Too many People have already been involved in the investigation,' said God, in his faraway voice. 'Switch on your terminal, I need to show you something.'

I wiggled the mouse, and the screensaver blinked out. The terminal's screen went blank, and a few moments later, a diagram of the Worldsphere appeared – an outline globe with a few continents and the spaceport sketched in.

'Two People have built a time machine,' said God. Benny sank her teeth into her lower lip and sucked in a breath. 'Let's not worry about the technical details, which I don't have the full information on anyway, and which I don't plan to have. Suffice it to say it created a conduit from a point inside the Worldsphere –' a yellow dot started flashing on the screen '– through space and time. The other end is anchored at their intended destination.' The dot became a line, stretching away from the sphere. It kept going, moving past stars, finally leaving the People's home galaxy behind.

I watched. I had a sinking feeling about where that line was headed. 'Do you know who did it?'

'Oh yes,' said God. 'We had a shortlist of suspects right

from the beginning, and all we had to do was confirm which of them had gone missing. If WiRgo!xu and !Ci!ci-tel are still on the sphere, they're very well hidden.'

'I met them both at the party.'

'Yes, you did.' The yellow line had entered a second galaxy; the scale zoomed as it approached another sphere. I wasn't surprised to recognize the outlines of Earth's continents. The line touched the surface of the planet, and stopped.

'Can you show me a close-up?' I said. 'And what epoch is this?'

'About three thousand, one hundred and sixty-four of your Earth years ago,' said God. 'Give or take five years.'

'So that's . . . about 570 BCE,' I said. The globe was expanding. 'More,' I said. 'More. Oh shit.'

'Where is it?' said God.

'Babylon,' I said. I sat back in my chair. 'WiRgo!xu must have made a copy of my notes when he was playing with my terminal. They've plonked down right in the Neo-Babylonian Era. Best time to visit.'

'More than visit,' said God. 'They probably plan to stay. According to the personality projections from APIG, it's likely they've been planning something like this for a long time. Leaving the People, going undercover on a barbarian world.'

'Would you have let them?'

'Of course we would have,' said God. 'But we'd have kept a careful eye on that world, and on them. Making sure of their safety. They know that.'

'So they wanted to go somewhere that you couldn't follow. Somewhere that's out of bounds because of the Treaty.'

'Exactly. The Milky Way, *and* a different time period. They probably expect us to hush it all up and forget about it. But we can't.'

'Why not?' I asked. 'Shut down the Path – they must be where they want to go by now. Hide any evidence that this ever happened.'

'We can't shut down the Path.' There was an embarrassed pause. 'We don't have the technology. Only WiRgo!xu and

51

!Ci!ci-tel know how, and they destroyed all of their research before leaving.'

'What about sending some agents along the Path to fetch them?' I said. 'No, of course, that would be *another* treaty violation. Grief, why didn't *they* switch it off? They could have sneaked off without anyone ever knowing!'

'Good question. APIG are working on it. In the meantime, we do have a brute-force method for getting rid of the Path.'

'Good.'

'Blow it up,' said God. 'Send a forced singularity bomb down the Path.'

'Oh, good.'

'The only drawback is that it would destroy a substantial area at both ends of the Path.'

'Oh, *shit*.' I glanced back at the screen, where a flashing yellow dot sat next to the ancient city of Babylon. '*How* substantial?'

'We calculated the minimum required to do the job,' said God. 'It wouldn't destroy more than a twenty-kilometre radius.'

I wish I could say that I was filled with righteous rage, the urge to protect Earth and its timeline, and clever alternatives to God's plan.

Instead, I was filled with a sort of panicked haze. 'You realize, of course,' I said, in an oddly high-pitched voice, 'that you would be changing history.'

'Yes.'

'Substantially.'

'Yes.'

'WiRgo!xu and !Ci!ci-tel haven't chosen any old backwater. They've chosen a pivotal time in human history. A population centre that can shelter a quarter of a million people. I know that doesn't sound like much to you, but it's the largest city in its era on Earth.'

God said, 'If we blow the Path away, we can claim it was a natural phenomenon. And the other parties to the Treaty can pretend they believe us.'

'Plausible deniability,' I said faintly. 'You don't care about the collateral, as long as your meta-arse is covered.'

Joseph's occupied shell rocked on the desk, as though agitated. 'Beni, if we get into a war over this, it's not going to mean a few planets getting singed. We're talking whole galaxies going up in flames here. Destroying one city, altering one bit of history – it's got to be worth it.'

I slumped. That couldn't be right, that couldn't be a rational transaction, a fair trade.

'I hope you didn't come here for my approval,' I muttered. 'I'm not even a historian. Why tell me at all?'

'There is an alternative,' said God.

My heart gave a little lurch of hope. 'I'm listening.'

'You walk the Path,' said God. 'You go back in time. You find them and bring them back again, and we make them shut the Path down.'

'What if they don't want to go back?'

'You explain that you've got five days to convince them, after which they'll be blown to little bits along with everyone else in the city.'

My terminal shut off. God watched me from Joseph's shell. I held the fate of hundreds of thousands of people, and of Earth's history, in my hands.

I wished I had drunk considerably more of the Crimson Star Lager.

'And all because of my notes,' I sighed.

'I'm afraid so,' said God.

And all because of my notes. I started packing.

There are certain things you should always take, whether you're visiting the People or a society of cave dwellers. Into the leather satchel went knickers and my toiletries bag – toothbrush, toothpaste, deodorant, sunscreen, condoms,[3] vitamins. Then some primitive-societies survival gear: aspirin, tummy tablets, two rolls of loo paper, bandages, some broad-spectrum antibiotics. I grabbed my hat and tossed it by the brim like a Frisbee. It landed near the door, where I wouldn't forget it.

I didn't have two essential items yet – God had promised money and a translator at the rendezvous.

[3] Erring on the side of optimism.

I topped the bag off with my diary and some pens. There was still a bit of room, so I tucked in a couple of miniature bottles of whisky. I'd been reading up on Babylon – everything I could find – and though I was looking forward to sampling the local booze, some of the real stuff couldn't hurt.

I gathered my standard travelling clothes, substituting a lightweight white shirt for the more sturdy brown one. I tucked sunglasses into the pocket of my leather jacket, wondering just how conspicuous they would make me. I was going to stand out, and I'd just have to deal with that. How hard could it be? At last week's seminar on death mythology, I'd been the only human being on a planet of slimy purple folks.

I put some spare socks into the satchel, which still had enough room for more stuff. I wouldn't need my official papers, tickets, moneyslot, phrase book . . .

I had a bit of a think about taking one of those disabling sprays with me. They had a rack of them at the chemist's, in designer cans, and I found myself weighing one of them in my hand. Normally I'd have relied on my martial-arts skills – the only thing I have to thank the military for. For some reason, this time, I felt as though I wanted to be armed.

In the end I dropped the can back in its rack and just bought the condoms. It had worried me how safe I felt, holding the can; if I felt that secure just because I had a pepper spray in my pocket, I might let my guard down. Besides, I'd probably manage to get the can backwards and spray myself in the head.

On the other hand, it might be a lot easier to walk up to WiRgo!xu and !Ci!ci-tel, Mace 'em, and drag them back. Easier than talking them out of their mad plan.

On the *other* hand, maybe the last thing I want to do is seem like a threat to a couple of troubled and desperate high-tech veterans.

One of my students caught me packing. I had hoped to slip away as unobtrusively as possible. Of course, it's difficult to disappear for a week in the middle of classes without *some-one* noticing . . . people are going to start wondering whether you're ill, panicking about your workload, having a mad affair, or sunning yourself on a beach somewhere.

My overdue marking paled in comparison with the immediate problem.

Anyway, Joseph – restored to his senses after his religious experience – let Anne-Marie Rose in while I was kneeling in the middle of my lounge, pulling everything out of the satchel and double-checking it all for the third time. I didn't even notice she was there until I looked up and saw her bright little eyes fixed on the packet of condoms.

I stuffed them blushingly into the bottom of the satchel and said, 'What can I do for you, Anne-Marie?'

'Um,' she said. She was dressed in the latest Vampire Cheek, thrift-ship Goth gear covered in colourful patches and silly badges. DRINK ME, said the pin on her black jacket, next to one that said HAVE A NICE NIGHT. It always made me smile. 'I heard that you were going away again,' she said.

'Just for a week,' I said, feeling a sudden haste to get away informing my actions. I shoved a packet of sticking plasters into the satchel. 'I'm sorry about the marking on your essays. I promise I'll get it done as soon as I get back.'

'That's OK,' she said, casting her eyes over the clutter on my floor. She tugged at her thick red leggings. 'Mark Mbangi's tutorials aren't that bad.'

I had to smile again. 'Even if he does seem to have personally received advice from every major archaeological figure this century. Just ignore the close-personal-friend stories and stick to the curriculum.' I pushed a hand into the pile of papers and handed her a stack. 'These are photocopies of the tute notes I was going to use. Hand them out for me, would you?'

'Yes, Professor, thanks,' said Anne-Marie, hefting the pile in her arms. 'Mbangi's notes are always full of little mistakes.'

'Mine aren't exactly perfect.'

'Yeah, but you make sure all the alien names are spelt right. With Mbangi you can never tell if it's a whole new species or just a typo.' My smile turned into a guilty grin. It was good to see the students could see through Mark's bluster too. They'd survive another week's absence on my part.

Anne-Marie was carefully pushing the notes into her shoulder bag. 'What's this, Professor Summerfield?'

I looked up. She'd caught the topmost paper before it went into her bag. It was a photocopy marked with my characteristic highlighting and scrawl, obviously not one of the tutorial notes. *'Beer Before Bread? A Theory Revisited,'* read Anne-Marie. 'By Edward Watkinson.'

'Oh yes,' I said. I held the Edward Watkinson Chair of Archaeology at St Oscar's, named for one of the century's most noted archaeologists, and a bit of a hero of mine. Even Mark Mbangi hadn't had the chutzpah to claim he'd met Watkinson, who was on his way to becoming a legend – not only because of his exploits on exotic planets but because he'd reputedly published more than ten thousand papers in his lifetime.[4]

Anne-Marie was perusing the paper. I said, 'Watkinson spent a year or two studying the origins of human civilization, and he came across an antique theory that grain was originally domesticated to make beer, rather than bread. It's an interesting argument, though it usually ends up in a bunfight over caloric intake.'

'Are we going to study this?'

'Uh, not in Mesoamerican Literature and Music,' I said. 'Though we might get to it in History and Philosophy of Archaeology. No, it's just personal interest . . .' I sighed, snapped back to the reality of the situation. 'Anyway, I'll make you a copy when I get back, if you like. Listen, can I trust you with something?'

Anne-Marie looked at me with those glittering eyes. 'What is it, Professor Summerfield?' she said, in a hushed voice.

'It's this.' I picked up a long envelope from the lounge.

---

[4] I did a bit of a literature search, and found nine hundred and thirteen papers with Watkinson's name – though he was co-author, often as part of a large team, on four hundred and seventy-two of those. That still leaves a substantial body of wholly original work, on every topic from ethnomycology to folsom points to Lvan glass megaliths – Watkinson was interested in everything. The fact that he had four arms makes me suspect he could type two papers simultaneously.

'It's possible I might . . . be delayed in getting back to work. If I'm not back in one week, will you give this to Dr Follett for me?'

Anne-Marie grasped the envelope as though it contained a map to El Dorado. 'Yes, Professor,' she said.

When she had departed, I sat on the floor, my back to the sofa and my satchel held between my ankles, fiddling with my fringe.

What I'd wanted the envelope to contain was an explanation of my predicament and detailed instructions on how to come and rescue me. Instead, I'd had to settle on an apology, instructions for the remaining part of the semester, and a copy of my will.

I knew Anne-Marie would take care of it for me, and deliver it as promised – some of my other students couldn't have made a simple deadline like that if their grades depended on it (as they often did).

If I didn't make it back, these kids I taught would never know why.

Suddenly, I felt terribly old. I went on restuffing my satchel with a subdued but determined air. As if anyone could see me.

PLANET MD 20879

Clarence carried me again. I found myself waking as we drifted down to the ground. The desert stretched away in all directions. We touched down, gently, dust puffing up around Clarence's feet. The desert was dark orange-red, almost Martian, all that iron in the rocks. It undulated gently, giving an illusion of smooth waves.

The sky was blue at the zenith, shading to bands of violet closer to the horizon, the air full of red dust. The ground was covered in the fine grit, punctuated by rounded stones of various sizes. Here and there I could see huge, worn rocks, taller than I was, partly coated by mosses. The tiny plants scattered the sunlight in psychedelic colours.

'It's beautiful,' I said.

Clarence put me down. He'd hardly said a word, a worried

frown marring his perfect face. 'I wish you could come with me,' I told him.

Clarence moped, wings drooping. 'So do I,' he said. 'I don't really know what's going on. But I can tell . . .' He ran a finger down the side of my face. 'This isn't good.'

I patted his arm, feeling lost. 'Will you take me home when I get back?' I said, sounding more like a little girl than I would have ideally liked.

'You betcha.' Literally from out of nowhere, Clarence produced a small envelope. 'Sealed orders from God. And no, I haven't tried to read them.' He looked around, as though feeling a bit naughty to still be talking to me. 'I have to go.'

I stood on tiptoes and kissed him on the cheek. 'Off you go,' I said. 'I'll be fine.'

I watched him take off. Or I tried to. For my benefit, he leapt into the air, flying a short distance using just the wide white wings, his whole body involved in the muscular movement. Then he blurred, shifting into something like hyperspace, and was gone.

I opened my sealed orders.

The Path intersected a particular area near the surface of this world for almost two weeks. I was five kilometres from that point, where I would find a technician waiting for me. They had to do something complex and mathematical to the Path to make it accessible – otherwise it would just be a sort of flicker, barely detectable.

MD 20879 was inhabited, but only by a small mining operation. They were on the same continent, but hundreds of kilometres away; there was little chance we'd be disturbed.

The sealed orders included a small tracking device to bring me safely to the technician: a clip-on earring that *murmured*. I snapped the small lavender-and-pink triangle into place.

At first it was disturbing to have this tiny voice whispering, 'That's right . . . keep going . . . keep going . . . left a little . . . that's right . . . keep going . . . keep going . . .' every fifteen seconds or so. After a while it became rather comforting. It would be terrible to wander in this beautiful wilderness, not knowing which way you were supposed to go.

Eventually I topped a gentle rise, and the earring said, 'Here we are . . . here we are . . .'

It didn't need to tell me. I saw the Path at once, standing out powerfully against the red soil. It looked like a huge, shiny metal ruler, perhaps ten metres long.

Something in my chest went *twinge* at the sight of it. I don't know if it was some sixth sense reacting to the time-mangling vibes of the thing, or just the familiar, sinking feeling that I'd rather be somewhere else.[5]

I started to walk down the slope, pebbles rattling down in tiny avalanches as I tried to keep my balance. As I got nearer, I could see that the ends of the 'ruler' were blurry, as though I was seeing them through a shimmer of heat. Next to each of the ends was a small gold-coloured pyramid etched with narrow lines, like printed circuitry.

The technician, a drone, was waiting for me, an orange-red oval hovering next to the Path. As I got closer, I saw it was camouflaged, its fields turned the colour of the rusty soil. 'Hi,' it said brightly. 'I'm O-Ran!Xing, and I don't want to be here any more than you do, so let's get on with it.'

'Right,' said Benny. 'What do I do?'

'You just step on to it and start walking. Towards this end,' said the drone, moving towards one end of the slice of Path. 'If you walk the other way, you'll eventually reach the Worldsphere. When you're ready to come back, it'll be obvious which way to go: the Path terminates at your destination. Keep the tracking device – it's also a translator.'

I thought of something. 'Will time pass at the same rate for me as it does for you?'

The drone nodded, rolling its head. 'I'm off as soon as you're away – if you're returning, you'll be returning to the Worldsphere. We can't leave this extrusion active.'

'You're not taking any chances,' I said.

'Yes we are,' said the drone. 'You.'

Fair enough. I took a deep breath and stepped on to the silver line.

The jolt up my spine reminded me of the time a practice dive

[5] The bath.

went badly wrong, and I landed in the water on my back. My whole body was jarred, the air knocked out of my lungs.

Instantly, I could see the Path as it really was – stretching away across the landscape, to the horizon and beyond. I looked over my shoulder, and it was just the same in the other direction. The inside of my head itched with the unnaturalness of the thing.

O-Ran!Xing was watching me, expectantly. Once I started walking, I'd have to keep going. There'd be no way to know where I was without stepping off the Path. I'd be on my way, nonstop, to Babylon.

I gave the drone a wave, and started walking.

Extract ends

BASKET CHASE

*While certain cultural cues (see Appendix III) indicate
a different origin for the Egyptian pyramids, the zig-
gurats of Central and South America and of Mesopotamia almost certainly show the influence of the
Ikkaba.*

*This is not to downplay the ingenuity of the human
beings who designed and built those great temples.
They were inspired by the alien visitors, but developed
their architecture and skills without their assistance.
(The poem often called 'The Wanderer's Lament' suggests that the Ikkaba came to avoid meddling in the
development of other cultures.)*

– Summerfield, Bernice S, 'Pointing to heaven:
Ikkaban cultural influence and architecture'.
In *An Eye for Wisdom: Repetitive poems
of the Early Ikkaban Period*, St Oscar's
University Press, Dellah, 2595.

BABYLON, 570 BCE

The sun was sinking when Benny stepped off the Path.

She stood for a moment, taking deep breaths of the cooling
air, the deep, clean taste of preindustrial times. She let it play
over her tongue for a moment, tasting desert dust, distant
fires.

She was a little distance from Babylon, near a road that led into the great city. Its walls, kilometres long, stabbed up from the flat plain; there were no houses outside, no urban sprawl, just a tight knot of buildings and population.

People and animals were going in and out through a huge blue gate that projected from the nearest wall. The Ishtar Gate, Benny knew, largest of eight around the city's perimeter. Babylon, *Bab-ili*, the gates of the gods.

The day after God's message, she'd crammed for hours, reading back through everything on her computer and haunting the Archaeology Department's library. She was already reasonably familiar with the period, but there was so much to remember . . . but if she couldn't remember, she'd wing it.

Just for these few seconds, while she allowed herself to relax into the new environment, she let herself be a tourist. Wishing she had a camera, or could pick up a postcard, say a snapshot of the city's most impressive component: Etemenanki, the House of the Platform of Heaven and Earth. The step pyramid loomed above the city, seven storeys, nearly a hundred metres tall. And nearby, the smaller Esagila, the Temple that Raises its Head.

A little touch of Ikkaba, she thought.

If WiRgo!xu and !Ci!ci-tel felt safe, this is just what they'd be doing: gawping. Checking the obvious tourist attractions might be a good way to start her search. Not used to work or danger, the People tended to regard everything as leisure. Was it possible the renegades were just here for a holiday?

Benny made her way down a little hill to the paved road, heading towards the city. Palm trees dotted the plain. To her right was the Euphrates, reed boats moving on the water.

There were hundreds of people on the road, almost all of them heading for the city. Servants and slaves hefted huge packs, merchants led donkeys and camels laden with goods. She joined the river of people. Most of them were too busy staring up at the Ishtar Gate to notice the odd-looking woman in their midst.

They were mostly Babylonians in their linen and wool tunics and turbans, but she spotted some Medes, a group of

Hittites, a wealthy Egyptian family riding horses, and others she didn't recognize. Maybe she wasn't drawing attention because of that rich mixture of clothes, skin tones, hairstyles.

Benny caught the eye of a merchant riding in a cart. 'Excuse me,' she said, 'I've been travelling for a long time, and I've lost track of the date.'

'It's the third of Nisan,' said the man, looking down at her.

Benny glanced at the crowds. 'The New Year's Festival,' she said. The celebration of the brief spring before the searing summer.

'Don't worry,' said the merchant. 'You haven't missed it. It's not over until the eleventh.'

'Thanks,' said Benny, letting herself drift away from the cart, through the crowd. Obviously, the translator was working just fine, using some sort of telepathy – their conversation had probably been in Aramaic.

The Gate was only getting more impressive the closer she got. It was covered in red and white lions and dragons, symbols of the gods. It funnelled the crowd as they walked over a ramp across the moat, between high, crenellated watchtowers. The slap of hundreds of sandals and the clop of hooves echoed on square stones as they passed through the thickness of the city walls and on to a wide paved road. Torches were being lit high on the walls, gushing red flame.

The Processional Way stretched into the distance, Babylon's main street, jammed with people. The babble – ha, the Babel – of voices was overwhelming, as was the smell of sweat and spices and camel dung.

Benny hoped the renegade People had been impressed, if only a little. Human beings, even Serious Primitives, could build big things too.

Maybe WiRgo!xu and !Ci!ci-tel had chosen this time of year because they didn't think God would be ruthless enough to kill so many people. The city was packed, the flow of traffic not letting up as Benny stepped on to the Processional Way, twenty metres wide. The edges of the road were jammed with beggars and buskers, adding their cries and songs to the noise of the crowd. Somewhere she could hear merchants shouting their wares. A small knot of people had formed around a town crier, reciting his messages from memory.

She had thought about trying to organize some kind of evacuation. Empty the known world's greatest city, hundreds of thousands of people displaced. Returning, after the disaster, to discover that city vanished, nothing left but a sharp-edged crater. Not even any ruins. If some miracle happened and she got them all out, she might save all those lives – but she couldn't rescue history.

Benny closed her eyes for a moment, standing still as the crowd jostled around her. If she couldn't save these people, all these people, was there any point in even walking home? Would she even exist any more?

After a while she got off the Processional Way, meandering through the narrow residential streets in search of a tavern. She hoped they weren't all packed with New Year tourists. She didn't fancy sleeping outdoors, even if the evening was warm and clear.

The houses were windowless, faceless, built to reflect the sun's heat. There was no way to tell one from another; anyone might live inside, from a fat merchant to a skinny laundryman. Smoke from brick ovens drifted through their high roofs. She passed people here and there, mostly men, the occasional solo woman. The crowds were away in the city's centre.

The stars were beginning to come out. Benny paused, leaning on a wall, watching the clear sky filling with lights. The stars made her feel weirdly homesick, surrounded by all this *humanity*, longing for St Oscar's mix of aliens. Wanting Joseph to bring her a cup of tea. Wanting to know where she was sleeping tonight.

THE WORLDSPHERE

!Cin-ta!x was making pancakes by hand. The recipe floated on a screen that followed him around the kitchen of his house, but otherwise he really was doing it by hand, whisking the batter while little flecks of the milky stuff lodged in his arm hairs and on the kitchen counter and window. Dawn was breaking over the mountains, a slow lightening from grey to red to orange to yellow.

!Cin-ta!x and his House lived just below the snow line, where his breath smoked in the morning when he went jogging on the trail. He had built it himself with the help of a flock of waldoes: a wide band floating above the tender young plants on antigrav generators.

The House fussed around after him, cleaning up the batter where he spilt or splattered it and generally busybodying. It had sulked for days when he'd first decided to join the Primitive Cooking Interest Group, pointedly doing lots of housework to make up for its lack of kitchen duties. In the end it had joined the IG itself, bitching to the other Houses in the Group and collecting obscure recipes.

!Cin-ta!x put the batter aside to sit, letting the House pick up and clean the whisk and spoons. He normally cooked in the nude, but for this recipe he'd decided to wear an apron to keep the pancakes out of his chest hair and his chest hair out of the pancakes. He headed upstairs for a wash. The House took the apron from him with a sigh of sarcastic thanks.

!Cin-ta!x grinned at himself as he splashed into the floating bath, a sphere of warm water held in place by a force field. His hair was pale blue, complementing the milk colour of his skin. He ducked his head under the water for a moment, and came up for air. The mirror peered back at him with eyes the colour of straw.

The House had developed its overprotective demeanour shortly after the fuss with God, and had never really got over it. They had been together since the House had been built; !Cin-ta!x fancied it had imprinted on him, like a baby bird mistaking a dog for its mother. Mostly it was affectionate, sometimes it was stifling, and he'd storm out in a huff to run on the trail until his dwelling was ready to quit nagging him. In their better moments they spent time discussing literature and playing very bad games of chess.

These days he spent most of his time in the House. A visit was only a solidigram away, but he didn't make, or have, many visitors.

It wasn't that !Cin-ta!x was a recluse. He looked forward to his weekly visits to the village at the base of the mountain, only a few minutes away by travel capsule. He knew most of the People down there, would knock on doors and say hi to most of them. They didn't know who he was, which was why he was here.

It had been difficult to find somewhere that the gossip hadn't reached. !Cin-ta!x wasn't surprised. One of his student projects had been to create a model of just how scuttlebutt travelled through the Sphere. He'd won an award for it. The model predicted that he had a few more years at least before someone in the village realized who he was. Then it would be time to move on, taking the House with him.

Only bad news travels faster than the buzz, his project had concluded.

It had been his own decision to be the Temporal Interest Group's spokesperson, their public face. They had been just like any IG, no membership lists, no joining procedure, nothing that would let the curious find out for certain who belonged to the group, who'd left, who'd been talking to them. But when God had found out about their experiments, someone had had to do the explaining. !Cin-ta!x had volunteered.

TIG no longer existed. That is, the members of the Group had voluntarily stopped discussing their Interest in the Temporal. !Cin-ta!x still kept in contact with most of them. Like them, he'd hooked up with dozens of other Interest Groups, keeping themselves busy with cooking, sports, alien languages, embroidery. Stuff totally unrelated to time, time travel, dimensional engineering, the whole cluster of technologies they'd been investigating.

The batter needed to sit for half an hour. Once he'd had breakfast, he'd wander down to the village, take some pancakes with him for the local kids to try. Maybe have a swim in the lake. It was a nice, quiet life, for the time being.

He was washing his hair when the call came.

Extract from the Memoirs of Bernice Summerfield

Every woman is born with an alarm bell. If we're taught to be too polite, we forget to trust that internal warning, that this-is-wrong feeling – and we ignore that instinctive voice at our peril. Years of adventuring has made me keep an ear out for that telltale ringing sound.

I spent what must have been half an hour wandering up and down those residential streets, wondering if I was ever going to find somewhere to stay. Just as I was resigning myself to sneaking on to someone's roof to sleep, a man leaning against a house wall gave me a smile from behind his bushy beard. 'You look lost,' he said.

Rrring! I took my hands out of my pockets, faced him, and said, 'I'm looking for a tavern. Do you know where I can find one?'

'A tavern, eh?' He pointed. 'There are a few along the next street. Go up to the end and turn left – *you* shouldn't have any trouble finding them.'

'Thanks,' I said. I took a couple of steps back, keeping the distance between us, and started walking away.

When I glanced back, I saw he was following me. I stopped and faced him again, keeping my hands up, my face calm and neutral. 'What do you want?' I said.

He looked me up and down. He was a head taller than I was, dressed in the usual wool tunic and sandals. He had terrible teeth. 'If you're looking for somewhere to sleep,' he said, 'there's a spare bed at my house. My wife's away, and it's lonely. Why don't you save your money and come back with me?'

'No, thanks,' I said firmly.

He kept looking at me, and I could read his tiny brain as he tried to decide how far he could go. Was I fair game because I was a foreigner, or because I was out by myself at night – obviously a sex worker, on my way to the inn and a night's work?

He took a step towards me. 'I'm not interested,' I said, loudly, wondering if my voice could penetrate the brick walls of the houses. 'Stay where you are.'

'Come on,' he said. 'I like exotic women. I'm wealthy. I'll give you a meal.'

'I'm not interested,' I said. 'Leave me alone.'

He lunged, grabbing my wrist. I turned my hand, grabbed his wrist from the outside, and spun out of the grip, smashing the heel of my other hand against the inside of his elbow. The same movement I'd had drilled into me in endless hand-to-hand-combat classes and later in self-defence lessons, as instinctive as catching a ball.

He yelped in surprise and pain, almost losing his balance. I took the opportunity to pull his arm behind his back and shove his face up against the wall of a nearby house.

'I wonder,' I said, pushing my knee into the small of his back, 'whether you think you can treat any woman like that.'

'Let me go, you whore!' he said, sounding gratifyingly astonished. The way I was holding him, he couldn't even turn his head. His free arm flailed, unable to reach me.

'Or if you think it's only all right to attack harlots. You'd never touch a woman of *character*, oh no.'

I'd fought off bug-eyed monsters and marauding knights in my time, but this was lots more fun. As well as being heart-thumpingly terrifying. But you don't think about that at the time.

'You dishonour the Goddess of love,' I improvised. 'Get out of my sight, and never touch another harlot unless she invites you. Do you understand?'

He didn't answer, so I gave his arm a little twist, and he grunted what I hoped was agreement. I gave him a shove so that he fell on the ground a little distance from me.

He looked at me, and I thought for a moment I was going to have to really thump him. But then he saw that a few people had come out of their houses, wondering what all the shouting was about. He got up, spat on the ground, and walked off, brushing the dust from his tunic.

I watched him go, until he turned a corner and was lost from sight. The people in the doorways were whispering, staring at me. They didn't have much time for harlots, either.

I sighed. Edward Watkinson hadn't had to spend all his time fending off sleazebags with his bullwhip. 'Welcome to

Earth,' I told myself, and went in search of a tavern and (relative) safety.

At least Mr Hands' directions had been right. After a couple of blocks I found myself on a thoroughfare, crowded with people, dancing and eating. It was a street party, lit by oil lamps and a big fire built in the middle of the road. Musicians were jamming a long, spiralling tune.

I watched them for a few minutes, rather wishing I could just join in. This was like the metaphoric Babylon – people stuffing themselves with dates and booze, necking by the fire or at the fringes, dancing underneath the stars.

They were king of the castle, and they knew it. The greatest city in the known world, the hub of an empire that stretched from the Red Sea to the Gulf to the Median empire in the north and east. They even threatened Egypt's borders. Plenty of wealth and slaves to go around, plenty to celebrate at the New Year's Festival. Later, it would be the Persians' turn, or the Egyptians', or the Greeks', but for now, the Babylonians were number one.

I moved along the edge of the party, keeping an eye out for any more trouble, but the crowd were too busy having a good time to hassle me. The leftover adrenaline was starting to make me feel shaky and ill, the way stage fright sometimes hits you after the actual performance. I was remembering a knife held to my throat in a truck on Jaris, remembering the struggle in the cramped space, the raw terror and the raw determination to survive.

I really just wanted to sit down for a bit.

There were a couple of taverns, their clients spilling out and merging with the street party. I headed towards one.

Then I saw the redhead.

It was his hair that caught my eye – dark ginger in a sea of black, catching the light of a torch flame. He was huddled against a wall, watching the party with wide eyes.

For a moment I thought it might be !Ci!ci-tel, with his wavy, cartoon-orange hair, and my heart gave a lurch of excitement. But the face was too sharp, and I saw that the man was wearing Victorian or maybe Edwardian clothes, a high-collared shirt under a dark suit with narrow lapels. Over the top he was wearing a djellaba, one of those loose white Arab cloaks, complete with headdress.

If I'd been a bit sharper, I'd have hidden before he could see me. But he looked up and spotted me, stared for several seconds with his mouth open. When I started to push towards him through the crowd, he bolted.

For the next minute we both ran in slow motion, bumping into and tripping over people, and in my case running right into a table and scattering persimmons all over the ground. Someone helped me up, both of us slipping in the crushed fruit.

For a moment, I thought I'd lost the redhead – then I saw a flash of white as he pushed free of the crowd and ran down a side street.

I pelted after him, staying close to the buildings, and turned down the street. It was another anonymous lane, squeezed between rows of blocky faceless houses. The djellaba billowed out behind him as he ran, making him look like a departing ghost.

'Wait!' I shouted, which isn't easy when you're running full tilt over paving stones. He didn't stop, just turned down another alley.

I dodged into the alley right before that one, and nearly collided with him – he'd turned again on to another of the narrow streets.

We stared at each other for about a quarter of a second, each of us probably looking as goofy and astonished as the other. He was in his late twenties or early thirties, with high cheekbones and a five o'clock shadow.

Then I grabbed for his djellaba, and he struggled, backing away with a little gasp of terror. 'It's all right!' I was saying, trying not to shout. 'I want to help you!'

He slipped out of the white cloth and was running again. I dropped the cloak and ran after him.

We ran in silence, our footsteps and the harsh sound of our breathing echoing back at us from the houses. I was gaining on him, a little at a time, as we twisted and turned like rats through a maze.

He turned one corner, and suddenly there was a loud splash. I jogged around the corner and skidded to a halt barely a metre from one of the great canals.

I bent over, hands on my thighs, breathing hard, and waited. In a moment he surfaced, looking as though he was struggling. How deep was the canal? 'Hey!' I shouted. 'Are you all right?'

He disappeared from view again. It was dark – all I'd been able to see was the paler colour of his face, standing out against the black water. Now I couldn't see anything, my eyes straining in the night. 'Hey!' I shouted again, but there was nothing.

There was a horrible, silent moment.

Then I saw him a few metres away, looking back at me, just his head poking up from the water. He turned and started swimming away.

For a moment, I almost jumped in after him, but there was a path that followed the canal – I didn't want to get my satchel wet, and besides, I could probably keep up with him. Splashing noises echoed from the high walls of the buildings as I followed.

He must have swum, fast, for five minutes. I had to jog to keep him in sight. After a while I saw him head for the bank, maybe a hundred metres ahead. I picked up speed. There were people and lights ahead – a small crowd outside one of the large houses. Yet another party.

I saw the redhead pull himself up into the garden in front of the house, squashing the onions. Some of the partygoers stopped their chatter as I ran up. They looked back and forth between us. Elegant ladies and wealthy men, puzzled by the pale and gasping creatures who had suddenly appeared.

The redhead saw me and pushed past them, shouting something I couldn't make out. He'd gone into the house by the time I reached the crowd.

'I'm so sorry,' I said, as the Babylonians stared at me. 'He's had far too much to drink. I'd better just pop inside and take him home!'

Inside, the doorkeeper was snoring gently, a beer bowl by his side. I squeezed through a narrow hallway full of the smell of cooking, past a couple of people snogging against a wall, and found myself in a large, square courtyard.

It was full of people, nobles sitting on wooden chairs and stools, or standing and talking, getting drunk on beer and wine. A small band played loudly in one corner, while a pair of jugglers stood in the centre, moving in time with the music. Doorways led off the courtyard to the rooms of the house.

I looked around. The redhead was arguing with a tall woman, while an amused crowd formed around the pair of them.

'Is he one of your entertainers, Ninan?' asked someone, sipping from a bowl.

The woman waved her hand at him, impatiently. 'Be quiet, Bel-ibni,' she said. 'The man's accent is almost impenetrable. Say that again, fellow.'

The man said slowly, 'May I . . . stay here . . . minute?'

Ninan, the lady, shook her head. 'I'm sorry, I just can't understand what you're saying.'

'Do you want me to send for the police?' asked a woman – a servant, I guessed.

Ninan shook her head. 'Look at him, the poor thing is half drowned and starved.' She reached out and touched his hair, fingering it as though she expected the odd colour to come off. He stared at her. 'What are we going to do with you, eh?'

I stepped up. 'Look,' said a woman, 'it's another of them!'

'I'm very sorry about this,' I said, in what was probably perfect Aramaic. The man stopped staring at Ninan and started staring at me. He was dripping, bewildered, and understandably, he was scared half to death. 'I'd better take him home!'

'What's going on?' said Ninan. 'Who are the pair of you?'

'Er,' I said, 'we're travellers.'

She looked me up and down. 'You have come from some country beyond the ones I know,' she said. 'One of the cold lands, beyond the sea?'

'Even further than that,' I said. I took the redhead by the arm, and he almost jumped out of his skin, staring at my hand. 'Calm down,' I whispered. 'She's right, your Aramaic is terrible. I'll get you out of here. You'll be all right.'

He nodded, but he was shaking so badly that I let him go. He gripped his arm, as though my touch might be poisonous. 'Will you come with me?' I said. 'Because let me tell you, I'm puffed from chasing you around this damn city. If you'd rather take your chances, I'll leave you to it.'

'I'll come with you,' he said quietly.

'You see,' I said, smiling at the partygoers. 'He just needs to sleep it off.' One or two of them laughed.

'I want to talk to you, young lady,' said Ninan. 'Come back here tomorrow.'

'Um, sure,' I said. 'In the morning?'

Ninan glanced around at the party. 'Late in the morning,' she said, and laughed.

Extract ends

!Cin-ta!x was talking to God, which was not something he did every day. In fact, ever since the Treaty problem, they'd had as little contact with each other as possible. Though for all !Cin-ta!x knew, God was monitoring everything he did. Well, he cooked pancakes, and he jogged, and he discussed poetry with his house.

He sat in his living room, wearing a brightly patterned dressing gown. The House was fidgeting, nervous as hell. God was a pleasant male voice, seeming to come from all around him. 'So you see why we need your help,' it was saying.

'What if I refuse?' said !Cin-ta!x. 'Just joking.'

'You're still bitter.'

'It was my decision to be the figurehead,' said !Cin-ta!x, 'of course. Sometimes, though, I wish People had shorter memories . . .'

'I wish I could offer to do something about it,' said God. 'But there are some forces even I can't control.'

!Cin-ta!x laughed. 'Yes indeed,' he said. 'And that's when you need to call in the experts. Just let me have breakfast, give me directions, and I'll be right there.'

'Bring the others,' said God.

'Can you guarantee their anonymity?'

'That much I can do,' God promised. 'Everything's got to be kept under wraps this time. I mean it. One leak and we're dead.'

'All right then,' said !Cin-ta!x. He towelled his damp blue hair. 'How many of us are there, God?'

'Members of the former Temporal Interest Group? My count was twenty-two.'

That was a couple more than even !Cin-ta!x had known about. He'd have to look into that later. 'I meant, how many People live the way I do – keeping on the run, trying to stay ahead of the past? It's like a wave that catches up with you, over and over . . .'

'Four million, twenty two thousand, eight hundred and six,' said God. 'Those are the ones I know about, anyway.'

'We ought to form an Interest Group,' sighed !Cin-ta!x.

Extract from the Memoirs of Bernice Summerfield

I found a tavern with a free room, and stuffed the redhead into it. He perched damply in the corner, arms clutching his bony knees, and stared at me as though I'd grown an extra nose. The brick floor was covered with rough reed mats. I sat down and sighed.

I really didn't need another problem. Not that I had a lot of problems, you understand, just one particularly enormous one. Tomorrow I was going to have to start searching for WiRgo!xu and !Ci!ci-tel. Tonight I wanted to make sure this chap wasn't going to do anything stupid – like run away or try to kill me – and get some badly needed Zs.

I decided to take the Sherlock Holmes route. 'All right,' I said. 'You look as though you date from the late nineteenth or early twentieth century.' I drummed my fingers on my lower lip, considering. 'You probably stumbled across the Path, though how you could see it or get on to it without technological help I don't know. Never mind that. Since you're obviously not a local, you're probably an explorer of some kind.' It struck me. 'An archaeologist?'

'Linguist,' said the man softly.

That explained his stumbling Aramaic – it had been good

enough for my translator to manage, but his pronunciation had been centuries out of whack. 'You're English,' I said, 'unless this thing is confusing me.' The translation device was starting to pinch my ear.

'You're also English,' said the man, and started, as though he'd caught himself talking.

'Not quite. I'm Bernice Summerfield.' I held out my hand. He flinched. 'Holder of the Edward Watkinson Chair of Archaeology,' I finished limply. He looked as though he wanted to tie himself into a knot and tighten until he disappeared.

'You haven't seen anyone else . . . out of place?' I asked. 'Anyone who shouldn't be here, like us?' He shook his head.

It didn't make sense. If *I'd* stumbled back in time by accident, I'd have been hugely relieved to find another time traveller – and possibly a way to get home. What was going on here?

I lit a sesame-oil lamp, and the small room began to fill with a warm stir-fry smell. He looked pale in the yellow light. 'Have you been here long?' I asked. 'Have you had anything to eat?' He shook his head. 'Well, do you *want* something to eat? It sounds like everyone's still up – I'm sure we could get something . . .' He didn't say anything. 'You could at least tell me your name.'

'Lafayette,' he said, automatically.

'Look, er, Mr Lafayette,' I said. 'I'm not going to bite. I promise I'll try to help you get back to your own time. Once I've finished what I came to do.'

Lafayette took a deep breath and said, 'Did you create the Path?'

'I was sent to find the two People who made it, and take them back . . . home.' I wanted to tell him more, try to get his trust, but it was hard to know what would be the right thing to do. I messed up my hair in frustration, making him jump.

'Can I ask you a question?' I said. 'Look, why are you so frightened of me? I'm used to intimidating my students, but I would have thought you'd be pleased to bump into another time traveller. Especially if you got here by accident.'

'You are on fire,' he said.

* * *

I didn't get much more out of him after that. I decided that, if he was going to run away or attack me, he would already have tried it.

In the middle of the night I woke up with a start, but Lafayette was lying curled up on the mats, snoring gently. He looked completely limp, as though he'd desperately needed the sleep. He'd probably been wandering in bewilderment ever since he'd reached Babylon – at least a day, long enough to start on a beard.

If he calmed down a bit, he could help me search for the People. I could use an extra pair of eyes. I was already having depressing thoughts about needles and haystacks.

And having a man with me would probably mean I wouldn't be hassled again. I had to smile.

Were WiRgo!xu and !Ci!ci-tel lying awake, out there somewhere, wondering if they'd done the right thing, wondering if they'd been followed?

Lafayette stirred in his sleep, muttering something. I think he talked more when he was asleep than when he was awake.

You are on fire.

What did he mean?

I decided to try to find out in the morning. I also decided that if I was going to search this crammed and noisy city, I was going to need help from high places.

Extract ends

3

LANGUAGE

*Every Babylonian woman must, once in her life, go
and sit in the temple of Ishtar, and have sex with a
stranger . . . she may not return home until a man has
thrown a silver coin into her lap, and taken her outside
the temple to lie with her. As he throws the coin, he
must say, 'In the name of the goddess Ishtar.' . . . Once
she has given herself up, her duty to the goddess has
been done, and she can go home.*

– Herodotus

Something went thump. Lafayette jerked out of sleep and
opened his eyes.

Miss Summerfield was awake, blinking and muttering and
looking for the source of the noise. Something heavy, falling . . . on to the floor?

They both saw the snake at the same moment. It was a
narrow, glossy length of brown, creeping across the floor.
They scrambled backwards, trying not to get the slithering
creature's attention.

They looked at each other, backs pressed to the walls.

'Look,' whispered Miss Summerfield. She nodded at the
grille high in one whitewashed wall, a series of oval holes
which let in the breeze. The snake must have entered through
it, Lafayette realized, then travelled across the rafters until it
lost its hold.

The reptile's head moved around, a curious tongue darting in and out. 'Don't panic,' said Miss Summerfield. 'Stay calm, I'll think of something in a moment . . .' She looked at the grid again. 'How did they know we were here?'

They? 'You mean the ones who built the Path?'

She nodded, her eyes glued to the snake. 'I think they're trying to kill us.'

'Then they're not making a very good job of it,' said Lafayette. He picked up the snake, which curled and wriggled in lazy annoyance. He pushed aside the curtain in the doorway and threw it out into the hall, prompting a yell of protest from outside.

Miss Summerfield was looking at him in surprise. He said, 'It's only an Aesculapian snake. They're not poisonous. One got into my tent last month.'

She slouched against the wall. 'Thanks.'

In the dim light, he could still see the flickering aura around her. It was not quite so spectacular as before, as though his eyes had adjusted to its light.

Her entire body was covered by a pale impression of flames. It reminded him of a beaker of methylated spirits, accidentally set alight during a chemistry class a dozen years ago. A soft, watery flame.

It gave her the appearance of an angel, or of some supernatural creature. But her speech, her rugged clothes, the way she moved more like a labourer than a woman – none of that was angelic. He half expected her to spit, or to take out a packet of cigarettes.

She made his spine and his scalp tingle. He had dreamt about the Path all night, sensing her gentle fire only a few feet away.

She grabbed her hair and forced the fingers of both hands through it, as though roughly combing it. It was cut in a very short, practical style, as mannish as her clothes. It served to emphasize her delicate face, her lithe body.

Lafayette stopped staring at her. While she remained an unknown quantity, he decided, she deserved no less courtesy than any lady.

Extract from the Memoirs of Bernice Summerfield

Lafayette and I had breakfast together – dates and onions and two different kinds of bread, both unleavened. And a jug of the ubiquitous beer. I wasn't quite willing to risk the water, and the thick beer was surprisingly good – tasting of barley, yeast, date juice, and the refreshing kick of ethanol. Not too much of it, though, so I could avoid seeing little pink drones for the rest of the day.

The theory Watkinson had been toying with – that civilization was created in order to ensure a supply of beer – was an idea close to my heart. Hunter-gatherers certainly would have noticed the interesting results when their stored grain fermented. The theory went that they liked it so much that they started planting and harvesting barley specifically to make beer, and all the other trappings of society like pottery, bureaucracy and alcoholism grew up around that industry. Even breadmaking had just been an offshoot of brewing.

The Babylonians were only the latest in a long line of Mesopotamians. The originals had been the Sumerians, millennia ago – and they'd used something like two-fifths of their grain harvest for brewing. Beer was still an important part of the local diet. The Babylonians had inherited their religion, their writing, and their penchant for the raising of the wrist.

The trouble with the beer-first theory was that it was hard to imagine bands of drunken hunter-gatherers surviving for long, as they fell off cliffs and tripped over mammoths. Still, I couldn't help but like the idea that the point of human civilization was the pint.

Pondering the point of human existence made me frown. I decided we'd take brekkie back to our room instead of eating in the kitchen. I didn't want to be surrounded by all those people, reminded what was depending on me.

Besides, every eye was on us. Despite all the tourists, we stood out, in our hopelessly anachronistic clothes and our sunburns. A little girl jumped up on a table and touched Lafayette's red hair, as though checking it was real, just as

Ninan had. Her mother shouted at her and she ran away giggling.

Maybe it would be useful to be conspicuous, hopefully get WiRgo!xu and !Ci!ci-tel's attention. It would be much easier if they came to me. They might arrive waving weapons, but at least I'd be able to tell them about the danger they were in. Surely the knowledge of imminently being blown into tiny bits is enough to sway any baddie.

Unless, despite all the personality projections and calculations, they were out of their minds.

But right now, I was worried about attracting the wrong attention. There were some very seedy individuals in the inn, guzzling beer for breakfast and looking like they'd enjoy eating a couple of foreign weirdos as a chaser.

So Mr Lafayette and I sat opposite each other, on our reed mats. He ate nervously, then hungrily, wolfing down the dates and leaving the onions. He was thin, with high cheekbones and watercolour-blue eyes. His red hair was a mess, despite his trying to arrange it, and his face was covered with orange stubble. He had long fingers with knuckles like knots – his hands looked too large to go with the rest of him.

I waited until he was slowing down a bit, and then asked, 'What date was it when you left?'

He hesitated, then answered, 'December the twelfth, 1901. That's Anno Domini,' he added helpfully.

I snapped my fingers, making him start. 'Sorry,' I said. 'But I'll bet you're part of Robert Koldewey's expedition.'

He looked at me in surprise. 'What was the date when you left?' he asked.

'2594,' I told him.

He nodded slowly, believing me. 'And yet you have heard of the Deutsche Orient-Gesellschaft expedition.'

'Of course,' I said. 'It's a landmark in archaeology. I studied it at school. The first properly scientific excavation of Babylon. Koldewey was a pioneer.' And was interrupted, after eighteen years' work, by World War One – sixteen years in Lafayette's future.

I frowned, waiting for the awkward questions. But he said, 'Then you took advantage of the Path. You used it to travel here in order to find its creators.'

Good sign – he was sufficiently over the initial shock that he was able to think about his situation. 'That's right,' I said.

'How many centuries does it cross?' he said. 'There might be many others who stumbled upon it by accident, and found themselves here.'

'I had to use special machinery to see the Path, let alone step on to it. It's invisible and unreachable without the right devices.'

Lafayette was shaking his head. 'One of our handlers found it,' he said. 'And I was able to see it with my own eyes.'

I didn't like the sound of that. 'I hope you were the only ones,' I said, 'because otherwise – oh, *wonderful*. We'll have to keep an eye out for anyone else who shouldn't be here . . .' *Another* problem.

'If you are from the twenty-sixth century,' Lafayette said, 'then you must know everything there is to know about the ruins of Babylon. We are still at the beginning of understanding.'

'I can't tell you,' I said. 'I can't give you any knowledge of the future, anything that could change my own history. D'you see?'

He thought about it, but looked disappointed. He'd be even more disappointed if I'd told him that, about eighty years later, Saddam Hussein would have Babylon restored as a sort of amusement park, bulldozing what was left of its walls and relics. Koldewey's expedition was part of a brief window of enquiry.

'Listen,' I said. 'The lady we met last night asked me to pay her a visit this morning. If I can win her over, she might be able to give me some help tracking down the renegades. But I'm afraid it's mostly going to be legwork.' He looked at me blankly. 'Like a police detective. Walking all over the city and asking questions.'

'Ah,' said Lafayette. 'Leg work.'

'Look,' I said, 'you'd better come with me. And work on that accent!'

He almost smiled.

* * *

We arrived at Ninan's house late in the morning, just as she'd said. I had to ask directions a couple of times, but when I mentioned her name, people knew just which way to point.

The light was brilliant, the sky a bright pale blue. We passed a shrine being rebuilt by a crew of slaves and labourers, freshly baked yellow-white bricks being slotted into place. Here, everything was made of mud. Mud they had, in truckloads. Stone they didn't have. But since it almost never rained, you could happily build your house from mud without it melting into slime in the next downpour.

King Nabu-kudurri-usur[1] was making his mark, vigorously building, rebuilding, reinstating traditions and religious practices that had fallen into disuse.

They sang as they worked. 'As I walked down the street, I saw two harlots . . .'

Lafayette and I both stared around at the great buildings, at the shrine and statues, at the crowds. We didn't speak, drinking in the city.

We were brought back to Earth by the details of the residential streets. We had to squeeze past donkeys carrying firewood or rubbish, even a camel laden with vegetables. More than once, hands reached out of the crowd to touch Lafayette's red hair. He jumped, every time, but they were only curious. I nearly tripped over a legless beggar who shook his crutches angrily at me.

At last we got there. Ninan's doorkeeper recognized me. 'How's your head?' I asked, smiling. He grunted, squinting in the bright light, and let us in.

Ninan was in the courtyard, wearing a long dress that hid the shape of her body. She was eating apricots and peaches from a bowl. 'Hello again,' she said. 'You brought your confused friend. I'm glad. Have a seat.'

I'd explained the translator to Lafayette. He had just accepted it, the inevitable result of the progress of technology. I hoped he really was coping, and wasn't storing up a huge charge of future shock. The conversation would be confusing – from his point

[1] Nebuchadnezzar, or Nebuchadrezzar.

of view, I'd be speaking in English, while our hostess would be using Aramaic.[2]

Ninan smiled, showing good teeth. She had large brown eyes and a high forehead. I guessed she was in her forties, round-hipped, small-breasted, healthy as a horse and thoroughly rich. 'What's your name, young woman?' she said.

'Bernice Summerfield, my lady,' I said. 'I'm usually called Benny. This is John Lafayette.' Lafayette looked up at the sound of his name. He'd been scowling and staring at the ground. Listening hard. I hid a smile. He probably wanted to be taking notes.

'Well then, Beni,' she said, offering me the bowl of fruit. 'You and your friend had all my guests talking last night. And talking, and talking,' she laughed. 'Where do you come from?'

'Oh,' I said, 'a long way away. You've probably never heard of it.'

She sat forward a little. 'Go on,' she said. 'Where were you born?'

'Well, have you heard of Beta Caprisis?' I said. Not surprisingly, she hadn't. 'These days I'm from Dellah. I travel a great deal.'

'You do?' she sighed. 'You must tell me all about it.'

Aha. 'A great lady like you must have visited many lands,' I said.

'I wish I had,' she said. 'I wish I had. I exchange letters with people from Egypt and Lydia and with many Assyrians, but . . . Go on, Beni. I don't have anything to do until this afternoon. Tell me about your travels.'

I had her interest. Now all I had to do was keep it.

Extract ends

---

[2] Language is, of course, one of the greatest obstacles to the explorer, especially anywhere off the beaten track – whether in space or in time. I'm terribly spoilt thanks to computerized translation. Still, you can't rely on it too much. A faulty dictionary file, and the mistranslations it caused, could have led to war between the explorers and the natives on the newly discovered world of Jalkejai, but fortunately for the explorers the natives used group sex to resolve their conflicts. (Rumours that the dictionary file had been deliberately sabotaged by the explorers are probably entirely true.)

Lafayette's forehead rested on his arms. He didn't dare look up. On the ground next to him, Miss Summerfield was also receiving a massage from one of Lady Ninan's servants. The servant wore a knee-length tunic, but Miss Summerfield was quite naked, not even covered by a towel. She did not seem concerned in the slightest.

Ninan had insisted they take advantage of her bathroom. Miss Summerfield had shooed him into the narrow room, translating all the while, overriding his protests. This was a luxury, he realized – he'd seen the ordinary people washing themselves in the canals. The soap was rough as sackcloth, but the water was blessedly cool.

After a couple of hours of listening to Ninan, Lafayette had begun to catch words and phrases, enough to follow the gist of the conversation. Aramaic had, naturally, changed considerably over the centuries; and he was chiefly familiar with it as a written tongue. He wondered, if he encountered a Greek somewhere in the city, if he would be able to hold a conversation with them.

He knew the feel of ancient things, and this Babylon did not feel as ancient as some of the tablets and bricks he had handled. Of course it didn't; it was centuries younger, and many of the buildings were new, part of the reconstruction. And yet, the city was old, old enough that its kings practised archaeology of their own.

His mind wandered as the servant mercilessly pummelled his shoulders. A breeze was blowing, cooling the noon warmth of the bathroom, and he was surrounded by the comfort of ancient things. Lafayette imagined leaving the city, travelling to Athens or a very young Rome, to the conquered Holy Land or even as far as Britain. Endlessly travelling, adventuring, never quite at home.

Benny.

There was no reason to doubt the extraordinary stories Miss Summerfield had told Ninan. Lafayette could tell that she was modifying some of the details of her journeys, the better to have Ninan understand them. But she had clearly travelled beyond the Earth, and through time. Perhaps, to her, this journey to Babylon was merely another trip, no more momentous than his own journey to Turkish Arabia.

Certainly she had come better prepared than he had. After two days of wandering the city, starving, sunburning and struggling to be understood, he had been cursing himself for not having the sense to turn back to the camp. He had taken the mysterious Path without proper provisions, with nothing more than a canteen of water, his pistol and the clothes he was wearing.

If he was able to return, he would have to invent a very good story to explain his absence.

He realized he had almost fallen asleep under the servant's soothing hands. He was about to look around for Miss Summerfield, and then he remembered. 'Ahem,' he coughed.

'You can get up,' he heard her say. 'I'm decent.'

She was decent, just barely – he glimpsed the white skin of her breasts as she fastened the last button of her shirt. She smiled at him – had she *meant* him to see?

Lafayette had insisted on keeping his trousers on during the massage, to the confusion of his masseuse. After chattering at him in Aramaic and then in another tongue he didn't recognize, the slave had shrugged, pushed him face down on to the mat, straddled his hips and gone to work. At least the slave had not insisted on assisting him with his bath.

Lafayette sat up. Miss Summerfield held her jacket and her hat, wearing only her shirt and trousers. Her feet were bare. Lafayette thought they were shapely, but then, he had no real standard by which to compare them.

He wished he could hide his face in his arms again.

'You can tell the hired help from the actual slaves,' Miss Summerfield was saying, 'by their tattoos. Did you notice?'

Lafayette said, 'I saw a rough tattoo on the wrist of my, er, attendant.'

Miss Summerfield nodded. 'She's the property of the Temple of Marduk.'

Lafayette struggled into his shirt. 'Did the lady Ninan say she would help you?'

Miss Summerfield frowned, pulling on her boots. 'Not exactly. I think she was convinced by my story – I told her I was searching for a pair of travellers who had stolen something of mine. She said she could talk to her friends in the police, but she couldn't promise anything.'

She sat back. 'Still, it's a start. We agreed that I should start by checking the popular sights.' She repeated her earlier gesture, combing her fingers through her hair in frustration. 'I wish I had a brilliant, clever plan, but I don't.'

'Legwork?' suggested Lafayette, after a moment.

'Legwork,' agreed Miss Summerfield. 'Let's get working. Oh, and by the way, we're invited to a party.'

Extract from the Memoirs of Bernice Summerfield

Lafayette and I spent the rest of the day walking around the city. Sometimes the streets were so jammed we had to hold hands, weaving slowly in and out between the families and the sightseers and the performers.[3]

The most important parts of the New Year Ceremony would be taking place behind closed doors – rituals in the temples, with the King and the most important priests and priestesses. But there would be plenty of processions and partying down to keep the population happy.

First port of call: the marketplace, where I spent half an hour haggling for silver. I'd brought a little bag of goodies, some old jewellery, some miniature gourmet foods. In the end I buckled and even sold my spare booze. But now we had plenty of local cash for the next few days.

'You want to go native?' I asked Lafayette. He'd been trying to follow the bargaining, scowling so hard with concentration that one pedlar asked if he had a headache. 'While we're about it, we could buy you some local clothes.'

'I'm comfortable as I am.'

---

[3] My diary says, 'Lafayette wasn't keen on this hand-holding thing, but he didn't object too strenuously. He's cute when he's embarrassed. He doesn't say much, but there's a lot going on under the surface, I think. Plus I caught him trying to get a look at me when I was putting my shirt back on, cheeky thing.'

'Suit yourself, ha ha,' I said. 'But let me know if you change your mind.'

I had a short list of places to visit, thanks to Ninan's suggestions. On our way to the first, I showed Lafayette the solidigrams God had provided. They were a circular base with a miniature power supply.

Lafayette took them from me and stared at them hard. They were projections, but solid, like statuettes, about fifteen centimetres high. Full-coloured and fully detailed. He held them at arm's length, as though expecting them to move or speak.

'Now look,' I said. 'Push your thumb into the control again.'

The little image of !Ci!ci-tel changed. His skin and eyes darkened, his hair became black and curly, and he developed the beginnings of a beard.

Lafayette stared at the statue. 'Oh,' he said. 'I understand. This is the same man, disguised as a Babylonian.'

'Spot on,' I said. 'With a bit of legerdemain we can show the shopkeepers and the beggars both versions.'

The crowds were thin as the locals went indoors to avoid the sun. I pulled down my hat as we walked. Lafayette said, 'Even if they have translators like yours, they may still say or do things which will give away their origins.'

'Very true. They only had access to the most basic information. You know, I really should tell you more about all this. I –'

We turned a corner, and both of us stopped.

'Well,' said Lafayette, after a full minute had passed.

We'd come to a sort of courtyard, beneath the northeastern corner of the King's palace. Despite the heat, there were a few tourists about, gawping up at the building.

'I really wish I'd brought a camera,' I sighed.

A series of narrow arches held up a terraced roof, rising in seven steps from the left to the right. It must have been twenty-four, twenty-five metres high at the top.

There was a garden planted on the roof. Palm trees, fruit trees, rising above beds of herbs and shrubs. There was a constant noise from inside the building, and you could see the water trickling down the terraces, just enough to keep the soil moist. There must have been holes in the roof – fingers of sunlight penetrated to the archways below.

'I wish I could get inside,' I said. 'I want a look at the irrigation machine. I want blueprints, I want photographs, I want to be able to *publish*. Ooogh!⁴'

Lafayette wasn't listening. 'It's actually them,' he said. 'The Hanging Gardens of Babylon. One of the Seven Wonders of the Ancient World.'

I was looking around the courtyard. No sign of either of the People, but there were some beggars and souvenir sellers I wanted to try asking. There were a few soldiers about – they'd be worth a try as well. I was glad of the extra cash I'd picked up.

'The Hanging Gardens of Babylon,' said Lafayette again.

I looked at him. I don't think he was blinking. 'Hey,' I said. 'Are you all right?'

He just kept staring. I touched his arm, and he grabbed my hand and nearly fell over.

'Calm down, calm down!' I said. He blinked, rapidly, and I thought I saw something shift inside his eyes.

'I'm all right,' he said, after a moment. 'It's just the surprise.'

I frowned. 'You're sure?'

He nodded. 'Yes, yes. Let's ask our questions.'

And a fat lot of good that did us. No one remembered seeing either of the renegades, or anyone acting in a memorably bizarre way.

The next stop on our list was Marduk's temple, but I dragged Lafayette into an inn for some lunch first. It was still stifling, but the worst of the day's heat was past. I insisted on putting some sunscreen on Lafayette's face. He let me, without comment, closing his eyes as I rubbed the stuff into his skin. He'd had a shave at Ninan's, and his skin was still pink with all that scraping.

We ate lentil and carrot stew, flavoured with cumin and

---

⁴ The last was a noise of intense academic frustration.

coriander, and drank more of the beer. 'All right,' I said. 'I'll tell you the story. Are you up to it?'

'Yes,' he said, with a small flash of teeth. A Lafayette smile? It changed his whole face: even his eyes lit up for a moment. 'I've seen the Hanging Gardens. Nothing can astonish me.'

'Fair enough. You already know that I'm from the future, that I've travelled to other worlds and met the beings who live there.' He nodded hesitantly. 'The two renegades we're looking for are both members of a race who call themselves the People. They're incredibly advanced; even their machines are intelligent.' But I'm not telling you about the Worldsphere, or God, not any of that. Not yette, Lafayette. 'They look close to human, but they're not human beings.'

The solidigrams were on the table between us. Lafayette thumbed the control, changing !Ci!ci-tel back to his original appearance. He was counting the tiny, perfect fingers on the image. Six on the right hand, seven on the left. And that oddly coloured skin, more like parchment than any human skin colour, and the bright orange hair . . .

'They can easily alter their appearance,' I said. 'Actually, there's not a lot they can't do.'

'Why are they here?' whispered Lafayette. 'Are they inventors, testing some new device for walking between the centuries?'

'There's more to it than that, I'm sure,' I said.

'What do they want here? What could such distant, strange people want with Babylon?'

'I wish I knew.'

'I wonder that this has not happened before,' said Lafayette. 'If such things are possible, then they should be commonplace. Travellers from future centuries ought to visit the King.'

'Time travel is rare,' I said. 'It's very difficult, and it's usually illegal. WiRgo!xu and !Ci!ci-tel are dangerous because they might change history.'

Lafayette's eyes had the flat, large-pupilled look I was beginning to associate with his *totally* understanding what I was telling him. 'They might try to influence politics, or the outcome of a war,' he said. 'Especially if they have some knowledge of history. Perhaps they plan to kill Nebuchadnezzar. Or provide his armies with new weapons.' He was catching on far too fast. 'But why? Why should it concern them?'

'I don't think they're here with a plan,' I said. 'I think they're running away. They're using ancient Babylon as a sort of hideaway. The People can't let anyone know this has happened – WiRgo!xu and !Ci!ci-tel probably think they won't dare send anyone after them.'

'Then – you are a sort of unofficial agent of these People.' I could hear the capital 'P' when he said it.

'That's right. I've got about four days to find them.'

'What will happen at the end of that time?'

I toyed with my hat. 'The People will destroy the Path. WiRgo!xu and !Ci!ci-tel will be trapped here. It's all right – I'll make sure you get home before that happens.'

We sat there in silence for a few minutes. I fanned my face with my hat, trying to keep the flies out of my nose.

Lafayette said, 'Why didn't Wir . . . Wirgo–'

'WiRgo!xu,' I said.

'Why didn't Wirgoku and Kikitel destroy the Path, to be sure no one could follow?'

'I don't know,' I sighed.

A few more moments went by. We both knew we had to keep on looking, but neither of us felt like wandering around in the heat, waving the little 'statues' and totally failing to accomplish anything.

'Perhaps they wanted to be followed,' said Lafayette.

I looked at him.

We spent the rest of the afternoon getting blisters on our feet. We visited eight temples in descending order of size, twenty inns, and a couple of marketplaces – the first two the renegades would have encountered on their way into the city. I was keeping count: we showed those bloody solidigrams to twenty-four soldiers, thirty-five buskers, forty-three shopkeepers, sixty-nine beggars, one hundred and thirty-six tourists and six harlots.

Sometimes I found myself just scanning the faces in the

crowd, hoping I'd stumble into them the way I'd stumbled into Lafayette. Hoping that luck and hard wishing would make the right, important thing happen. Like if you wish hard enough, Santa will bring you the present you want for Christmas.

By the end of my second day in Babylon I was slightly tanned, quite exhausted and thoroughly depressed. We were both wrecked, and Lafayette was sunburnt, despite the sunscreen.

I was starting to think I'd been fooling myself. I'd raced back in a panic, with no proper plan, expecting to find, confront and sort out WiRgo!xu and !Ci!ci-tel and still have time to get Nebuchadnezzar's autograph.

But what else could I have done? I was the only hope we'd had. Which meant, I thought as I sat in our stifling room, that we were very probably knackered.

I was thinking maybe I should try to evacuate the historical figures. Nabu-kudurri-usur and his court. Oh heck, and some of the Hebrews, if I can remember which ones. And find them and convince them in time. Oh God, forget it, it's hopeless, and what about the other quarter of a million people?

I'd made up my mind. I wasn't going to give up, yet, obviously, but I believed it was a lost cause.

If I couldn't save Babylon, I wouldn't leave it.

I suppose I was frightened of getting home and discovering that everything had changed. A squashed Babylon would mean a lot more than a squashed butterfly. I might get back to discover that the human race has been wiped out by the Caxtarids, or that St Oscar's is a military school instead of a university, or that I'm the Divine Empress Gloriana. Or I never met Jason. Or I'm an alcoholic. Or I never found my missing dad. Or I beat my children.

In my diary – written by the flickering light of an oil lamp, I wrote: 'I'm scared of letting all these people down. Like the whole human race. At least if I get blown up as well, they can say I died heroically. Assuming I ever existed at all.'

Extract ends

4

THE PARTY'S OVER

*Curiously – or perhaps understandably – cultures
influenced by the Ikkaba did not usually copy their
propensity for self-sacrifice. The temple complex on
Yemaya was clearly used by the Ikkaba for their
ritual suicide. Central American cultures such as the
Aztecs sacrificed other people on their Ikkaba-inspired
pyramids; the Mesopotamians merely had ritual sex
there.*

*We still don't understand why the Ikkaba burnt
themselves alive, but Watkinson's theory that they
expected reincarnation has interesting parallels with
the Mesopotamian story of the descent of Inanna (later
Ishtar) to the underworld, and her triumphant return.
Perhaps the Ikkaba believed, as the Sumerians did, that
you can't keep a great goddess down.*

– Summerfield, Bernice S. 2595, *An Eye for Wisdom:
Repetitive poems of the Early Ikkaban Period*,
St Oscar's University Press, Dellah.

The young woman was a slave; Lafayette saw the tattoo on
her wrist as she led him and Benny to a pair of stools in the
courtyard. She offered them cups of sweet-smelling wine.

The courtyard was already beginning to fill with people.
The centrepiece for this evening's celebrations was a live
apricot tree. There were great jars of water, half sunk into the

courtyard; one had been removed, and filled with soil to accommodate the tree.

Perhaps Ninan was imitating the Hanging Gardens, in her own small way. Fashion? Paying a compliment to the Queen who had inspired them?

Miss Summerfield dipped the tip of her tongue into the wine. 'Watch it,' she warned, 'this is fermented palm sap. It'll melt your brain.'

'*Shalom; mah shlomeich?*' Lafayette said to the slave.

She looked at him in surprise. '*Shalom. Ani tov, mah shlomcha?*'

Miss Summerfield was fingering her earring. 'Was that Hebrew?' she asked.

Lafayette nodded. He turned back to the slave. 'Do you belong to the Lady Ninan?'

'Yes, lord,' she said. She still looked surprised, and perhaps a little alarmed at this unknown foreigner who could speak her tongue. She couldn't be older than fourteen. That was a tender age to be taken into slavery.

'I've studied many languages,' he said. 'It's my trade. I'm very pleased to meet you. My name is John Lafayette.' She gave a quick, nervous little nod. 'What should I call you?'

'Miriam, lord,' she said.

Miss Summerfield said, 'Oh. She can translate for you.'

Lafayette nodded. 'I could probably improve my Aramaic given a few weeks, but my Hebrew is far better.'

'Oh good.'

'Miriam!' called Ninan, clapping her hands.

Miss Summerfield put down her bowl. 'There are certain things you shouldn't say. You know the history of this time, right?'

'Of course.'

'Well, just don't tell anyone about the future,' she sighed.

Lafayette thought about it for a moment. 'Of course,' he said.

'Just tell 'em you're from a mysterious foreign land,' said Miss Summerfield. She had a wild-eyed look, but her shoulders slumped down. 'You've heard me do it, you know the sort of thing.' She leant back against the wall, the cup of wine held between her knees, and looked around vaguely.

Miriam had returned. 'The Lady Ninan asks that the Lady Beni joins her,' she said.

Beni drank the rest of the wine in a gulp. 'Right,' she said. 'Eat, drink, and be merry, Mr Lafayette.'

He watched her go, frowning. There were clearly facts she was keeping from him, troubling facts. Although if she continued to consume the strong palm-sap wine in that fashion, they wouldn't remain secrets for long.

Extract from the Memoirs of Bernice Summerfield

After half an hour, I was starting to run out of travel stories. If this had been the twenty-sixth century, I could have told Ninan rather more without sounding like I was entering the realm of mythology. As it was, I was entering the realm of tipsiness.

On the other hand, an ancient Babylonian would probably accept stories about strange creatures, right? I could tell her about the Ootsoi and the Goll and all the different Kapteynians – strangely shaped and coloured beings from distant realms who turned up late to my tutorials – and she wouldn't blink.

And anyway, did it matter a damn?

I was just going to start telling Ninan about the time I shagged that Citdbtbed[1] when she said, 'Oh! I forgot to tell you. Do you see that fellow over there?'

I turned, nearly falling off my stool. 'Which one?'

'Wearing the tunic,' she said, and helpfully added, 'He has a beard.' I looked around vaguely. 'Watching the musicians.'

'The portly chap?' I said.

'That's him. The merchant Itti-Marduk-balatu. Well, I was telling him about you earlier in the evening, before you got here, and he started boasting about how he'd met an even stranger pair of foreigners.'

---

[1] I wasn't to know the Citdbtbedani reproduce by shaking hands, was I?

My heart attempted to lodge itself in my sinuses. 'He did?'

'Yes. He said my foreigners might *look* strange, but his *acted* strangely. When they went into his house, the first thing they did was take all their clothes off!'

Lady Luck had just whacked me over the head with a canoe paddle. I said, in an oddly squeaky voice, 'I must talk to your friend.'

'Later,' said Ninan, 'I'll introduce you. Remind me. Go on with your story.'

I tried to remember where I was up to. 'There were six of them, all criminals of some kind. Thieves and cutthroats.' I kept glancing at Lafayette, who was deep in conversation with Miriam, until he finally looked up. I jerked my head in a come-here signal.

'I couldn't show them I was frightened. So I walked right up to the table where they were playing dice. And I grabbed one of their beers and gulped it down.' Lafayette got the message after a couple more jerks, and wandered over, bringing the slave with him.

'And I said, "Tastes the same as a camel smells!" Oh, hello, Lafayette. How's your new translator?'

'She's very helpful,' said Lafayette, in Hebrew.

'I'm very helpful,' said Miriam, in Aramaic,[2] and covered her mouth with her hand, hiding a smile.

Ninan smiled too. She was dressed to kill, in a long linen frock, wearing silver rings and golden earrings, her eyes made up with kohl. 'Have a seat, Lafayette.'

I jumped up as he sat down. 'I'm, um, just going to run to the loo,' I said. 'Lafayette, why don't you talk to the Lady Ninan for a few minutes. Won't be long.'

'I'm sorry,' said Itti-Marduk-balatu. 'I haven't actually met those people – but I do know someone who has.'

'You do?'

---

[2] The translator was clever enough to let me hear the words in my own as well as in the original language – no more confusing than watching a subtitled film. By this stage I was cluey enough to tell Aramaic from Hebrew and so on.

'Indeed,' said the merchant. 'A friend of mine had a long conversation with them. They were very peculiar. Did you know they took off all their clothes when they got inside his house?'

'Goodness, they did?'[3]

'Indeed,' he said again.

'It's terribly important that I find them,' I told him. (He could probably tell that, from the way I was vibrating like a gong.) 'Is there any chance of talking to your friend?'

'Of course,' he said. 'But right at the moment, my mind is filled with a business difficulty.'

'It is?'[4]

'It's a delicate matter,' he said. A passing servant offered us pomegranate seeds. 'I'm in need of a scribe. Someone trustworthy.'

'Someone discreet?' I asked, biting into one of the sharp-sweet seeds.

'You're following my thinking exactly,' he said. 'I need a business letter written, but I'm afraid my usual scribes are being paid by my competitors to pass on information.'

I wondered if Lafayette could write Akkadian. He might have translated plenty of cuneiform documents written in the Babylonians' official language, but had he ever tried pressing cut reeds into mud?

Luckily, that wasn't what Itti-Marduk-balatu had in mind. 'Do you see that chap over there?' he asked me.

'The one with the beard?'

'The skinny fellow next to the fat fellow,' said the merchant. 'I've heard he'll do the kind of work I need. Write a letter, take his fee, and then forget all about it. Obviously, I can't approach him myself . . .'

'I've always wanted to meet a Babylonian scribe,' I said. 'It

---

[3] Sudden, shattering hope renders me inarticulate, as does too much palm-sap wine. It worries me that I gave up so easily. I mean, I didn't actually ever give up, I still had several options to try. But I was far too ready to accept defeat – to punish myself for failure, I suppose. The Ikkaba would have understood.

[4] Argh! Pull yourself together, you fool!

must be a fascinating job, handling such a complicated language. In fact, I think I'll go and talk to him right now. If you'll excuse me?'

Extract ends

'You are terribly lucky, Lafayet,' said Lady Ninan.

'I am?'

'Travelling so much,' she sighed. 'I was born in Babylon. Do you know, I have never left the city?'

'Never?'

'Not once,' she sighed. 'I've never been beyond the city walls. My sacred duties keep me continually busy. And if I was to leave my post at the temple, I'd never be able to return.'

'Why is that?' enquired Lafayette politely. He felt slightly panicked to be left on his own, but at least he had Miriam. He caught glimpses of Miss Summerfield in the crowd . . .

'It's traditional,' Ninan was saying. 'I am consecrated to Marduk – I cannot leave his house.'

Miriam translated, and added, 'She's the god's chief whore, didn't you know?'

Lafayette stared at her. 'What?'

'The temple's stocked with harlots, and she's the queen of them all,' said Miriam.

Ninan frowned, but she obviously wasn't following. Lafayette was suddenly remembering everything he'd ever read about Babylonian religion.

His hostess said, 'The best I can do is to invite as many guests as I can. I'm obliged to hold all of these parties, so I send messages to Ur and Nippur and Kutha, to Media and Egypt and as far away as Greece. I must live my travels through other people's accounts. I have visited the Great Pyramid and the Parthenon without ever leaving this courtyard.'

Miriam translated and added, 'And if I wasn't needed to fetch and carry, I'd have been forced to be a harlot. Earning silver for their temple.'

Ninan reached out and took Lafayette's hand. He managed not to jump. 'I still have many years ahead of me,' she said wistfully. 'I have sufficient money. I would love to travel along the Nile, to journey relentlessly. Imagine waking up in a different bed every morning!'

'Imagine,' said Lafayette.

Extract from the Memoirs of Bernice Summerfield

The scribe was a thin-limbed fellow in a baggy tunic, with a long beard cut in a rectangular shape. He was busily stuffing himself with food, and he looked as though he needed every bite. His name sounded like something falling downstairs: Nabu-zuqup-kemu.

Between mouthfuls he said, 'Couldn't possibly.'

I glanced back at Itti-bitty-duck, or whatever his name was, who was pretending not to watch us, and wished I wasn't quite so drunk. 'Why not? I'm sure the fee –'

'Not the fee,' he said, pushing another hunk of bread into his gob. 'I can't concentrate on writing, I can't concentrate on anything.'

Except eating, evidently. 'That's a shame,' I prompted.

He swallowed hard, and sighed, 'It's the harpist.'

I looked over my shoulder at the band. Which one was the harpist? Oh right – a tiny, plump woman with greying hair, almost entirely hidden by her long dress. She sat with the harp in front of her, plucking its strings with a plectrum. There was a distant smile on her face as she played, as though her hands were operating on their own as she dreamt a happy dream.

'Isn't she gorgeous?' sighed Nabu-zuqup-kemu.

He was right, she was. 'Does she know how you feel?'

He nearly spat out a date. 'No, no, no,' he said. 'I couldn't possibly speak to her.'

'Why not?' I tried to smooth out his tangled hair. 'There's nothing wrong with you. She's not married or something, is she?'

'Widowed,' he said.

'She's probably just waiting for a handsome young man like you, with a respectable profession, to take an interest.' I straightened his tunic. 'Go on, go and say hello.'

'I couldn't possibly,' writhed the scribe. 'Couldn't you . . .?'

* * *

Speaking of writhing, Lafayette looked as though his chair was covered in ants. Ninan had paused in her interrogation to talk to an elderly Egyptian woman. I switched off my translator and murmured, 'Would you rather be somewhere else?'

He glanced at me. 'Sometime else,' he said. 'Or even someone else, at the moment.'

'Ninan's not that bad,' I said. 'She's just bored and lonely. Haven't you ever known someone who was stuck in a dull job?'

'Ah,' he said. 'Not exactly like this, no.'

'Having any trouble keeping up with the conversation?'

'Not with Miriam's help.' He smiled at the young woman, and turned to me. 'Tell me that in your time there are no more slaves.'

I sat down, thinking about it. 'Slavery's illegal throughout Earth space. But then, laws have never stopped slavers. You hear about it from time to time, but it is rare. Is she treated well?'

'I think so,' said Lafayette. 'Some of her friends have been forced into prostitution.'

I nodded. My head was starting to clear a bit. 'Common enough. Everyone uses slaves in this era – they haven't got machines to do the work. And slave women have the worst of it. Come to think of it, you're only around thirty-five years past emancipation, aren't you?'

'Closer to seventy,' he said stiffly. 'You're thinking of the Americans.'

'Oh sorry, I get a bit fuzzy before the twentieth century.'

'Tell me,' said Lafayette, 'that there is no more prostitution in your century.'

'Um,' I said. 'Um, attitudes have changed a bit since your time.' Ninan was saying goodbye to her Egyptian friend. 'Let's talk about this later. I need to get back to the chase. Can you keep her chatting for a few more minutes?'

'She is also a harlot,' Lafayette hissed, glancing at her.

I looked at Ninan. 'We definitely have to talk about this.' I got up. 'Just a few more minutes.'

'What do I say if she wants my custom?' Lafayette stage-whispered.

'I don't think you need to worry about it,' I said. 'Stay calm, she won't bite.'

I had to wait until the band were taking a break, drinking bowls of beer and laughing among themselves. I edged up to the harpist.

'You're Nigutu, aren't you?' I said, sotto voce. 'There's a chap over there who fancies you.'

'Is there?' she said acidly. 'You can tell him that I make more than enough money playing my instrument, without needing to play his as well.'

I couldn't help it. I broke up laughing.

A little circle of astonished silence formed around me, the crazy foreign woman with her hands on her knees, bent over, laughing her head off. God knew what Lafayette was thinking, let alone the poor scribe.

After a moment, the musician joined in, cackling at her own joke.

When we'd stopped laughing, and everyone had stopped looking at us, I said, 'That wasn't what I meant. I think he's in love with you.'

She raised an eyebrow at me. 'What makes you think that?'

'Look at him.' I nodded my head in the scribe's direction. 'He's miserable. Just look at how thin he is. He hasn't eaten for weeks, pining for you.'

The scribe smiled and waved at us, making me wince. But at least he was following instructions, and had stopped stuffing his face.

'I've seen him before,' Nigutu said.

'I'll bet he goes to every party where you play,' I said. 'Why don't you go and say hello? It won't hurt.'

The musician sat down on her stool and gave a heavy sigh. 'I'm sure he's very sweet,' she said, 'but there's someone else I've got my eye on. Actually, I was wondering if you could introduce us?'

She looked over to where the Lady Ninan was sitting, chatting with – oh my God.

'The man with the reddish-coloured hair,' she said. 'Isn't he gorgeous?'

* * *

I didn't get back to Lafayette for another twenty minutes. Ninan had gone to greet a late-arriving party of guests, and had taken Miriam with her, leaving him sitting on his stool with his arms folded and an apprehensive frown on his face.

He relaxed visibly when I appeared. 'Hello again,' he said.

'Hi.' I sat down on the stool next to him. 'Damn, these things are uncomfortable.'

'Did you make any progress?'

'You could say that,' I said. 'I don't suppose you'd be interested in getting married?'

Lafayette's folded arms tightened. His eyes had that flat look again.

'Sorry,' I said. 'Badly timed joke. I don't mean me. One of the musicians has a crush on you. I think she thinks you're exotic.'

Lafayette gazed in vague panic at the band. 'I am surrounded!' he said.

'Don't stare,' I said. 'If it's worrying you, I don't think you're even a bit exotic.'

'Thank you,' said Lafayette. He frowned, opened his mouth as though he was going to speak, frowned some more. My head was starting to pound.

'Miss Summerfield . . .'

'Mmmmffff?' I was leaning forward with my head in my hands, wondering if it really was going to explode.

Long pause. Then, 'Do you remember when I told you that you were on fire?'

'It is the sort of thing that tends to stay in one's mind,' I said in a muffled voice.

'I can still see the flames,' he said. 'They cover your body, burning without harming you.'

I looked up at him. 'I look like that all the time?'

'There's a tradition that my family has the second sight,' he said. 'I'd never thought about it before. Maybe this is what was meant.'

He did something that surprised me. He reached out and took my hand.

He turned it over, looking at my sleeve. Looking at invisible flames. 'Burned with fire and was not consumed ...' he murmured.

'Lafayette,' I said, 'I wonder if you're a time sensitive.' He was staring at my hand as though it was a precious artefact, and holding it just a little too tightly. He had strong hands. I was surprised to feel the colour starting to rise in my cheeks. 'I mean, you might be able to see objects which have been displaced through time.'

He didn't look up, still gazing at my fingers. 'There is someone else here who is also burning.'

I grabbed his shoulders. This time he didn't jump, but just turned his head, looking into the crowd.

'Lafayette,' I hissed, 'which one is it?'

'That man, standing by himself beside the apricot tree. Look.' He pointed.

I looked. It was the merchant Itti-Marduk-balatu.

Extract ends

5

PAST SHOCK

You, Traveller,
Come in under my terrible wing.

You mover, you roller, you leaf in a stream.

Give me an hour of your whirling clock
Give me an hour of skin and sandalwood
Give me the hour of the rose.

Held to me
Bound to my breast
Never resting
You mover, you roller, you leaf in a stream.

You, Traveller,
Come in under my terrible wing.

Give me your name
And your bruised feet
And the cities and the roads and the empty places
And the deserts and the mountains and the dust in your
   hair.

Take my hand
Take my hands and the shapes of my body
I your Calypso, your Circe,

Your stopping place, your sleeping place.
Take my hands and the shapes of my body
And my lethal moment,
The moment of the rose.

You mover, you roller, you leaf in a stream.

Take me with you
In the back of your mind
In the beat of your blood
In the moment of the rose.

You, Traveller,
Come in under my terrible wing.

– Yemayan poem, c. 1450 BCE, reproduced with
permission from Summerfield, Bernice S:
*An Eye for Wisdom: Repetitive Poems of
the Early Ikkaban Period*, St Oscar's
University Press, 2595.

Extract from the Memoirs of Bernice Summerfield

We were woken by the sound of a woman wailing. I opened my eyes, lying still on the mat, listening to the sound rise and fall.

It was profoundly eerie, echoing wildly from the walls of the buildings, like the cry of some wounded animal lost in the mountains. As I listened, the little hairs standing up on the back of my neck, the voice was joined by another. And then another.

Lafayette woke up with a violent start, sitting bolt-upright on his mat and looking around madly.

'It's OK,' I said, sitting up and waving my hand at him. 'It's all right, I think it's some kind of procession.'

Lafayette was shivering all over. I passed him my leather jacket. 'Stay here,' I said. 'I'll go and take a look.'

He huddled in my jacket. Neither of us had had much sleep, but he looked profoundly exhausted. The five o'clock

104

shadow had returned, and his eyes almost looked bruised.

I didn't feel that wonderful myself. I walked through the narrow halls of the inn, squinting against an incipient headache, until I came to the front door.

The doorman was watching the procession. A group of young women and men – street performers? professional mourners? priests? – were wandering along the road, wailing loudly. Their eyes were huge and reddened; they staggered and swayed.

They looked as though they had just found out the world was about to end.

'What is it?' I whispered.

'The day of penance,' said the doorman.

Lafayette and I ate in silence. Even the drunks in the tavern seemed cowed – each time they would start one of their bawdy conversations, another shriek or wild strain of music would sound from outside.

Lafayette looked like he could use a couple of days' sleep, but when I suggested he stay at the inn and take a nap, he just shook his head. He was wearing his own jacket now. His head was bowed over the table, his eyes open, but heavy with bags. I was starting to wonder if he was ill.[1]

'This is no different to any large-scale religious celebration,' I said. He raised his head slightly. 'It's not as jolly as everyone putting up Christmas trees, but it operates on the same principle – everyone's part of the ritual.' I flinched as another wail started up outside. 'Whether they like it or not.'

Lafayette picked up a date, bit off a little, leaning his elbows on the table. I went on, 'The noise and the running about

---

[1] The average time traveller has to face a similar problem to the traveller in exotic lands or on exotic planets: bugs. You probably have reasonable immunity to the diseases of your own time, and you'll have been immunized against some of the worse ones. But even if you avoid something hideous like smallpox, the local water flora can still get you. And the further back in time you go, typically, the worse the sanitary arrangements and medical technology become. The Shugs were wiped out after developing time travel because one of their scientists brought a lethal plague back from a previous century.

symbolize the primal chaos before the gods created the world.'

'The Deep,' said Lafayette.

'Ti'amat,' I said. 'That's right. The ocean, the dragon mother of the world. The younger gods felt threatened by her and her consort, so they elected Marduk to protect them. In the end he killed her in battle and used her body to create the world. This whole festival commemorates that. They recite *When On High*, the King pledges his allegiance to Marduk.'

There was shouting outside, the sound of a fight. Lafayette seemed to shrink further into his jacket. He rested his forehead on his hand.

He was frightening me. 'So,' I said, 'tell me about this second sight of yours.'

He rested his chin on his hand. 'One of my ancestors is supposed to have been a drac. A sort of French water fairy.'

'Is there a story about it?'

'Yes there is,' said Lafayette listlessly. 'My great-great-a-lot-of-greats-grandmother was washing clothes in the Rhône river one day, when she saw what looked like a golden bowl floating downstream. She waded in to try to catch it, and the dracs caught her and pulled her down under the water.' He sighed, putting down the half-eaten date.

'But she didn't drown,' I prompted.

'No,' said Lafayette. 'They kept her in their underwater palace for seven years. They made her serve them as a maid, and she had three sons by her master. One day she was eating an eel pie, and she got a little of the fat in her left eye. Suddenly, she could see perfectly clearly under the water.'

It was a classic fairy abduction story – I could guess the ending. But it had got Lafayette talking. 'Go on,' I said.

'They let her go, after the seven years were up, and allowed her to take just one of her sons back with her. He became my great-something-grandfather. One day, she went to market, and she met the drac who had kidnapped her all those years ago. When she greeted him, he asked which eye could see him. And when she pointed to her left eye, he poked it out with his finger.'

'But her child still had the sight?'

across the top of the courtyard. Plenty of bright sunshine, but cool air.' The last words turned into a groan as he rolled over. The reed mattress of the bed was stiff and scratchy. 'Sleeping fields,' he said.

'How many is that?' asked WiRgo!xu.

!Ci!ci-tel thought about it for a moment. 'Seventeen,' he said. 'Though there might have been one or two improvements that we mentioned twice.'

WiRgo!xu reached for the ladle again. 'Air conditioning,' he said, 'is worth mentioning twice.'

'It can be got used to,' said !Ci!ci-tel.

'Of course,' said WiRgo!xu. 'You can get used to anything. The war taught us that.'

'Did I ever tell you about that group of kids who accompanied the raid on !Qa!xaR?'

'I don't think so.' WiRgo!xu took a mouthful of the water.

'Oh, that was hilarious. They'd just hooked up with the Xenocultural Relations (Normalization) Interest Group. They spent the trip there swimming in the Ship's pool and chattering about battle strategies and weapons ratings. When we got to the planet, we gave them a map and a mission objective and dumped them in a swamp. After two days up to their collective arse in freezing mud, wandering around looking for the enemy base, they lost all interest.'

WiRgo!xu laughed. 'Now the question is,' he said, 'were they smarter than us, or vice versa?'

'I'd never thought about it that way before,' admitted his companion.

'We got used to the mud.'

'Some of us did. But we always knew there was a hot shower waiting for us,' said !Ci!ci-tel. 'We knew that if the job was important enough, you held on through whatever was necessary.'

WiRgo!xu waved away a fly. 'We should have just dropped a tub of antimatter on to the All of Us home planet,' he said.

'What!'

'I'm being sarcastic,' said WiRgo!xu. 'It was never necessary or important to pound on a civilization that technologically inferior.'

116

'Of course. He was half drac, after all. Ever since then, my family has supposedly been able to see fairies, if only out of the corner of our eye.'

I smiled. 'Have you ever seen one?'

He almost smiled. 'If such creatures ever existed – and my mother was certain of their reality – they must long since have become extinct.'

'But you can see the fire,' I said. Lafayette nodded, his head dropping back down again. I wondered just what was in his family tree.

We sat in silence for a few moments. Then I said, 'There's no sign that the son et lumière is going to let up. I think we should brave it. I want a word with the merchant Itti-Marduk-balatu.'

Lafayette didn't shift when I got up. 'Come on,' I said gently, putting my hand on his arm. 'You can come with me and keep me safe. All right?'

Extract ends

Clarence was tempted to fly over the area, just to see what was going on. Instead, he headed for Whynot.

He cleared the spaceport, transmitting hellos to a dozen Ships he knew, and kept going until he was well beyond the atmosphere, high above the Worldsphere's surface. A blue floor stretching away in every direction.

Then he turned, tracing a great arc through the vacuum. Whynot was a wide disc of blue and green and white, its complex orbit taking it close to the spaceport as it passed over every part of the Sphere.

No matter where you looked, you saw sphere: below, continents and oceans; further away, sky and clouds; further still, just a dark-blue wall that curved and curved until it met itself again.

It was hard to believe the whole world was in danger.

Clarence had hazy memories from his former life as a Ship. They included the cloud patterns of real worlds. He had a clear image of a tight spiral of violent air moving slowly across the face of a helpless ball. But he couldn't remember anything more, not even the planet's name.

There would never be a tornado on the Worldsphere, never

a hurricane. Not unless someone asked for one.

Bernice, like all barbarians, lived without guarantees like that. Not just when she was away on some mission, but all of the time. He didn't even know whether they had weather control on Dellah. She said it always rained there – surely that couldn't be intentional?

Clarence ruffled his feathers as he soared through the Sphere's inner space. No one lived in perfect safety, in perfect control over their lives, even on the Worldsphere. Accidents still happened. The day he'd left to see Beni, some poor woman had managed to burn her studio down while experimenting with fire sculpture. She was in regen, but it had been close – she might have wound up dead. Centuries of plans suddenly interrupted.

Among the People, old age was the main killer, followed by murder and suicide, and then the stuff that the Freak Accidents Interest Group thrived on. Clarence sighed in the vacuum. They were always trying to interview him.

His vague memories included that repeated moment of shock, the discovery over and over that something had happened to him and everything was different now. Occasionally, even now, he would be hit by the astonishment. Small things. *I have fingers!* Big things. *Shit! Where's my hyperdrive?*

Beni's whole life must be a series of surprises.

She had given him his name, some obscure cultural joke, no doubt. He could hardly call himself Business Before Pleasure Principle any more: there wasn't enough of Business Before Pleasure Principle left.

Clarence fell through Whynot's atmosphere, decelerating as he arced down over the island continent of Righteye. He turned in the last few moments, landing feet first in a plaza. A few People nearby applauded. He gave a little bow.

It was pleasantly warm, the sky pleasantly clear. The sun was slightly larger and brighter than it was on the surface of the Sphere. Clarence padded across the plaza towards a travel-capsule station. There was a huge map of the continent next to it, showing all the transport options.

Clarence realized he was blushing. He looked around, hoping no one was watching. Once, his brain had held the entire Home Galaxy in digital detail. Now there was just enough room for his next flight plan.

He left the city behind, let his wings carry him over the small towns and random bits of landscape. God had been redecorating, as usual; the public map had updated as he'd watched, adding a small island here, shortening a mountain there.

There were more lakes than he remembered, and a part of the continental shelf had been reclaimed, adding kilometres of flat land to the east coast. He wondered if anyone would be brave enough to try to build there, or if they figured God would get bored and dump it all back in the ocean.

A lot of People lived here, despite the inconvenience of God's incessant tinkering. Clarence had always assumed they had some kind of masochistic problem. But maybe, he thought as he touched down in a lightly forested area, they were in it for the surprise.

The trees were mostly bare, a few new leaves showing against dark trunks. A cool mist was moving over the ground. There were no birds or insects, and the air rang with silence.

There was a terminal in one of the trees. He knew just where to look for it; this area moved around, but it never changed.

This was where you came to talk to God when you wanted to *know* no one else was listening.

Clarence hefted himself up on to a branch and said, 'Hi.'

'Hello, Clarence,' said God, speaking from the tree trunk. 'Did everything go well?'

'No problems,' he said. 'I stayed to make sure everything went the way it should.'

'That's good news.'

'I wish you'd let me go with her.'

'Come on,' said God. 'Your new body is patterned on contemporary mythology. You'd cause a riot.'

A few moments' silence. Clarence started wishing there was the odd bug or nightingale about the place.

'You guilt-tripped her into going,' he said, running a sensitive fingertip over the bark.

'I activated our simulation of her,' admitted God. 'She responded almost the same way it did.'

'It wasn't her fault that they read her files.'

'It had to be one of our agents,' said God. 'Not one of us.'

'*Why* couldn't it be one of us?' said Clarence. 'It's our problem.'

'You know why,' said God. 'We can't be seen to act in this. If *they* discovered one of us in another time period . . . Besides, she's the obvious choice. She's already an expert.'

'What do I do now?'

God said, 'Come down to the site. I'll give you the coordinates. There's not much to do, but at least you'll know what's happening.' Clarence moped. 'Try to look at the big picture,' said God.

'That's easy, from up here.' Clarence looked up, to the second sky of the Sphere floor. 'You can't see any of the people.'

Extract from the Diary of Bernice Summerfield

The crowds were much thinner than the previous days, but they were wild – a mix of performers, painted and dishevelled, and ordinary people caught up in the madness. We had to push our way through jerking dancers, flinching as singers shrieked in our ears. Someone bopped Lafayette in the head with a trumpet. We ran, our arms thrown up to protect us from any more manic musicians.

The residential streets were a little quieter, only the echoes of distant cries and shouts reaching us as we walked down a thin road. Suspicious eyes watched us from doorways. We kept our gaze on the road, trying to be invisible by dint of not making eye contact.

'About Ninan,' I said, without looking up.

Lafayette glanced at me. 'I have studied the religion of Babylon.'

'I think you're a bit confused, mate –'

'You agreed that there were prostitutes in the temples –'

'There were. There are. They're for raising revenue, the same as any slave for hire. No different to the weavers or field workers. It's not part of their religion, it's pure economics.'[2]

'But Herodotus said –'

'You've been reading the cuneiform sources,' I said. 'Have any of them confirmed what he said?'

That got him. He had to shake his head. 'What about Ninan?' he asked.

'She's dedicated to the god. She can't have sex with anyone else.'

He stopped, frowning. 'That is what she meant when she said that if she left she would not be able to return.'

'That's right. They wouldn't be able to guarantee her purity.'

Lafayette blinked. 'Is she a virgin?'

I started walking again, and he followed. 'As far as human beings are concerned.'

Lafayette's eyes were doing that strange thing again. I was starting to wish I hadn't brought the subject up. 'Just try not to be so nervous around her,' I said. 'She's on our side. She thinks we're amusing.'

'I ought to behave towards her as to a lady . . .'

'Yes,' I said, trying not to grind my teeth. 'Without her, we wouldn't have this lead.' I grinned evilly. 'You can always ask her about ritual sex – I'm sure she can clear up all sorts of things for you.'

A great shriek came from somewhere in the distance. Lafayette started. I touched him on the arm, without thinking about it. He stared at my hand.

'I am so afraid,' he said. 'I will say the wrong thing.'

'You've been doing fine,' I said. 'Everyone thinks you're amusing or cute. Don't worry.'

He looked at me with those flat eyes. 'Do we have the power to change history, Miss Summerfield? With our fore-knowledge? Could we alter the flow of events?'

---

[2] Lafayette is confusing 'sacred prostitution' – a misleading name for religious practices that include sex – with common-or-garden prostitution. Both went on in the Mesopotamian temples, which made buckets of money out of the latter. They were a bit like medieval monasteries, powerful and wealthy with land, slaves and offerings.

'You mean accidentally.' He nodded. 'Almost certainly not,' I said. I held on to his arm, wanting to steady his mind as much as his body. 'Unless you make exactly the right change at exactly the right moment, it's nearly impossible to shift the major events.'

'Why am I here?' he said. 'Why did this happen to me? Why am I able to see the fire? How did I bring this on myself?'

'Mr Lafayette,' I said, 'sometimes things just happen.'

At last we reached Itti-Marduk-balatu's house, a large building in a wide, clean street. It was almost quiet here. I wondered if some of the wealthier citizens had bribed the dancers and musicians to keep away.

That made me smile. This wasn't some outbreak of mass hysteria: it was an official parade to keep the people happy, to purge their feelings of guilt and fear. All of it washed away by the priests' incantations, the blood sacrifices. Marduk wins again, and he and his buddy the king will keep away the demons. All you have to do is stay loyal to them. Happy New Year.

Lafayette stopped at the doorway. 'How can you be certain this man will help you?' he said. 'Surely we don't have enough silver to bribe him. From the sound of it, he will not help out of the goodness of his heart.'

'You're right,' I said. 'But don't sweat over it. I've got something on him.'

Lafayette gave me an odd look. 'I mean,' I said, 'don't worry, because I know something Itti-Marduk-balatu doesn't want anyone to know.'

Itti-Marduk-balatu was talking to a scribe, both of them sitting on stools in the courtyard. The area was bare and functional, unlike Ninan's, though I caught glimpses of good furniture in the adjoining rooms. Two little girls were playing with wooden toys, laughing quietly, and through a doorway I saw a woman working a loom. An apparently tame ibis strutted about.

The air hung in hot curtains, and the scribe wiped sweat

from her forehead as she took dictation. The merchant said, 'Come in, come in, sit down, I'll serve you some refreshments in a moment. This heat! This noise! How is anyone supposed to do business? Where were we?'

The scribe's eyes moved over the cuneiform. 'Son, don't let anyone touch the dates we promised the oil-presser Shamash-eriba without my permission,' she read back. Lafayette tried to peek over her shoulder. The scribe didn't seem bothered, probably assuming he couldn't read.

Itti-Marduk-balatu said, 'Don't neglect your work, or the farmer's work. Don't you know you have to drive people like that?' He thought for a moment. 'That's everything.'

The scribe ran her eye over the last few characters and smiled. 'All it needs now is your seal, lord,' she said.

Itti-Marduk-balatu took his seal out of its box and rolled it on to the clay. The cylinder added a little scene with people and animals, his personal mark. 'I'll give it to my messenger when it's dry,' he said. 'Thank you. That's everything for now.'

She nodded politely at us, packed up her equipment, and left. 'She's my record-keeper as well as writing all my business letters,' Itti-Marduk-balatu told us. 'She's scrupulously honest. Which makes her an excellent accountant and translator, but does mean she's not suited to certain work . . .'

'Exactly the reason we're here,' I said smoothly. Itti-Marduk-balatu gestured to a hovering slave, and moments later, a bowl of fruit and a jug of beer appeared.

Lafayette caught my eye and gave a tiny nod.

'I was hoping you could bring Nabu-zuqup-kemu with you,' said our portly host, as his slave poured the drinks. 'I need to settle this matter fairly quickly.'

Lafayette was fidgeting, once more stuck with being able to understand only half the conversation. 'We thought it might be too conspicuous,' I said. 'You know, the two strange foreigners and the dodgy scribe sneaking into your house . . .'

'I take your point,' said Itti-Marduk-balatu. 'At any rate, what did Nabu-zuqup-kemu have to say about my proposal?'

'Oh, he's willing to do the job,' I said. 'In fact, he's known for a while that you need the occasional letter done on the

113

quiet. We had quite a chat at the party last night.'

Itti-Marduk-balatu bit into a peach, looking nonchalant. 'I wonder who he's been talking to.'

'Other scribes,' I said. 'He didn't name any names, but he had some interesting stories to tell. My favourite was the silver from Kish that you managed to bring into the city, disguised as a shipment of barley! You clever fellow.'

My first guess had been that the merchant was a disguised time traveller – maybe even one of the People. But everyone at the party had known him for years. That left one possibility.

Itti-Marduk-balatu had put down his peach. 'My competitors are forever brewing up stories about me,' he said.

'Nabu-zuqup-kemu said he'd even read a copy of the letter to your friend in Ur.'

'Did he, now?'

'Of course,' I said quickly, 'none of that is our business. All we want is to find the men I'm looking for.'

Itti-Marduk-balatu ate the rest of his peach, very slowly. I didn't say anything more, letting him think about it. Lafayette sat very still, his hands clenched on his knees. We heard the city shrieking, somewhere far away.

At last he said, 'I have met them personally, you know.'

I smiled. 'I thought you might have.'

'An extraordinary pair.'

'That they are.' And you touched them, and a little of their aura of displaced time rubbed off on you. You, mate, have too much time on your hands.

'They were dressed as Babylonians, and they could speak as well as you. They called themselves Wirgaku and Kikitel.' Lafayette reacted, recognizing the names. 'But they had no manners at all. One of them propositioned two of my servants, and both of them took off their clothes, right in front of my wife!'

'What did they want?' I pressed. 'To buy or sell?'

'They said they had ample silver. They didn't even try to bargain – that was another peculiar thing. At least you know how to do that,' he said wryly. 'What they wanted to buy was land. Good farming land, somewhere close to the city – something they could make a living from.'

114

'Could you help them?'

'Not directly.' He took a long pull on his beer. 'I don't deal in land, but I gave them the names of a few merchants who could get them what they wanted.'

'Are they staying in the city?'

Itti-Marduk-balatu looked at me thoughtfully. 'Just what are you planning to do?' he said. 'If you don't have proof of their crime, you might find it difficult to get the police to help you.'

'I just want a quiet word with them,' I said. 'I'm sure I can talk them into doing the right thing.'

He stroked his beard. 'I wish I could help you, but they wouldn't tell me where I could find them – they insisted that if they needed me, they'd contact me. You can imagine I wasn't in a hurry to have them visit again!'

I laughed. 'Coincidentally,' I said, slapping my hand on Lafayette's shoulder and nearly giving him a heart attack, 'my friend here is quite interested in local farming land. Maybe he should talk to some of those land merchants you mentioned.'

'Of course,' said Itti-Marduk-balatu. 'In fact, let's make a bargain.'

Extract ends

Somewhere, surprisingly close by, in the dimness of a Babylonian living room, two figures lay on long beds. The screaming had died down a little in the midday heat.

One of them snored gently. The other reached down to a bowl of cool water, took a ladleful, and tipped it over his head. The water ran down into his hair and his growing beard, trickling pleasantly down the back of his neck and into his linen tunic.

He put the ladle back in the bowl and lay down again. The other man's eyes flickered open. They looked at each other for a moment.

'Air conditioning,' said WiRgo!xu.

'Mmmff,' agreed !Ci!ci-tel.

'You could install a variably permeable field across the doorway.'

'Why stop there?' said !Ci!ci-tel. 'You could stretch a field

'I've already rejected the wargame hypothesis.'

'Well, I think it's a good explanation of the War,' said WiRgo!xu. 'We could have either ignored the Hive Mind, for the most part, or squashed them like –'

'– bugs?' said !Ci!ci-tel. 'We're supposed to be here to learn . . .'

'I know, I know.' WiRgo!xu rolled over. 'With no natural frontiers, these people can't even defend themselves properly. They're used to being captured, and recaptured. Hence the ethnic mix. Not that I can tell any of them apart.'

'They can tell,' said !Ci!ci-tel, 'and that's what counts. Anyway, think of it as a spotting game.'

'What if I spot a bunch of hairy invaders on the horizon?'

'That's their problem,' !Ci!ci-tel muttered. 'We're not here to change things, either.'

'To be changed.'

'Yes.'

'I don't think I'm ever going to learn to cook, though.'

!Ci!ci-tel laughed. 'I thought those slaves were going to strangle you.'

'I was doing my best,' protested WiRgo!xu. 'If I'd been able to use my feet . . .'

'They probably *would* have strangled you.'

WiRgo!xu mournfully wriggled his disabled toes. 'I'll learn.'

'Why bother?' asked !Ci!ci-tel. 'We didn't come here to bake bread. There'll always be slaves to do it for you. Think of them as the force fields of the house.'

WiRgo!xu grunted. 'It's easy for you,' he said. 'You don't have ghost pains in your feet.'

Both of them dozed for a few minutes, but the merciless heat pestered them awake again. They lay still, letting their minds move slowly.

'!Ci!ci-tel?'

'Mmm?'

'What will we do if someone *does* come after us?'

'I don't know,' said !Ci!ci-tel. 'Kill them.'

WiRgo!xu said, 'Are you sure?'

'Think about it. It wouldn't add to our punishment,' said

!Ci!ci-tel. 'Even if they did catch us and take us back, they wouldn't do anything worse to us than ostracization.'

'They could kill us,' said WiRgo!xu. 'You know, off the record.'

'Why bother?' said !Ci!ci-tel. 'After a few decades of living alone, we'd kill ourselves.'

'I still don't like it,' said WiRgo!xu. 'The point is to help People, not kill them off.'

'It's amazing what you can get used to,' said !Ci!ci-tel.

Silence in the heat for a few minutes.

'They're all going to want air conditioning, you know,' said WiRgo!xu.

Extract from the Memoirs of Bernice Summerfield

Nabu-zuqup-kemu had a small, neat house, not far away. We walked there, cooking in the afternoon sun. The streets were mostly empty; sensible Babylonians would be indoors, trying to sleep.

Lafayette trailed silently behind me. I'd gone over the conversation with him, making sure he knew what was going on, but all he did was nod a little and keep his eyes on his feet.[3]

The doorkeeper asked us to wait in one of the rooms for a few moments. The dimness inside the building was striking after the burning sunlight. He went into one of the adjoining rooms. I heard a shout, some noisy giggling, and after a couple of minutes Nabu-zuqup-kemu emerged, smoothing down his tunic.

I raised an eyebrow at him. 'And how is Nigutu?'

He blushed to his ears. 'She's very well, as far as I know, thank you. What did Itti-Marduk-balatu have to say?'

'He was very helpful. Actually, he was positively garrulous. We're one step closer.'

'Marvellous,' said Nabu-zuqup-kemu. 'Can I offer you a cup of wine, to celebrate?'

'I think I'm still recovering from last night's party,' I said.

---

[3] You'd think I'd have seen it coming, wouldn't you? (As it were.)

He grinned. 'But we couldn't have done it without your help.'

'It was a real bargain,' Nabu-zuqup-kemu said. 'A whole poem in exchange for a little bit of dirt on Itti-Marduk-balatu. Leap like lightning/ Leave this place/ Of dust/ Of death . . . You're good, you're very good.'

'Oh, it's not original,' I said.

'That doesn't matter,' said Nabu-zuqup-kemu. 'It's quite different to the usual stuff you get around here. I'll find a noble in need of a really striking bit of poetry, and sell it to them. Hey, I've got lots more dirt where that came from, if you've got more poems . . .'

'I'll let you know,' I said. One Ikkaban poem, dropped into Babylonian society, probably wouldn't do any harm, but two or three could confuse future archaeologists terribly.

From one of the rooms, the sound of a harp rose, playing a merry tune. I grinned. Nabu-zuqup-kemu blushed again, but he had to grin too.

Lafayette just stared at the tiles.

Extract ends

The Coping Team was hard at work when Clarence arrived. God had to guide him through some of the safeguards he'd set up to prevent People wandering into the area, from bogus warning messages to a heavy sprinkling of itchy plants.

Not that the area wasn't uninhabited, isolated – which was presumably why WiRgo!xu and !Ci!ci-tel had chosen it. There were no transit terminals for hundreds of kilometres, no habitations for thousands; it was a genuine wilderness area. Soaring down, he'd seen it as a blur of yellow, green and purple – short and long grass, the odd shrub and bursts of hardy flowers.

It was raining as Clarence touched down, a constant, itchy drizzle. The angel suspected it was another way of keeping People away from the area. He could also sense a deadness in the air – some kind of suppressor field, keeping the Path's temporal signature hidden from nosy sensors.

The actual Path was hidden by a hologram, a dome over the Coping Team's camp, just as its extrusion on MD 20879 had been hidden. No one was going to stumble over it.

Walking into the solidigraphically protected area was like walking into a tent. The rain stopped, reflecting from a roof of solid illusion.

The first thing Clarence noticed was the remains of some kind of aeroplane. A huge, clear bulb, and two detached wings. They were a little distance away from the centre of the camp; the wings had been neatly stacked beside the fuselage. Whatever could be learnt from the craft had been learnt, and now it was just junk.

A series of temporary dwellings had been set up, just comfy-bubbles with the usual amenities. The bubble houses would have a basic intelligence, just enough to run the cooking and cleaning programs. As the saying went, non-sentient Houses tell no tales.

The Path was in the centre of the camp. Clarence had to pass the bubble houses before he could see it, but he could *feel* it, with whatever Shiply senses he still had. It was like a steady buzz, an irritation, jarring against the space around it.

It didn't look that impressive. A rectangle of silver perhaps three metres long, about three-quarters of a metre wide, cutting through the flowers and the grass. There was a small machine next to the Path's end, as there had been at MD 20879, keeping it visible.

The short extrusion was surrounded by People, talking, walking about with various devices, or just staring thought-fully at the thing. Each of the People – drone, insect and humanoid – was surrounded by projected terminal screens, flat rectangles that moved with them as they walked. One woman was almost hidden inside a flock of the things, her fingers stabbing at them as she talked herself through some complicated calculation.

A tall, willowy man in a camo jumpsuit came up to Clarence. 'God said you'd be coming along,' he said. He had blond eyes and blue hair. 'I'm !Cin-ta!x, with TIG.'

'Hi,' said Clarence. Probably most of the Coping Team were from the now defunct Temporal Interest Group, although a group from XR(N)IG were quietly doing projections about the war. Clarence thought they were getting ahead of themselves –

but, then, forewarned is forearmed and all that. 'So,' he said, 'how's the bomb going?'

'Actually,' said !Cin-ta!x, 'our first priority is to find a method of shutting the Path down. If only there were sensor records from its creation . . . extrapolating backwards is proving very difficult.'

'If you can shut it down, what then?'

'We'll need to do it as quickly as possible.'

'But you'll wait until Beni returns.'

!Cin-ta!x shrugged. 'Not my decision – God's running this show. But do you really think a barbarian and a couple of renegades are worth endangering the entire Worldsphere?'

Clarence loomed over the man, despite his height. Now he spread his wings to emphasize the size difference. !Cin-ta!x had slitted pupils, like a reptile's, and they widened as the angel suddenly put him in shadow. 'We told her she had five days,' said Clarence. 'Besides, wouldn't you like to talk to the engineers who built this thing?'

'Not particularly,' said !Cin-ta!x, 'as I don't want God suggesting I have bits of my memory erased for the good of the People. Anyway, you asked about the bomb.'

Clarence furled his wings, glowering. 'I suppose you've got that sorted out.'

'It's a lot easier to blow something up than find out how it works,' admitted !Cin-ta!x. 'We're just refining the calculations now. It's a forced temporal gravitic pulse, generated by the Path's own terminus under chronosynclastic stress. Once we've got the maths, we'll build the stressors. But we're not starting on the hardware until we're sure there won't be any backlash of energy to the Worldsphere.'

'What about the other points along the Path?' said Clarence. 'Is it only that Earth city that gets blown away?'

'Interesting you should ask that,' said the scientist. He waved a screen closer to himself. It was covered in orange scrawl. Clarence felt he should understand it, but he got lost after the first couple of equations.

'Let me explain it,' said !Cin-ta!x. 'We got some peculiar data from MD 20879. It suggests some kind of ripple effect. When the Path was extruded so that Beni could enter it, it's possible it triggered a series of extrusions at certain points along the structure's length. Possibly millions of them.'

'Then other people might have been able to get on to the Path. Oh heck! Even you-know-who might find it, and then we'd really be up the spout.'

'It's possible,' said !Cin-ta!x, 'but it's unlikely. The majority of such extrusions would occur in empty space, or for infinitesimal periods. However, the Path is so long that there would still be a significant number of usable extrusions.'

Clarence stared at the Path's terminus. 'Then anything could have followed Beni back.'

!Cin-ta!x raised a finger. 'Only if they have equipment which could sense the Path. Without that technology, it would remain invisible to them – they'd have to literally stumble across it. So I think we're all right there.'

'Why did they do it?' sighed Clarence. 'What could be worth it?'

'Everyone's been waiting for TIG to do something like this for years,' said !Cin-ta!x. 'But we'd never be so stupid.'

'Because everyone's waiting for you to do it,' said Clarence.

'Yes, that's true,' sighed !Cin-ta!x. 'WiRgo!xu and !Ci!citel had no connections with us, and from what God could tell us about them, I doubt they'd have the nous to build anything more sophisticated than that ridiculous plane. Someone told them how to build this. And it wasn't someone in TIG. Which means either there's a mathematical genius on the loose, or the information came from an outside source.'

Clarence said, 'You mean, this could be sabotage? Someone trying to cause a war?'

'It might even be our honoured co-signatories to the Treaty,' said !Cin-ta!x drily. 'After all, we know they have the technology. In fact, it could be a sort of test. How much do we know? Do we have the maths to stop this thing?'

'That might mean that war is inevitable,' breathed Clarence.

Extract from the Memoirs of Bernice Summerfield

Lafayette and I left the residential area. The noise swelled until it was a street away, around a corner, and then we were in the thick of it. And thick was the word – I hadn't seen a crowd that tightly packed since Stonewall 625. Arms and legs and faces, swinging by, more than a parade and less than a riot.

We took a step back, watching the procession from the side street. 'Isn't there some way we can go around this?' shouted Lafayette over the noise.

'I wish I knew,' I said. 'We can't risk getting lost. We've got to talk to those land merchants. There isn't time.'

I grabbed his hand, and after a moment, he closed strong fingers around mine. We stepped into the crowd.

It was like stepping into a fast-moving river. I raised my other arm, warding off bodies and faces as they loomed in. The crowd was a tangle, limbs and shrieking mouths. You couldn't tell the official performers from the citizens swept up in the mourning.

I gave up trying to squeeze between people and started shoving them out of my way. I pulled Lafayette along with me, feeling his grip on my hand tighten with panic as the crowd closed around us.

If I remembered Itti-Marduk-balatu's directions correctly, we only had to make it through a few blocks of the chaos, then push our way into a side street, and we'd be heading in the right direction.

Everything was back on track. We were zeroing in on the bad guys. We wouldn't lose any more time floundering around – we'd find 'em, confront 'em, talk them out of their crazy plan, and take them home.

A fat man flashed me. I stiff-armed him out of the way and pushed between a couple who were screaming epithets at one another. Get out of my way, Babylon, I'm on a mission from God.

I felt Lafayette's hand pull at mine, hard, and again, and suddenly his fingers slid out of my grip.

'Shit!' I stopped dead, turning, pushing someone's arm out of my face. Lafayette had already disappeared into the crowd.

I pushed my way back, looking around. 'Lafayette!' I shouted, but I could hardly hear myself. I raised one hand way up, hoping he could see the fire. 'Lafayette!'

Someone jostled me, and I almost lost my balance. I found myself stumbling sideways through the crowd, pushed and shoved, trying to keep on my feet. Someone hit me in the back, hard, and I yelped with pain.

I staggered against a wall, pressed up against the bricks by the sheer weight of bodies. I stared around wildly, trying to spot Lafayette's red hair in the mass of black curls.

Shit, shit, shit. I didn't have time to spend the rest of the day looking for him. And he was bewildered enough as it was – he needed me, and it made it *very hard* to think with all these people shouting and screaming and wailing!

I saw him!

He was running, or trying to run, battered and buffeted by the crowd. He was running back the way we came – no, he veered, and veered again. He was running at random.

I saw his face for a moment. His eyes were closed, his arms thrown up in front of his face, his mouth open. I think he was screaming.

I fixed my eyes on his hair, hardly daring to blink as I squeezed my way down the side of the crowd, shouting his name. My voice was just part of the noise, so loud it was like being deaf, like the roar at a rock concert that becomes a ball of sound pressing against your head.

I pushed a woman out of my way with both hands, then had to stop to help her up before she was trampled. Before she could say anything to me, I plunged into the throng, fighting my way through to Lafayette.

I grabbed him by both shoulders. He yelled and struggled, ripping free of my grip, and batted at me with his hands.

He was shouting, short, sharp sounds of panic, and I could tell he had no idea who I was or where he was or what was happening. I grabbed him by both his arms and dragged him sideways through the crowd, heading for a doorway. If someone would let us in, maybe I could get him out of the riot, get him to calm down.

We slammed up against the wall of a house. Lafayette was still shouting, trying to pull away from me.

I slapped him.

It stopped him. At least he was standing still and staring glassily at me. For a long moment he held my eyes like that, and I could see he was watching me burn, burning with displaced time, out of place, out of joint. Were the flames a tiny trickle, or were they a gout of fire rushing up from my hands and hair? Did I look like an angel or a demon?

He grabbed at his head, fingers clenching, trying to cover his ears. He backed away from me, his eyes still staring, and I could see something inside his skull was about to break.

I pulled his hands away from his face, pushed him back against the wall, and kissed him.

He gave me such a marvellous look of wounded Victorian propriety that I did it again.

It turned into a totally insane hair-clutching shoulder-grabbing snog, while Babylon screamed around us.

I don't know what possessed me.

In the holovids, if two people kiss, they always immediately end up in bed. It's a plot convenience. In real life, it's usually nothing like that. Our heroes might plunge between the sheets, or they might have an embarrassed discussion about their work schedule, or laugh and go for coffee, or just neck and then stop, or smile dreamily and go home. They might shag like bunnies months later when they've got to know each other better, or they might never get past that first peck. In a holovid, there isn't time to include all of that real-life messy stuff, not when your audience is shouting for skin.

When I was younger, I think I was scared by those holovids. If you admitted your affection for anyone, they seemed to say, you immediately had to fuck them. No options, no choice. You'd given the game away and now you had to give *you* away. Part of growing up was learning that I still had the choice.

Of course, Jason and I might as well have been a holovid story.

And then there was John Lafayette.

I got him back through the crowd, through the still, hot air, to our inn. Most of the tourists were staying inside, watching from doorways or rooftops, or just keeping out of the way.

There was weeping and wailing and gnashing of teeth. Here and there people were fist-fighting in the streets. I saw more than one couple, in a door or against a wall, tearing at one another as they stroked and bit and kissed.

Lafayette was panting when I half dragged him into the dimness of the tavern. We stumbled together through the thin hallways and into our room. He fell to his knees on a mat. I dragged the curtain across the doorway.

I knelt down beside him and took his face in my hands, trying to see through his eyes into his head, see what was going on in there. See what he was seeing. He looked as though his brain was boiling, as though he had been left on the heat for days, new and incomprehensible ideas stuffed into the pot one after the other until he was boiled dry.

'I'm so sorry,' I said.

He didn't know what to do with his hands. They ended up resting on my shoulders. He was shaking like a house in an earthquake. His voice came strangled out of his throat. 'Will you please kiss me again?' he said.

There's a particular trick to snogging, like a martial-arts exercise, concentrating your whole body's energy on your opponent's mouth. Everything else you're doing keeps spiralling back to that centre. He didn't move, paralysed by the heat, but I was pushing his shoulders into me with my palms, and then holding his hips and pushing them against me and sliding my hands up his back to his hair again. He tasted like panic.

I wonder if he felt those invisible flames, if my hands and my tongue burnt him.

He didn't know what to do. He took his jacket off, but that was because it was hot inside the room, the air hanging on our bodies like melted wax. I took hold of his collar and fumbled with the top button, stiff in its buttonhole.

He shut his eyes and knelt there, with his head slightly bowed, as I worked my way down the shirt. Inside he was pale and thin, with just a tuft of reddish-blond hair breaking the smoothness of his skin.

I pushed my hands into his open shirt, running them over him and around to the back, holding him to me. He was a nice shape, easy to get your arms around. He leant on me, and I could feel the shaking slowing down, the stiffness in his back and arms unravelling. His hands were fists, the wrists pressed against my back. His cheek rested on my shoulder. I stroked his back, very gently.

'Better?' I said, after several minutes had passed.

He nodded, a tiny movement. I decided his sensibilities had been sufficiently offended for one day, and took my hands out of his shirt, and sat back.

He looked at me, looking small and human and normal, a speck of matter caught up in this cosmic mess. It wasn't fair. It wasn't his fault he'd landed back here. And he'd been doing so well. 'All right?' I said.

He took my hand and kissed it, softly. I thought it was sweet.

I didn't expect him to start unbuttoning *my* shirt.

I stayed still, watching him in surprise. It took him nearly a minute to manage the first button, but after that he'd learnt the trick. He glanced at the curtain, nervously.

I did the sleeve buttons myself, and shrugged out of the shirt, glad to get some air on my skin. Lafayette stared at me, and then he stared some more, and stared and stared. I actually started to blush under the intense scrutiny. I wanted to make some witty apology for the small size of my breasts.

Then I realized that he was watching the flames.

I took his shoulders, gathering him up, holding him against me. He made a little sighing noise, discovering what skin on skin felt like. I echoed it, a happy noise deep in my throat. We leant on each other, our hands gently stroking each other's back, and I could feel the fear and the dreadful weight running out of me, soaking into the hard tiles of the floor and draining into the earth.

We stopped there – that was far enough. Both of us needed that touch, needed to know there was still comfort in the world, that we weren't alone. That was all we needed. No need to take this any further.

Outside the inn, an insane wail went up. Another voice picked up the sound, and rose, and swelled, and then another, and then another, the sound of cats warning one another they're about to fight, the sound of the chaos before Marduk beat it down, the sound of the world ending.

It broke over us like a wave, making us stroke and clutch and grab and drop on to the mats, with me forcing my tongue into Lafayette's mouth and with him holding on as though I was a life ring and he was drowning, except that I was what was drowning him.

Meanwhile, in the temple Esagila, a priest sliced off a ram's head, smeared the temple's walls with its blood, and watched the body and the severed head sink into the Euphrates, the dirty water sucking down another year's worth of sin.

Extract ends

6

THE EVENING AFTER THE
AFTERNOON BEFORE

*You have to assume God always tells the truth. Let's
face it, if God lies to you, you'll never know about it.*

– AgRaven, Interpersonal Dynamics Interest Group

Lafayette dreamt of the river. He rushed along with it,
helpless as any leaf or twig, freezing-cold water in his mouth
and eyes.

The countryside was a wet green blur. A morning mist
hung in some of the low-lying fields, fat white droplets
obscuring dark trees. The water carried Lafayette past it,
slowing as the river became wide and fat, the current turning
into a tidal pulse.

Finally the river became the ocean. Lafayette whirled and
bobbed on its surface, soaked through, squinting up at the
sky. It seemed to him that the sky lay on the sea, pressing
softly down on it, each of them reflecting the other. Neither
of them noticed him, a spot of flotsam rising and falling with
the waves.

He floated.

Benny dreamt of the ocean. She was standing on the shore,
watching the surf.

Further up the beach, her parents were trying to keep the

sand out of the picnic food. It was the late afternoon, and the worst of the crowds had dispersed for the day, jamming the single transport rail back to town. Beta Caprisis was sinking behind the buildings, turning them into square shadows against the orange sky.

She hadn't liked swimming in the ocean, knocked over and thrown up the beach by the breaking waves. The water tasted bad, and the sand hurt her feet, especially where tiny purple shells had collected in a long line, rolled over and over in the same spot. She could see the line from where she stood, just out of the reach of the water. She was collecting shells, especially ones with holes in them which she could string on a necklace, but she didn't want to wade into the surf to pick them from that purple and black line.

A little further out, she could see a round, dark shape. She squinted at it, wondering if she had imagined it. Then a long, black spike broke the surface of the water, a hint of back or shell rising above the surf and then disappearing again.

Benny stared, taking a few steps back. She could see the dark shape clearly now, moving under the green water, heading away from the shore. They had been on holiday for a week, but this was the first time she had seen anything living in the ocean. Everything else was dead, washed up, clumps of seaweed or bits of wood, the limitless shells.

Another wave broke, forcing the round thing back up the beach. Its whole body lifted out of the water for a moment, turning. She got a glimpse of a brownish underside, thick, stubby limbs struggling against the water.

The whatever-it-was patiently turned and started heading out to sea again. Benny realized that it had come too close to shore, and now every time it tried to get back out into the sea, the waves would push it up the beach. It might be stuck there for ever, always trying to get started, never managing to get where it wanted to go.

There was no way a little girl could help it, especially if she didn't want to get yelled at for playing with an alien sea creature with spikes. She watched it until some other kids and their mum came along and started screaming that there was a stingray coming up the beach, and then she went back to her parents, and forgot all about it.

Clarence soared over the sea, wings spread, enjoying the sunshine. As he travelled, the light smoothly faded, until he could see the lights of boats skimming across the calm water.

The turtle island was paddling in slow strokes in a tight circle. God had asked her not to leave the area while its investigations proceeded.

Clarence swooped in over the island, and saw her mighty head rise slightly to greet him. He fluttered down on to the beach, a great eye rolling to look at him.

'It's been a while,' said the turtle.

There was a seat like a throne of rock, looking out to sea. Clarence draped himself across it. 'Um,' he said. 'I'm told we know one another.'

'We knew one another,' said the island. Her voice boomed, blending with the roar of the waves. 'Only I wasn't a turtle then, and you weren't a phoenix.'

'I wish I could remember you,' said Clarence. 'I'm always meeting people I can't remember. It's the limitations of the new body.'

'Never mind. I prefer it this way,' said the island. 'Anyway, you're all right now.'

'Am I?' said Clarence. 'Are any of us?'

'Hmmmmf,' hmmfed the turtle, sending seaweed flying in all directions. 'At least you're not a suspect.'

'What?'

'Asking me to stay put is just a psychological ploy,' said the turtle. 'God could find me in about two seconds, wherever I was on the Worldsphere. It just wants me to know it's got its eye on me.'

Did it, now? 'Do you know what's going on?'

'No,' said the turtle. 'All I know is someone tried to blow me away. Does God think I'd try to do that to myself?'

'There's not a lot that could kill you, is there?' said Clarence. 'I mean, unless there's an even bigger island around that eats turtles.'

The island snorted, sending huge plumes of steam into the

air. Fortunately, the wind was blowing in the opposite direction to Clarence. 'That doesn't mean it's attempted suicide. God knows what my psychological profile is. I'm very happy as I am. No, this is the work of someone holding a grudge. Someone who's found out who I used to be.'

'Well,' said Clarence, 'it wasn't me.'

'The angel returns to the scene of the crime,' said the turtle. 'No, I don't think it was you, not if your memories are as fragmented as I'm told.'

'How did you find out about me?'

'Grapevine,' said the turtle. 'Lots of chitchat about your accident.'

'Oh,' said Clarence. 'You should have come and said hello.'

'I told you,' said the island. 'I'm happy as I am.'

Extract from the Memoirs of Bernice Summerfield

OK, maybe we could afford to waste the rest of the day.

I woke up in the early evening. The intolerable heat had ebbed away; there was a cool breeze coming in, the curtain softly waving. I wanted to reach over and open it just a little wider, but I didn't want to wake up John.

I was in that strange state of mind where you're full of questions, but you don't really care what the answers are. Why did we do that? Should we have done that? What now?

John was sleeping with his head resting on the curve of my left breast. His hip touched me, his arm was thrown across on my belly, one foot crossed mine. It was as much contact as we could stand in the heat. His hair was a mess, damp with sweat.

He hadn't had the foggiest idea what to do. It didn't matter. He let me guide him, guide his hands, position his body, whispering orders underneath the sound of the rioting. He let me do it all, fell right into the trembling-virgin act. I felt like bloody James Bond.

I don't think I want to know what was going through his Victorian mind. I only kissed him to try to snap him out of his hysterics.

It would be nice to hypothesize that the renegade People directed some kind of lust-inducing psychic attack at us, to keep us out of the way. They could leave it on, trapping John and me in a permanent state of shag. What a *horrible* thought.

I wondered if he'd decide I was worth treating like a lady. Or if he thought I'd shown my true colours. What would he be like when he woke up? Affectionate? Chivalric? Revolted? Not that I needed his approval, damn it. It wasn't a love affair. I didn't know what it was. Maybe it wasn't anything at all.

How to reconcile this with my vague distaste at my students' one-night stands? With the romantic or prudish or something conviction I have that making love ought to mean something more than having sex? But then, what about my own near miss with one of those very students? What about a certain angel of my acquaintance? Or the way Jason and I fell together?

But that wasn't like this. For one thing, Jason knew what he was doing. For another, it was like we fused at some perfect, hidden level, like it wasn't just our bodies joining, but everything, everything.

And yet, in the screaming afternoon, stretched across John's sweating body and pinning his ankles down with my toes, I wasn't thinking, I was past thinking.

I didn't know how to think about it. Sex means different things, at different times, during different historical periods, to different people. Pick an attitude, any attitude. The Babylonians were relaxed, if not positively enthusiastic; their greatest goddess is an outright slut. In John's lifetime, prostitutes were illegal and despised, and Jack the Ripper tore them apart.

But here ... Ninan shags the city's god, Ishtar shags Tammuz, the harlots bonk for silver, boy goats and girl goats go at it in their pens, men and women dress in drag for the festivals, wives and husbands and lovers touch and tease and envelop and entwine ...

Thinking about it, I started coming over rather funny. I decided to wake John up and get my clothes on before it started all over again.

* * *

John turned his back on me to get dressed. I had to giggle, and I saw him trying not to blush.

I left my shirt untucked, flapping the fabric to send air on to my stomach. 'We should at least try to see the first land merchant tonight,' I said, pulling on my socks. 'If WiRgo!xu and !Ci!ci-tel paid him a visit, you ought to be able to tell, right?'

Lafayette mumbled something, embarrassed that I was even acknowledging his naked presence. I had a great view of his naked presence, too, as he bent over to pull up his trousers.

Oh God, he was going to pretend that it hadn't happened.

I pushed my hat down on my head. My hair was damp. 'It'll be more difficult this time,' I said crossly. 'I don't have anything to bargain with. We'll know if they've met the People, but how can we get them to tell us how to find them? Is there time to watch a house in case they come back, and if so, which house? Jump in there any time, John.'

He finished buttoning his shirt, and turned around at last, sitting cross-legged on the mat. 'I don't know,' he said. 'Perhaps you can bluff them, tell them that Nabu-zuqup-kemu gave you information about them as well. Or perhaps you can convince them of the importance of your mission. Perhaps they will simply be friendly, and willing to help.'

I hadn't heard him say so much at once since I first met him. 'You might be right,' I said, after I got over the shock. 'By this time tomorrow, we'll have them, or my middle name isn't Surprise.'

Extract ends

Clarence couldn't blame the turtle for being ticked off. After all, she had reported the bomb herself. But if God didn't think the turtle had tried to kill itself, then why was she still under suspicion? Suspicion of what?

Oh, thought Clarence, as he made his way up the beach and towards Beni's house. The bomb had been a distraction, something to keep God busy – and to blind its local sensors – while the renegades switched on their Path. The turtle might have planted and activated the device itself, or allowed it to be planted, in order to help WiRgo!xu and !Ci!ci-tel get away.

If that was so, it was facing a long life spent swimming alone in the ocean. It must have owed them a hell of a favour.

He had expected another Coping Team, but there were only a couple of People hanging around outside the house – a pair of forensic drones chatting with each other. To Clarence, their high-speed communication was like an itch in the air. For a moment he longed to be able to join in.

He walked up to them, and waited for them to finish their conversation, which took another tenth of a second. 'Hi,' he said. 'I was just visiting the turtle, and I wanted to see how you were getting on.'

'We'd tell you,' said one drone, 'but the island keeps planting bugs.'

'We've destroyed three in the past day,' said the other drone, 'and I don't mind it overhearing what a nuisance it is.'

'We've had to stick to encrypted direct communication. Can we put you in the loop?'

Clarence's wings drooped. 'I'm afraid not,' he said.

'Sorry,' said the drones. 'We're outta here, we've got to go report to God.'

'Well then,' said Clarence brightly. 'I'll come with you.'

Extract from the Memoirs of Bernice Summerfield

I decided not to try to hold Lafayette's hand.

The crowds had thinned to a trickle, the performers finished for the day. Even the worst of the heat was gone, leaving Babylon resting, getting its breath back after the day's exertions.

I'd visited so many big cities, and they had so much in common, no matter how advanced or primitive. They had traffic problems, and refuse problems, and the separate worlds of the haves and the have-nots crammed close together.

I felt good. A cool breeze was blowing on my face, we were going to find the People, my body had that pleasantly massaged feeling you're left with after a really good session of bumping uglies. I had to stop myself from whistling jauntily.

'I wish to apologize,' John murmured.

He said it so quietly that I made him say it again. 'I wish,' he coughed, 'to apologize to you.'

'Good grief,' I said, 'don't worry about it. Anyone could have lost their head in that crowd.'

'That is not what I meant,' he said. He was walking quickly, keeping up with me, his eyes on the ground. 'I took advantage of you. There is no excuse for such behaviour.'

I managed not to laugh. 'You took advantage of me, Mr Timid Virgin!' I said. 'I seem to remember –'

'Let us not speak of it!' he said sharply. 'There is no need to speak of it. No one need ever know that it happened.' He stopped, and glanced at me, just for a moment. 'I give you my word as a gentleman – if you can still accept it – that I will never disclose what happened between us to another living soul.'

My jaw sort of hung open for a moment. 'Tell whoever you like!' I said. 'Put it up on a billboard, publish it in *The Times*! Good grief!' I put a hand to my forehead. 'Sorry. Look. Mores change, John. In my time it's generally acceptable for an unmarried couple to have sex, as long as they do it responsibly, which we did. I'm not ruined, or anything. You didn't do anything wrong.'

I could just about hear the gears in his mind grinding together. He continued staring at the ground. After about a minute, he said, 'I am prepared to marry you, if required.'

'Gaaaah!' I said. 'Why is it you can comprehend time travel, and this simple idea is so difficult?' A couple of harlots were walking past, laughing at our lovers' tiff. I made a face at them. 'I suppose I should be grateful you still consider me marriageable material.'

'Of course!' He glanced up at me, almost panicked. 'You're not like –'

'Can't work it out, can you?' I said. 'You know, I teach a course in historical attitudes to sex, and yours is practically antediluvian. Either I'm chaste or I'm a brazen strumpet. It's all the same to you, isn't it? The streetwalkers, the slaves forced into prostitution, my husband –'

'Your husband!' he shouted in alarm.

I pointed to my ringless left hand. 'Former husband and former male prostitute. They're all part of a quagmire of moral opprobrium. Ruined. And now there's me.'

'No!' Lafayette shouted. 'I am trying to tell you that I do not think you are ruined!'

'Then look at me, for God's sake!'

He managed it, lifting his head and meeting my eyes. 'Even if I cannot accept your moral attitudes,' he said, 'I believe you are an exceptionally brave and capable woman. Given our mission, those qualities are more important than modesty.'

Modesty. Suddenly I knew why he had turned his back to get dressed. He was trying to preserve my modesty. Stop me from feeling embarrassed or cheap.

I blew out a breath. 'Coming from a stiff-necked Victorian prude, that's quite a compliment.'

Lafayette raised a finger. 'Edwardian,' he corrected.

I grinned. 'C'mere.'

He didn't c'mere, so I put my hands on his arms, gently, and he let me hold him in an entirely chaste and proper hug.

Extract ends

For security, the drones decided to make their report in space. Clarence followed them through hundreds of thousands of kilometres of vacuum to the rendezvous. Travel capsules whipped past the trio from time to time, en route to Whynot or shortcutting to the opposite side of the Worldsphere.

God sent a stellar maintenance bot to meet them, downloading a tiny portion of its consciousness into the mindless drone. Clarence was amused to see that God had remodelled the front of the drone into its characteristic yellow ikon, presumably so they wouldn't forget who they were talking to.

God took a moment to reconfigure one of the bot's antenna arrays so Clarence could eavesdrop on the conversation. The drones patiently paused between bursts of data so that it could be translated for Clarence's slower mind. Standard practice when conversing with an organic, he knew, but it still made him feel stupid.

'The forensic evidence is clear,' said one drone.

'The conclusion is inescapable,' said the other.

'The island-turtle placed the device itself, manipulating the house's own fields.'

'However, we believe the device was provided by some other person or persons.'

'The island-turtle subsequently activated the device and then warned God, confident that it could be removed in time.'

God's face ikon frowned. 'And the motive?' it said.

'The obvious one,' said one of the drones. 'It was assisting WiRgo!xu and !Ci!ci-tel in their escape.'

Clarence's wings were suddenly dragging him across space, accelerating to a sizeable percentage of lightspeed even as his brain tried to catch up with what the hell was happening.

He decelerated, almost as sharply, as a ripple of raw terror slammed up and down his body. Without any responses built in by evolution, he didn't know whether to scream or curl into a foetal ball. Instead, he spun for a moment in three dimensions, his eyes and mouth wide, his mind paralysed by primal terror.

Hundreds of thousands of kilometres away, a flare had leapt out of the sun, an almighty gout of flame and radiation. It was currently washing through the area where he had just been.

Clarence stared. The flare was already dissipating, its work done. It had been very specific – a puff long and slender enough to wipe out everything in a specific area of space, without doing significant damage to the Worldsphere or to passing travel capsules. The radiation was dispersing in a series of waves.

It must have looked pretty bloody impressive from the ground, thought Clarence, as his spinning slowly stopped.

The raw panic had been an expression of his sensor's instant response to the threat. It was diminishing, now he was clear. He did two scans, one on himself, one on the area where he had been a few seconds ago. He was all right, if in need of a few repairs after the sudden acceleration, but his internal systems were already taking care of that.

The drones and God's bot were gone, instantly consumed in the fireball. It must have been the bot that triggered the flare.

For a moment, Clarence fervently hoped that it had been a massive malfunction on the part of the solar maintenance bot. Perhaps wear and tear, perhaps the result of having to host a subdomain of God's intelligence.

But he knew it wasn't true.

There was nothing to do but float here, and wait for death. Clarence closed his eyes.

A few minutes later, one of God's yellow drones skimmed up to him. Clarence opened his eyes again, surprised.

'Who the *fuck* did that?' said God.

Lafayette walked with his hands in his pockets. He did not pretend to understand Bernice's thinking, her passionate defence of their coupling. He had little choice but to stay with her, assist her in her mission. Without her help, he was lost in this city.

On the other hand, why did he need to stay with her? He was reasonably certain he could find the Path again. It was only a matter of locating the Processional Way once more, passing out through the Ishtar Gate, and then searching a little area of desert. There – he had a plan. He could leave her at any time.

Bernice was striding ahead of him, probably still scowling. Her mannish clothes only emphasized her fine figure, particularly her strong, slender shoulders. He sighed. She seemed so confident, so determined, so very used to her life as an adventuress. He remembered how she had smeared that sunburn ointment on his face. Her pursed lips, her small frown of concentration.

And yet he remembered her slumped against the wall in Lady Ninan's courtyard, a bowl of beer held in her lap as she despaired of completing her mission. And he remembered, in a disjointed manner, her plunging into the swirling riot and dragging him free.

Lafayette made a face. He could not simply abandon her. He had the sight, and she did not. And, despite his efforts to smooth over the entire business, a bond had been forged between them that would not easily be broken.

He was about to say something when she stopped, standing very still in the road. She waved her hand at him, signalling that he should also stop. He stood as still as he could, trying not to breathe too loudly.

In the dimness, he could see someone walking down the road towards them. No, two people. White tunics standing out in the dark, white grins flashing.

'Run,' said Bernice.

But she didn't run. She stood with her feet slightly apart, raising her arms, like a boxer readying to fight.

'I said run,' she said, without turning around.

'Don't be afraid,' Lafayette said. 'I will not leave you.'

'Then you'd better look behind you,' she said.

Lafayette whirled. There were two more of the ruffians coming up behind them.

He drew his pistol, pointed it at them, remembered to release the safety catch, and said, 'Stay where you are, or I'll fire!'

They kept coming. It suddenly struck Lafayette that they had no reason to be afraid – they had never seen a pistol, they had no idea what it was.

He pointed it at the sky, and fired off a warning shot, the gun kicking back in his hand with surprising force.

The sound was deafening in the evening quiet. The two men stopped in their tracks, gaping with fear. He heard Bernice exclaim a very unladylike word.

He lowered the pistol once more. 'This is a weapon,' he warned them. 'I can kill you where you stand. Don't come any closer.'

'John,' Bernice hissed, 'put that thing away before you kill someone.'

'I will protect you,' Lafayette said, 'even if you do not believe you require protection.'

She said, 'John –'

One of the men leapt at him. Lafayette shot him through the body.

He had never killed a man before. In fact, this was only the second time he had fired the pistol – if you counted the warning shot. The recoil seemed to slam back up his arm and into his shoulder, again leaving him feeling bruised and winded.

The man simply dropped, his body pushed back by the impact. He fell on the ground, tried to rise once, and then lay still.

All hell broke loose.

While Lafayette was staring at his victim, the other man leapt at him, shouting in rage, and grabbed his gun arm. Lafayette tried to pull away, and found himself circling backwards, with the man clinging to him in rage, screaming incomprehensible abuse.

Lafayette glanced at Bernice, who was fighting with the other two men. He ought not to have been surprised that she could fight – some kind of oriental technique, by the look of it, almost like a dance. If he had not had a crazed Babylonian hanging off him, he might have stopped to admire it.

The man hit him in the face. Lafayette staggered back, his entire field of vision turning white. A moment later he realized that he was sitting on the ground and the Babylonian had his gun.

The thug pointed the weapon at him. Lafayette felt his entire body clench, involuntarily, waiting for the lethal shot.

But the Babylonian kept pointing the gun, making little jerking motions of his arm. He had no idea how to make the weapon work. He wasn't even holding it with a finger inside the trigger guard, but as though it was a stone, jiggling it in his hand as the hot metal burned his skin.

Lafayette stood up and punched the man as hard as he could. The ruffian yelped and fell down, the gun skidding out of his hand. Lafayette snatched it up. The man said something that sounded frightened. 'Stay there!' Lafayette commanded, gesturing with the pistol. The man raised his arms, as though in supplication.

He couldn't see Bernice. He ran up the street, calling her name, but she was not in any of the side streets.

Lafayette turned back to see if the ruffian was pursuing him. Instead, the man had abandoned the body of his fallen comrade and was leaving the scene as quickly as he could.

Something glittered on the ground, catching Lafayette's eye. He crouched down. It was Bernice's earring, her translator. He closed his hand around it for a moment, then slid it into his pocket.

To his surprise, the local citizenry had not emerged to see what the matter was. Did they assume it was part of the festival? Or were they simply terrified?

It did not matter. He must find Bernice.

He turned around.

There was a metallic sphere hovering two inches from his face. It was three feet across, and a strange glyph was inscribed on its dark surface, two dots, a dash, and a curved line.

'Holy cow!' said the sphere. 'Who the heck are you?'

Lafayette cried out and ran.

7

HEAD ABOVE WATER

While the exact cultural relationship between the Ikkaba and the D'nasians remains unclear, there is one certain link between their literature: the repeated theme of death, change and renewal. In over forty per cent of the D'nasian stories we translated, the hero's companion (often a comic or comparatively lightweight figure) is obliged to take over as the story's protagonist when the hero succumbs to tragedy.

The 'moral' or theme of such stories is one of the child growing to replace the adult. Just as one cannot be a child for ever, one cannot be a companion for ever: eventually one must step forward and become the hero of one's own stories.

– Watkinson, Edward, *Ninshubur, Cosmo, K'tiansolnerilii: the Role of the Hero's Best Friend in the Literature of the Milky Way*, St Oscar's University Press, Dellah, 2537.

God escorted Clarence to a space station to complete the angel's repairs. It was exceptionally functional, meant for bots and the odd drone, mostly open girders exposed to space. A couple of expert systems looked him over, gave his internal systems a quick twiddle, and pronounced him fit.

Clarence sat on a crossbeam with God's drone. The yellow sphere was doing little spins of anger. 'That is the first

143

intentional act of solar sabotage since the Dyson Sphere was constructed.'

'I wish I had the full data from those poor drones,' said Clarence.

'Believe me,' said God, 'you've told me more than enough. I've sent a team to surround the island-turtle with communications dampeners. Nobody messes with my sun!'

Clarence didn't mention that, for a long frightened minute, he had assumed that God himself had blown the drones away – the only entity with the tools to manipulate the sun, and a powerful motive to keep the forensic investigators' results secret.

'What I can't work out is *how* she did it,' God was saying. '*Why* isn't a problem – things wouldn't be any worse for her if she threw in a couple of murders to boot. No, I can't work out how she reprogrammed my solar bot, took control of it. The same flare that blew away the investigators wiped out that piece of evidence.'

'Wait a moment,' said Clarence. 'The drones were in direct, high-speed communication with the bot. Both ways. Surely the turtle couldn't have handled the drone-speed talk with an organic brain and a two-light-second delay.'

'Good point,' said God.

'Could the bot have achieved sentience?'

God wobbled a 'no'. 'Not in a million years. It just had some extra memory put aside so I could inhabit it from time to time. No, it was being used by someone.'

'Well, if it wasn't the island-turtle,' said Clarence, 'who was it?'

Lafayette ran headlong through the narrow streets, between the blank-faced houses, in near darkness. He fell twice, and each time he scrambled to his feet and kept running, glancing back just for a moment.

The ball floated idly along behind him, as though unconcerned by his efforts to escape. He realized it was simply waiting for him to give up.

A part of Lafayette's mind was trying to work out what it was – something from the future? From another world? But most of his thoughts were consumed by an utter, unreasoning terror. Lost, said his brain over and over, lost and alone, lost and alone.

He ducked into an alleyway, turned left sharply, and turned again. Perhaps he could confuse the thing, lose it in the labyrinth.

He found a shadow and dived into it, gasping as he tried not to breathe audibly. The ball did not appear at the mouth of the street. He waited, crouching against the wall, but the ball still did not appear. Had he escaped it?

He thought of the glimpse he had had of Benny, moving in elegant patterns as she fought the ruffians. Had a flash of metal been a belt buckle, or a dagger? He had not heard her cry out. Presumably she was still alive – if their intention had been to kill her, they would probably have left her body where it fell. No, they had overpowered her and carried her off.

The thought made his scalp feel as though it was burning. He reminded himself once more that there were no romantic feelings between them, she was not his wife, that he had no special duty to her.

It made no difference. She was his friend and protector, and now he must do whatever he could to rescue her from their attackers.

Lafayette looked up with a start. There was something moving in the darkness – above the roofs. He had a glimpse of the smooth shape as it glided over the alley, and then it was gone.

The ball had lifted high into the air, and it was searching the streets for him. Ought he to try to remain hidden? It obviously had not seen him as it passed overhead. Or should he try to escape, before it returned?

It was back! And descending rapidly. He was sure no human eye could have made him out in the shadow – he could barely see his hand in front of his face. But that was no guarantee that this thing, whatever it was, could not somehow sniff him out.

If it slew him, or somehow captured him, he would not be able to rescue Benny. For a moment he considered allowing the ball to catch him – he might become Benny's fellow prisoner, and be able to look after her. No, there was no reason to believe that the ball and the ruffians had any relationship. He must remain free, and seek help.

The ball was drifting over the alley, as though puzzled. Lafayette prayed fervently that whatever futuristic powers it possessed, it could not use them to detect him. He lowered his head, hugged his arms to himself, and prayed to God Almighty to make him small, dark, invisible.

Lafayette didn't know how long he stayed curled in on himself. After a while it became comfortable. His head rested on his knees, his back against the wall. He wasn't there. There was nothing for the searching ball to find, nothing for it to see. He thought no thoughts, his body was transparent as water, an empty, silent space. Don't see me, don't see me, I'm not here.

After a while, he felt himself awakening from the strange, pleasant state of nothingness. He moved a little, leaning his head back against the hard mud of the wall. His eyes had grown used to the darkness.

There was no sign of the ball. Perhaps it had stayed for a while, trying to convince itself that it could make out his shape in the shadow. Perhaps it had simply hovered silently past him, without ever seeing him.

Whatever had happened, he was free of the mysterious thing.

He stretched, stood. Now he must find his way to the house of the Lady Ninan. She was the only one who could help them now.

He walked for hours, asking directions whenever he could make himself understood. He tried to stay in streets that contained crowds, both to hide himself and to avoid attack. There were many people enjoying the early evening cool, dancing while musicians played, or spilling out of the taverns into the night air.

Outside a tavern, he spoke in Hebrew until he found an expatriate Jew who could understand him. For the price of a drink, the man asked around the inn until he found someone

146

who could point Lafayette in the right direction. He had almost reached Ninan's house; just a few more streets.

As he turned a corner in the maze, a lone harlot called out to him. He didn't mean to look, but the cry startled him, and he turned his head. She took the opportunity to pat his face and admire his hair, chattering all the while.

She wasn't a Babylonian, by the look of her. She was thin, hungry, and her eyes held a glimmer of desperation. Perhaps she was one of the hundreds of thousands brought here as captives, perhaps the wife of a slave – she was certainly not youthful, though she had dark eyes and a distracting, red mouth.

Lafayette stared at her, wondering what she was saying to him as her fingers curled through his hair. She ought to have repelled him. But was he morally any better than she, after what he and Bernice had done?

It was entirely possible, he supposed, that her difficulty was not insufficient moral fibre, but simply a lack of money. Despite the insistent, murmuring voice, he suddenly felt utterly alone. Lost in the foreign city, helpless, a terrible distance from his home.

He disentangled himself from the woman as gently as he could. 'I'm sorry,' he said. 'Please, leave me alone.'

She gave him a bitter look and turned back, seeking the comfort – and the potential clientele – of the tavern. Lafayette frowned, put his hands in his pockets, and continued walking.

The ball found him one block later.

After a rest, Clarence dropped in on the Coping Team. Their flocks of screens had proliferated until they looked like an angular forest.

God had decided to leave the turtle under island arrest until its role in the affair had been clarified. Clarence had worried that the island would try to get its story on to one of the news networks in protest. But God doubted the turtle would risk its secret getting out in the blaze of attention, even now.

He'd flipped through various channels on the way here. The news media were mercifully free from information about the whole affair. He knew them – if they picked up even a small detail, they'd fetishize it, and before long there'd be chat shows about the unannounced solar flare and sitcoms about the island.

It was only a matter of time before everyone knew.

The Coping Team seemed unaware of the whole turtle thing, intently focused on their dual missions of blowing the Path up and shutting the Path down. !Cin-ta!x, his hair sticking out in all directions and his eyes slightly glazed from too much *wakey wakey*, took almost half an hour to even realize Clarence was there. The angel waited patiently, perched on one of the bubble houses, not wanting to interrupt the work.

At last !Cin-ta!x turned from the Path, saw the angel, and came and sat cross-legged on the ground. Clarence looked down at him.

'Sorry,' said the scientist. 'I haven't slept and my House keeps calling me every ten minutes to ask if I'm all right. We think we know where they got the equations. There are some telltale harmonics in the Path's transtemporal envelope. We think it's the bloody Ikkaba.'

'I thought they were extinct,' said Clarence.

'Oh, they are. Very extinct. The whole civilization is supposed to have committed suicide, millennia ago. But not before they got about a bit. Ikkaba relics are found in at least three different local galaxies.'

Clarence whistled. 'They did get around.'

'They must have rivalled the People, technologically,' said !Cin-ta!x. 'But nobody knows what went on in their heads. Why they never built a Dyson Sphere, or an empire. All they ever seemed to do was write poetry and kill themselves.'

The angel's wing feathers bristled. 'If they could time travel . . .' he said. 'Are we seeing some kind of incursion?'

!Cin-ta!x shook his head, wearily. 'Nothing like that. No, it's the Ke Chedani.'

The name went 'ping' inside Clarence's head. 'Hey, I remember them. Those teddy bear people from the rim.'

'That's the ones. Insatiably curious little buggers. They've been crawling all over the Ikkaba relics in their region, looking for technology and science they could rip off. TIG and the Ke Chedani Interest Group have been keeping a close eye on them, in case they turn up anything serious.'

'What will you do then?' asked Clarence.

'If they learn anything which might lead to time-travel technology,' said !Cin-ta!x, 'TIG has agreed to sabotage their research. Either that or bring them into the People, so that they'll be stuck with the treaty as well.' He sighed. 'Thing is, they haven't learnt anything they can actually use – they've got the maths, but it'll be centuries before they have the power sources. Hmm. We should have never let them get the maths.'

'WiRgo!xu and !Ci!ci-tel stole it,' said Clarence.

!Cin-ta!x folded his arms. 'That's the theory,' he said. 'They might have come into contact with them on one of their missions during the war. The question is, where did they get the expertise to turn those equations into the Path?'

Clarence glanced around the work site, at the members of TIG.

'Don't look at us,' said !Cin-ta!x. 'Most of us are also members of the Immortality Through Not Pissing Off God Interest Group.'

The sphere came shooting down into the alley, heart-stoppingly fast. Lafayette almost fell over as it swooshed up to him.

It stopped about ten feet away. He could not hope to outrun it.

He pulled the pistol out of his pocket. The thing had spoken – presumably it could understand him. 'Stay away from me,' he ordered it. 'Do you understand what this is?'

'It's a projectile weapon with a chemical explosive propel-lent,' said the ball. Its voice sounded frighteningly human, perhaps the voice of a young man, with a hint of an accent. 'I only want to know who you are, and how you got here.'

'My name's John Lafayette,' he said. 'Where is Bernice? Have you harmed her?'

The ball hesitated, then darted towards him. He shot it.

The bullet *stopped*. For a moment, he thought it had

ricocheted off the smooth surface of the sphere – but where was the sound? Then he saw it hovering, a few inches from the object's surface.

The bullet moved up and down a little, as though the ball was examining it. Then it clattered to the ground.

'Oh dear,' said Lafayette faintly.

'How did you do that before?' said the ball.

'What?' said Lafayette. He was backing away, looking for some avenue of escape.

'You disappeared from my sensors.'

'I wish I knew how.' I wish I could do it right now. 'Tell me where Bernice is.'

'Sorry, can't do that,' said the ball cheerfully. 'I'm going to do a contact scan now. Hold still.'

Lafayette had no intention of holding still. When the ball charged him, dashing through the air, he turned to run.

The ball simply knocked him in the back, hard, sending him stumbling to the ground. It drifted down as he struggled to rise.

Abruptly, he found he could not move. It felt as though cold blankets were being wrapped around him, tightening to trap his arms and legs. He panicked before he realized he could still breathe without difficulty.

'I'm just going to take a tiny tissue sample,' continued the ball in its pleasant voice. 'It won't hurt a bit.'

The front of the ball opened wide. A dozen metal arms extruded themselves like the legs of grasshoppers, each one tipped with a variety of sharp surgical instruments.

Lafayette let out a yell which could probably be heard in every street in Babylon.

The ball reached down, through the invisible blankets, with one of its legs. Lafayette felt the cool surface of the instrument brush against his skin.

'Oh *no*,' said the ball.

Lafayette felt cold and hot and felt something rushing up inside him, as though he were a pane of glass and some huge and unstoppable figure was running towards him, intent on breaking through and shattering him into pieces. He drew a deep breath, feeling the flood bursting through him.

* * *

He saw, clear as crystal, the caves of the dracs deep in the river Rhône. He felt the water buoying him up as he rose towards the surface in a cloud of bubbles. The water was his home, his friend, cool and sweet.

At the surface, dracs were playing, unseen by the women washing their clothes on the shore. They needed those women, needed their strong bodies and their fertile wombs. He was only a little child, but even he understood that. The dracs had few children of their own. Human blood was strong, human flesh was fecund.

The women must be brought over into their world, taken down through the living water into the caves. They would be cared for, treated well, returned once they had borne drac children. Sometimes, he knew, clear as crystal, they took men as well, surrounding their boats; but it was easier to take the women while they washed.

Together, the dracs broke the surface of the water, breaking free into the other realm. His lungs cleared themselves of water, sucked in the clear air.

The dracs laughed among themselves. The humans went on washing, gossiping and giggling, quite unaware of the eyes that watched them from the water. Oh, perhaps sometimes they guessed, perhaps they caught a glimpse of that other, hidden world living side by side with their own. Sometimes, when a human was returned to the surface after their seven years' captivity, their warning and their stories were believed. And then the women stayed away from the water, and keen eyes watched from the men's ships as they travelled down the Rhône.

But not today. One of the drac women took a bowl from her sleeve, a fine bowl set with lines of gold. The metal flashed and glittered in the warm sunshine. One of the washerwomen looked up, the yellow light moving across her features.

Lafayette jerked awake, violently, still trying to struggle free, to get away from the horror that was tormenting him. His back and head slammed against the mud wall as his arms flailed.

After a moment, he realized that the ball was gone.

What had the thing done to him? What had it done? He looked at his hands, stretched his body out, looked for cuts in his clothing or skin. But he could find no mark, feel no pain.

Perhaps whatever had happened had not been the sphere's doing. Perhaps it had been frightened away.

Perhaps it would be back. Lafayette pulled himself to his feet. He felt ill, he felt as though he had been travelling for ever. He leant on the wall, drawing deep breaths, smelling the smoke and sewage and the dried mud.

Ninan's house was dark and quiet, for once. For a frightening moment, Lafayette thought that the priestess had left. But the same doorman was there, peering at him, an oil lamp held in one hand. He shouted something, and a few moments later Miriam appeared, also holding one of the small lights.

'*Shalom*,' she said. 'How can we help you?'

'I need to speak to Lady Ninan,' he said.

'I'm afraid she is engaged in preparatory meditations and prayer at the moment,' said Miriam.

'It's terribly urgent,' he insisted. 'Bernice has been kidnapped.'

Miriam nodded. 'Come inside. But we had better wait until the Lady Ninan has completed her prayers.'

Lafayette followed her into the darkness of the house. It was noticeably cooler indoors. The girl's face was lit by the flickering yellow flame of her Aladdin's lamp. She took him through one room to another. 'This is the guest bedroom,' she said. 'You can wait here. I will bring you to the Lady Ninan in a little while.'

She lit one of the lamps hanging from the ceiling, and left him there. There was a low table and chair, and a bed, a wooden frame stretched with reed matting.

Lafayette realized he could hear chanting. He peered out through the door across the courtyard. The sound was coming from behind a curtain, lit from behind with lamplight. It was Ninan, intoning the ancient Sumerian words in a singsong voice. Most probably from memory – beyond the scribes, few could read Akkadian, let alone the dead language reserved for the liturgy.

Lafayette listened for a little while, wishing the ancient words were clearer to him. He stretched out on the low bed, a luxury after the reed mats of the inn, and let his eyes close.

As a child, he had loved to watch the rain through the window, safe and warm inside the house. He would sit in the window seat and read, or put jigsaws together, listening to the steady sound against the glass. Ninan's chanting reminded him of that comforting sound.

Perhaps his parents had hoped for great works from their scholarly son – either in the diplomatic services or at some dramatic excavation in Egypt or Arabia. But Lafayette had no such plans for himself. There was a mountain of work to be done, more tablets were being found every day. But while it all needed translating, there were surely no more remarkable discoveries to be made. Lafayette would do as much of the work as one man might do in a lifetime, and retire into comfortable obscurity.

Always assuming he survived this adventure. With a guilty start, he realized that even if Bernice was lost, he could still almost certainly get home again.

Still . . . he imagined being one of the linguists who had first translated the *Epic of Gilgamesh*, the first eyes in centuries to read those words. The story of the Deluge emerging from a Mesopotamian document.

Here, in the flat plains between the two rivers, the flood did not bring life the way it did in Egypt. It brought chaos and disaster, even with the canals to direct the annual rush of melted snow from the mountains that engorged the Tigris and Euphrates until they spilt free of their banks, muddy water swirling over the farms and houses in a torrent that never seemed to end –

'Jonlafayet?' said a voice. He was suddenly awake, sitting up on the low bed and running his hands over his face, dusty with sleep.

It was Miriam. 'The Lady Ninan is ready to speak with you now.'

Miriam sat between them, translating quietly.

'When I turned around again, Bernice had gone,' said

Lafayette. 'I searched for her, but they had spirited her away. I hope – I believe – that she is still alive.'

He decided to leave out the part about the mysterious ball. Ninan might interpret it as some kind of demon or monster, striking fear into her heart, making her unwilling to help.

Ninan was quietly furious. 'I will do everything in my power to secure her safe release,' she said. 'I will send a messenger to the head of this city ward at once, and have him contact the other heads of wards. I want as many police as can be spared to investigate this. Can you describe those who attacked you?'

Lafayette nodded. 'I think so.'

'Excellent. Then we should be attended by the police within the hour. Once we have dealt with them, you must take a bath and some rest. And I will pray for Bernice's safe return.'

'As will I, madam,' he said.

8

THE SHORTEST-LIVED PROFESSION

I did not desire your death
yet you died
I did not raise my hand against you
yet you died
I did not see, I did not know
Only my desire,
firm & bright as pomegranate seeds

I poured out before you
rivers of silver, fountains of gold
rich wine and apricots, blood-red pomegranate seeds
Ancient wealth, made new
Your welfare my desire

I did not desire your death
I did not raise my hand against you
I did not see, I did not know
And you died

Because of my desire
your death is on my hands
Because of my desire
your blood ran red as pomegranate seeds
Because of my desire

(This poem, sometimes called 'The Pomegranate
Lament', was not written by the Wanderer, as some

have theorized, but is far more likely to have been
written by a student or follower of his.)

– From Summerfield, Bernice S., 2595, *An Eye for
Wisdom: Repetitive poems of the Early Ikkaban
Period*, St Oscar's University Press, Dellah.

Morning.

Lafayette lay on the roof of Lady Ninan's house. He had a
good view of the wide street below – but anyone looking up
at him would have been half blinded by the rising sun.

Already, the traffic was thick: plenty of visitors, as well as
locals on their way to work. He had watched as the beggars
squabbled over positions, as the pedlars set up their wares at
the edges of the street. A snake charmer mesmerized a
tired-looking serpent, gaining a small audience and a few
copper coins. A cross donkey had got away from its owner,
and he had watched, trying not to laugh, as it was chased up
and down the street and was finally placated with a carrot.

He wondered if he had walked down this street, or the
remains of it, half-hidden lines in the sun-baked plain. In his
own time, perhaps this very building swarmed with wall-
tracers. Or perhaps it had been totally lost, mined for its
bricks over the centuries, plundered until it was nothing.

Nebuchadnezzar had spent his silver more on architecture
than on war. Perhaps he knew that the boundaries of the
country were a temporary thing, but that great walls could
stand for ever. Not that the mighty walls he had constructed
around Babylon would save it. The Persians had got in by
walking the bed of the Euphrates at low tide.

The beginning of the end for the city was less than a
century away; there were children in the street below who
would live through the Persian conquest. In the end, even
their occupation came to an end, as politics and trade routes
changed. Alexander would attach Babylon to his empire, and
die in the city itself, and after that, it would be abandoned to
the sands.

But now – in this now – it was abuzz with life. He could
smell the crowd, smell their sweat and perfume.

As he watched, eyes resting comfortably on the people as they flowed beneath him, he wondered what would become of him if he did not get home. Perhaps he could find training as a translator, or as a scribe. Possibly the Lady Ninan could assist him.

Perhaps it would be best to leave now, this moment, and find the Path.

But he had already made his decision.

He wished Bernice was here, with some of her 'sunscreen' to rub into his face and hands. It would not be too long before the heat here on the roof became intolerable, and he must retreat into the house.

But for now, he watched the crowd.

An hour later, when he was starting to have intense fantasies about apple cider, he saw what he was looking for.

There. A man walking among the crowd, looking little different from any other Babylonian but for the size of him. He was tall and broad-shouldered, and his beard was long and shaggy.

Lafayette recognized him at once. For a moment, he was back in the alleyway, the tall man screaming into his face as they struggled.

The ruffian stopped to haggle with a pedlar. Lafayette put his hand in his pocket, feeling the comforting shape of the gun, and headed for the ladder into Ninan's courtyard.

The man spent the entire morning meandering, sometimes shopping. He argued with a tavern keeper over the price of his lunch, pushed over a beggar who approached him too closely, and was generally obnoxious to everyone he dealt with.

At least he didn't notice Lafayette, trailing behind him at a good distance. In fact, the linguist speculated, the man had probably been sent to try to find him, and was wandering at random in the hope of spotting the pale foreigner. He stayed well back, hidden by a moving wall of people. Sometimes Lafayette lost his prey in the throng, but he would always pick the fellow out again. The man shimmered with the flames of time.

Not a strong fire – more a light similar to that which had marked the lying merchant, the result of a brush with someone who had travelled the long road of the centuries.

Lafayette followed the trail, watching it swirl through the crowd in pale colours. It was strange to remember that only he could see it. How could he have come by such a rare talent? Or did thousands of people have the same ability, and time travel was so rare that almost no one realized?

He lost the man, once, colliding with a family group chasing a pig. He had seen more than one of the animals roaming the street, scavenging in the garbage. This one was on its way to becoming supper for the man and his dozen children. Lafayette bumped into them, wove between them, almost tripped over the pig, and looked frantically around. The thug was nowhere to be seen.

He ran down the street – there! The man was taking fruit from a skinny merchant's cart, laughing at the vendor's ineffectual protests. Lafayette let out a breath, and allowed himself to blend in with the throng once more.

As the crowds began to thin, the man headed towards the residential section of the city. Presumably he intended to take his afternoon nap. Lafayette stayed well back, but the man was no longer looking around, just stumping along the streets, stretching and scratching, ready for sleep.

There! The man stepped into a doorway. The house looked like all the others in the street. But Lafayette had come prepared. He stepped up to the house, took a small container of Nabu-zuqup-kemu's ink from his pocket, and let the dark fluid run on to the wall at its base. There – a mark that he would recognize, but that the villains hopefully would not see.

He replaced the ink bottle in his pocket and took out his gun. Then he took a deep breath and stepped into the doorway.

He was expecting a doorman, and was ready to threaten the man, put a hand over his mouth if necessary. But there was no one. Carefully, he took a few steps into the narrow passageway, listening hard.

He heard snores coming from a room somewhere to his right, so he stepped to the left. At once he was in a sort of narrow cloister looking on to the courtyard. He stayed in the shadows as best he could, but if anyone happened to look through a doorway, he had no doubt they would see him.

Then he must complete his recce as quickly as possible, and escape. He made his way along the cloister, treading softly on the flagstones, until he reached the house's main room.

He was ready with his pistol, but there was no one there. Two other doorways led off from the living room, besides the door to the courtyard. If he –

He heard a thump from the room to the left. He pressed himself against the wall and worked his way around to the doorway.

He peeked around the door, just for a moment, pulling his head back at once.

Bernice was sitting on a bed, tied and gagged with strips of cloth, and there were two of the thuggish men guarding her. Her eyes had widened as she saw him.

He slid the earring from his pocket, and clipped it into place, awkwardly.

The thugs were discussing just what they could get away with doing to her without having their pay docked.

It was time to screw his courage to the sticking place.

He stepped into the doorway, lowering the pistol. 'You know what this is,' he announced, as the men turned to look at him in astonishment. 'Untie Miss Summerfield at once, and let her go.'

One of them stared at the gun in terror. One said, 'Don't kill us. I'll do what you say.' He stepped up to the bed.

'Take out her gag,' ordered Lafayette, gesturing with his free hand. The ruffian fumbled with the knot at the back of Bernice's head.

The cloth fell away. Bernice shouted, 'Behind you!'

Lafayette didn't have time to turn around before something hit him in the head.

The first blow didn't render him insensible. He staggered into the room, trying to turn around, his head ringing like a church bell.

It was the tall man. Evidently, his sleep had been interrupted. He punched Lafayette in the face.

Lafayette's field of vision turned white. He stumbled

backward and fell over the bed. Bernice was shouting, but he couldn't make out the words. He was aware that the pistol was no longer in his hand.

From somewhere came a foot like a steam hammer, colliding with his ribs. He heard a dreadful sound, like wood splintering, and tried to curl up around the damage.

Someone kicked him in the head. He felt his neck snap forward, and for a moment he thought it must be broken, nothing could withstand such force.

He did not try to rise; he could not have done so in any case. He felt the tips of sandals, in strange detail, as they struck at his arms and legs and back. He actually felt someone's little toe fracture, they kicked him so hard.

He could not feel the things inside him that were breaking and bursting. He could only imagine them. He wished he could see the Rhône again, be wrapped in the safety of that cool water, but he tasted blood and mud and finally nothing at all.

9

HELPLESS

Leap like lightning
　　Leave this place
　　　Of dust
　　　Of death

Here only the Turtle has triumphed

Lost the laughter
　　Silent now, and still
　　What did we do?
　　What did we say?

The wind has blown it all away

　　Amber ash and agony
　　Bleeding air
　　Stunned as silence cracked the sky

Leap like lightning
　　Leaving empty footprints
　　　Of dust
　　　Of death
　　What did we do?
　　What did we say?

The wind has blown it all away
Here only the Turtle has triumphed

– Ikkaban poem. *c.* 2500 BCE, reproduced with permission from Summerfield, Bernice S., 2595, *An Eye for Wisdom: Repetitive poems of the Early Ikkaban Period,* St Oscar's University Press, Dellah.

Extract from the Memoirs of Bernice Summerfield

There have been many times in my life when I have felt helpless. Helplessness comes in different flavours.

One flavour is the helplessness of discovering that you should have taken care of something long ago, or that you've made some terrible mistake, and suddenly it's all caught up with you. I felt that awful if-only, why-didn't-I feeling when God first told me about this whole mess. If only I hadn't brought those notes; why didn't I take more care?

Another is the helplessness of watching some disaster happen, knowing there's no way you can stop it. I watched a starship crash once, a drunken pilot missing the spacedock by a few degrees and smacking his solar yacht into the side of a freighter. It happened in slow motion, and you knew it was going to happen, saw the ship drifting wide of the mark more than a minute before the impact, but there was no way anyone could have done anything.

It didn't stop people from rushing to the viewing wall, faces pressed against the glass as the tiny, fragile ship spun and ricocheted and shredded. They weren't rubbernecking – the morbid voyeurs came later. They needed to get to that ship, to help, and they couldn't.

You do what you can. The staff of the spaceport took up a collection to buy flowers for the pilot's widower. People volunteered to go out in suits and help clean up the debris.

When the hired thugs started to kill John, I did what I could. Which was bloody nearly nothing. My ankles and my wrists were both bound with thick cloth. At least they'd taken out the gag. 'Stop it!' I shouted. 'WiRgo!xu and !Ci!ci-tel will be furious if you hurt him!' And then I remembered that they couldn't understand me; I didn't have the translator.

They weren't interested anyway. They were terrified of that pistol, and they hadn't forgotten how he'd killed a friend of theirs.

One of them kicked the gun into the corner. I dived for it, but the big fellow saw me, and caught my arm in a hand like a bunch of bananas. I twisted and tried to kick him in the leg, but all I could do was wriggle.

He picked me up and held me in a bear hug. I turned my head. They were pounding John into a pulp on the floor.

'Leave him alone!' I yelled. 'Just leave him alone, for God's sake!'

One of them grinned at me, and then kicked John in the back. He had stopped moving, and I could see a spreading stain of blood moving out from his body across the tiles.

That was when the cavalry arrived. Just after the nick of time.

The room was suddenly filled with armed men in tunics. Some of them were tattooed with the mark of Esagila, and all of them had drawn swords.

One of the men beating John stopped instantly, staring at the guards with huge eyes. The other man pulled a dagger out of his belt, and was instantly skewered. It was a stupid gesture – there were already four of the guards in the room, and I could hear more of them in the house.

The big guy dropped me. I hit the floor, trying to avoid smacking my head on the tiles. I had a huge bruise on my arm, along with the bumps and cuts I'd got when they captured me, but I was basically OK.

Unlike John.

The translator came away from his ear covered in blood. I wiped it off on my jeans. I stopped them from moving him, made them send for a surgeon. The little man arrived very quickly, by which time I'd already got John into the recovery position and stopped the worst of the bleeding with torn strips of cloth.

My would-be rescuer was breathing shallowly. He didn't move or react as we worked on him. I'd taken off my shirt, and my skin was completely smeared with blood.

All I could think about was yesterday afternoon. John

holding absolutely still, so still he was shaking with anticipation or fear, not knowing what I would do next.

Between the two of us we set his broken leg, and the surgeon set and bandaged four mangled fingers as best he could. I remember one of the thugs stomping on them, the terrible crunching noise.

I wish I knew whether he wrote with his left or his right hand.

We bound up two broken ribs, and the surgeon applied some kind of salve to John's swollen eye and lip. As far as the surgeon could tell, there was no skull fracture, which I think is a minor miracle. But he thinks there's internal bleeding, and by the look of John's gums, he's right. Gods know what's broken inside.

The surgeon apologized to me afterwards. He said he'd done everything he could, and that he'd come and stay the night tonight, but he didn't think John would live very long. He probably wouldn't even regain consciousness.

I was wrestling with the usual ball of grief and guilt. I'd been in this situation too many times. Of course, sometimes, it's been me lying there close to death, and someone else doing the watching, the waiting.

Once, when I was trying not to fall in love with Jason, he played a rotten trick on me. Pretending to be lethally wounded at the bottom of a pit. He let me cry for a while, holding what I thought was his dying body in my arms, and then let on that he was wearing a bulletproof jacket. The swine.

It had exactly the right effect, forcing me to realize how I felt about him. We fought and fought, Jason and I, but sometimes I would remember those dreadful minutes. But more, I would remember the mixture of rage, surprise, and overwhelming relief and joy when I realized it was all a joke, he wasn't really dying.

My mind kept waiting for that moment for John. Waiting to be told it was all a trick, he was pretending to be beaten up, the fight and the surgeon's visit were all staged as part of some bizarre plan.

Ninan had sent a couple of temple guards to keep an eye on him, and they followed him as sneakily as he followed the thug. They recognized the big guy from John's description, as well as from having messed with him before. He was, as they say, known to the police.

As soon as John followed them into the house, one of the guards ran for reinforcements while the other kept an eye on things. They responded very quickly. It was just a shame that John Lafayette decided to be a hero.

I didn't need to be rescued. WiRgo!xu and !Ci!ci-tel weren't going to kill me, or it would have been farm-buying time the moment they saw me. They were astonished, and then they were frightened, and then they went all calm and started discussing things. I think they had some kind of plan for me. I reckoned that if I waited, I'd find out what it was.

Maybe I did need to be rescued. The guards were getting more and more bored and drunk, and they'd been giving me odd looks all day.

The renegades looked well. They'd disguised themselves as Babylonians, as we suspected, and they're working on tans and proper beards. From what little I saw of the house, they'd gone native – assuming that was their base of operations, and not just a safe house.

Ninan was outraged. She was terribly upset to see poor John when we brought him in on the improvised stretcher. I needed to speak with her, try to work out what to do next. She insisted on my having a bath and some dinner first, and I couldn't argue with that; I was wearing my shirt loose over the dried blood. When I was presentable, we sat in her main room and talked it over.

'As far as I know, every one of the hired muscle was either arrested or killed,' I said.

'Excellent. I will have the house surrounded with guards,' she said, 'and four guards will wait inside for the strangers' return.'

'It might be better,' I suggested, 'if we don't make a big show of it.' I drummed my fingers on my lower lip. 'In fact, I'll bet they don't even know I've escaped. We can use that.'

'You're right,' said Ninan. 'But how?'

'We could search the house before they get back. Or rather, I could.'

'And discover the goods they took from you!' said the priestess.

'Er, yes,' I said. 'The other thing I want to look for is . . . medical equipment. They might have something which can save John.'

Ninan nodded, seriously. 'The surgeon promised to return this evening, so we could find out if he could use their instruments or drugs.'

If they had what I had in mind, I'd be able to do it myself. But I said, 'The sooner the better, my lady. I'll set off for the house at once.'

'I will send a guard with you,' she said, gesturing at a waiting servant. She raised a hand before I could protest. 'You must have protection.' She was right, of course, and the truth was I'd be glad of the backup.

'I have a duty to perform this evening,' she continued. 'So I may not be here when you return. But I'll put Miriam in charge of providing you with whatever you need.'

'Lady Ninan,' I said, 'I don't know how to thank you. I don't know how we would have managed without your help.'

'Just keep telling me your stories,' she said, smiling. 'This is more interest and excitement than I have experienced in a long while.' Her smile faded. 'I'm only sorry it's taken such a tragic turn. I will pray for your friend's recovery.'

'Thank you, lady,' I said.

John's only chance was for me to find, and work out how to use, some People medical thingummy or other. I couldn't believe they'd journey back here without the high-tech equivalent of band-aids.

If WiRgo!xu and !Ci!ci-tel had returned, maybe I could negotiate with them. Or maybe they'd help us as a matter of principle.

But then . . . I'd been assuming that they were still People, still basically good-natured and civilized. That they wouldn't let someone die just because they tried to rescue an enemy, that it was the ruffians and not their employers who stepped over the line.

What if I was wrong?

The temple guard arrived after half an hour. He looked like he was about nineteen. I hoped he knew how to use that sword, because I didn't fancy getting soaked in anyone else's blood.

It was early evening. We'd missed the grand procession of the gods, as the statues from around Babylonia were paraded down the Processional Way to the Temple of the New Year. That must've been one hell of a sight. I wasn't sorry to miss the crowds, though.

As I made my way through the residential streets, trailing the young bodyguard, I wondered what it would be like to come here as a tourist – to have the time to just relax and see the sights. Or, in my case, to take copious notes and video a lot of stuff and get rich from the resulting coffee-table book.

That's the trouble with adventuring – you're so busy getting the alligators off your legs with a canoe paddle that you don't have time to admire the river.

Was that what WiRgo!xu and !Ci!ci-tel had in mind? Tourism? They were risking the fabric of the universe, and cosmic war, so they could get some holiday snaps? Typical of the People to take an unimaginable piece of technology and turn it into a lark.

I had two days left before God's wrath descended on Babylon. But as I turned into the street and saw the ink-stained house where I'd been held, the only thing I was interested in was saving John's life.

If that isn't an argument for travelling solo, I don't know what is.

I made the guard wait outside – mostly because I didn't want him getting killed, but partly because I didn't want to have to explain any awkward bits of high-tech junk I came across.

The house was cold and silent; there was obviously no one at home. I found a lamp and lit it, the sesame oil sputtering.

I searched, room by room. Where had the renegades got to? What was their plan? Risking everything for the sake of an exotic holiday was insane, and it was hard to believe they were both gripped by the same madness, one that had escaped the People's psychological profiles.

Nothing in the storerooms but spiders, nothing in the bedrooms but a few sticks of furniture. Was it some kind of bizarre vengeance – ensuring the destruction of the World-sphere while they escaped into the unreachable past? That was a terrifying thought. Did they want to see the People destroyed – revenge for not being invited to their parties?

And if so, how the hell was I going to talk them out of it?

In a sense, I was nothing more than God's messenger. Tell them to get out, and then stand back while the fire and brimstone hit. There was a good chance there wasn't anything more I could do.

The Babylonians felt helpless before their fickle gods; there was always a chance the New Year wouldn't come at all, that the chaos would return. Human beings had been created only to serve the gods – we weren't the centre of the universe, the purpose of creation. All of Babylon could be swept away in a flood, and the gods would notice only that the noise level in the neighbourhood had gone down.

I knew just how they felt.

Damn it! Nothing anachronistic in the house at all. Where were the entertainment consoles, the reference files, and, sod and bugger, where was the medical equipment?

It didn't make sense. There's no way they would have come back here without it – unless they really were bonkers. I leant my forehead against the wall in the courtyard. It was more likely that they simply had their goodies stashed some-where else. If I couldn't find them, John was dead.

I turned, my heart suddenly thumping. The water jars!

They were huge vases, set into the floor of the courtyard to help keep them cool. You could have hidden anything in them, up to and including a small human being.

I stepped up to the first of the three storage vessels. The surface was slightly damp; porous, to help keep the water cool by evaporation. They had wide mouths, wider than your arm, with a ladle tied on to one of the handles. I pulled out the stopper.

I held the lamp close to the surface of the water inside, but

I couldn't see into it. I grabbed the ladle and started banging it around inside the vase. Nothing.

I pulled out the second cistern's stopper. It was empty. I held the lamp right down inside it, trying not to burn my arm.

One more chance. I tugged loose the stopper on the third cistern.

Empty.

I sat down suddenly, my back to the huge vase. 'Sorry, John,' I whispered.

When I got back, he was awake.

He gave me a watery smile when I walked in. I knew better than to assume this meant he was all right now. The surgeon was fussing over him in slow motion, checking every inch of him, but the damage was where Babylonian medicine couldn't get to it.

I pulled up a chair and sat down. 'Should have brought you some flowers,' I said.

'I am glad to see you are all right,' he said. His voice was tiny and hoarse. 'That means it was worthwhile.'

'It was not worthwhile,' I said. I wanted to take his hand, but it was a swollen, bandaged mass. 'It wasn't worth this. Why did you have to start waving that pistol around? Oh, shit.' I wiped at my eyes. 'Sorry about the language.'

'I do not believe I will survive my injuries,' he informed me gently.

'I tried to get you some help,' I said. 'I mean . . .'

'You must put me out of your mind,' he said.

'What?'

'You have a mission to complete. And I am certain it is of greater importance than you have told me. Am I right?'

I nodded, tasting a whole new flavour of helplessness.

'Then you must forget about me until you have finished what you must do,' he said softly. 'I am only here by chance. Soon I will be . . . irrelevant.'

'Bollocks,' I said, but he still refused to be shocked.

'The nearness of death has given me a new perspective,' he told me. 'All my life, I have merely reacted to events. I have drifted as a leaf drifts down a stream. Even when I walked the Path, I was merely responding. But you – Bernice, you make things happen.'

'I spent a lot of my time reacting as well, you know,' I said. 'We all do. Most of the universe isn't under our control. We just have to cope with it the best we can.'

'What of the renegades?' His voice was fading. He looked as though he was falling asleep. 'Are they reacting, or are they causing others to react?'

'First the War, now this,' I muttered. 'You're right. They're different from the bulk of the People.' I'd been assuming that this was the last step of their plan – but what if it was the first? What if there was something they wanted to make happen?

The destruction of the Worldsphere?

'You must keep your focus on them,' said John. His eyes had closed. 'You must not think about me until it is all finished.'

'Bollocks,' I said again, which wasn't exactly a productive line of argument, but it did express my opinion succinctly.

'Tell me about the future,' whispered John.

I wiped my eyes again. My sleeve was gritty with dust. 'I work at a university on another planet,' I said. 'It rains all the time.'

He laughed, faintly. 'Then some things will never change.'

'A lot of things haven't changed,' I said. 'There are still stupid wars. You can still get your heart broken. But it's a good time to be an archaeologist. There are whole new planets to explore.'

He thought for a moment. 'Have you seen the canals on Mars?'

'I've even met the Martians,' I said. 'I've visited more worlds than I can remember, scattered all through the universe.'

He sighed. 'Unimaginable.'

'If you lived in my time,' I said, 'you'd be deciphering alien languages. Or you could be helping me with my research into ancient poetry. I'm writing a book.'

'There are still books?'

'Oh yes – all kinds of books. You'd love the libraries. They're all connected electronically – you can obtain a copy of almost any book, anywhere, using special machines.'

'These People,' said John. 'They are even more advanced than you.'

I nodded. 'On their world, even the machines are People.'

'Ah,' he said. 'Are they friendly?'

'I have a few machine friends,' I said.

He smiled a little. 'It sounds like befriending a steam engine, or a spinning jenny. But I believe you.'

'Great Marduk,' said the surgeon, softly.

I glanced up at him. He was staring at someone at the door.

I looked, but there was no one there.

Then my eyes adjusted to the darkness in the doorway, and I saw the drone. It was half a metre across, almost spherical, a dark gunmetal grey. It had its face on sideways.

'Oh my God,' I said. 'And then there were three.'

'Um,' said the drone. 'I think your friend is in need of medical attention.'

John said hoarsely, 'Spinning jenny.'

The surgeon was staring at the drone with gigantic eyes. 'It speaks,' he said.

'You'd better leave,' I said, thinking fast. 'This kind of demon is common in our country, and usually friendly. But it might not be as friendly with a Babylonian.'

The surgeon just nodded, stepping away from his patient. 'There is nothing I can do for him,' he told me. 'If this demon has magic that can heal your friend, it needs to be applied swiftly.'

'Right,' I said. 'You'd better go home. Thank you for everything.'

The drone hovered into the room, floating silently down to John. The surgeon edged around it, wary but not panicked. He gave me a final look, and then went out the door.

'Don't be, don't be frightened,' the drone told John.

'I am not,' he said. 'I certainly do not believe you can worsen my situation.'

* * *

The drone's name was I!qu-!qu-tala. It took one minute to save John's life.

It hovered half a metre above him, silently. I stood well back, feeling subtle changes in the air pressure as I!qu-!qu-tala manipulated its external fields.

John gasped sharply, twice. I felt a vast urge to touch him, but I kept out of the way. I saw his eyes close.

At last the drone rotated so that its sideways face ikon was pointing at me. 'He'll be fine, fine,' it said. 'I've used a minor suppressor field to put him to sleep for a while, to speed the healing process.'

'You didn't use any instruments,' I said.

'None you could, you could see,' said the drone. 'Lots of broken blood vessels and smashed bones. Small-scale precision work. But he's fixed from tip to toe. He's going to be terribly sore for a few days, though. Be gentle with him.'

I was appalled to discover I was blushing. 'I promise,' I said. 'Look, were you sent to help us?' The drone tilted slightly, which I'd come to recognize as unwillingness to answer a question. 'If God didn't send you, you must have come down the Path with WiRgo!xu and !Ci!ci-tel. Where are they?'

The drone's face ikon blinked out. It started backing away.

'No, listen,' I insisted. 'I've got an urgent message for them. It's life or death.'

'Can't stay, can't stay,' said the drone. 'He'll be all right. Let him sleep.'

It backed out of the room. I rushed out into the courtyard, but it was already zipping skyward, dwindling into a dot.

I rushed right back into the room and crouched down beside John's bed. He was breathing easily, and I could see his fingers flexing inside the bloody bandages.

I pressed my head against the wood of the bed frame, so relieved that it was almost a physical pain.

Then I fell asleep for ten hours, and woke up with an agonizingly stiff neck.

Extract ends

172

10

LOOKING

The wise traveller is prepared for all sorts of eventualities – a loose button, lost luggage, a broken limb, falling in love. The archaeologist is prepared for anything, because the past, like the future, may contain anything. There are a limited number of unexpected events that our traveller might encounter, but the archaeologist could discover anything. Even with a good knowledge of the site and of the civilization under investigation, the archaeologist is prepared to be shocked. Shock is rare – most archaeological work is slow, steady, even dull – but shock is always around the corner.

– Watkinson, Edward, *Glory Under the Mud*,
St Oscar's University Press, Dellah, 2524.

No joke, mate.

– Bernice Summerfield, graffito in pencil opposite the above
paragraph, Capella 4, 2563.

From the Memoirs of Bernice Summerfield

The bath was just a little too short, but I wasn't complaining. Ninan's slaves and servants brought me hot water and soap, and left me to soak. Once I got them to stop scrubbing me, anyway. I think better when I'm alone.

John was in the courtyard, consuming a vast breakfast. I wondered if I!qu-!qu-tala had done more than just the necessary repairs – I didn't know what subtle alterations it might be able to do with those fields. That was a slightly creepy thought.

Presumably medicine was the drone's major function. Another drone had once fixed my knee, expertly using its fields to push the dislocated bits back into place. I!qu-!qu-tala had known what it was doing. In fact, it had obviously come to the house with the express purpose of saving John.

How did it know he was hurt? Had I missed surveillance equipment in the safe house? Had it been watching, lurking in a corner? If so, why hadn't it stopped the ruffians when they attacked John? And how much did WiRgo!xu and !Ci!ci-tel know?

I was going to confront them today. There wasn't any more time for this messing around. Even if John hadn't tried to rescue me, they might not have heard my message in time. For all I knew, they'd fled the area in panic – but then, why leave the drone behind? Was I wrong, and it hadn't come to heal John, but to spy on us?

My feet hurt from all the trudging around. And, despite the moisturizer in the sunscreen, my skin was drying out really badly. The Babylonians put some kind of oil in their hair and on their skin to combat the desert heat – maybe I should try that.

I tried to sink down in the cooling water, but the bath was too awkward. I should be trying to relax, but today was the day, and I couldn't get my brain to stop.

Instead I sat up, my arms flung over the sides, and looked at myself.

For a while I'd been worried about cellulite, until I'd looked it up and found out it was invented by chemical companies selling anticellulite creams. No, I was in good shape for an old lady.[1] I tried to keep reasonably fit, in order

---

[1] Old as compared with John Lafayette, anyway.

to avoid the aches and pains of unprepared muscles when I went into the field, but I wasn't worried about a bit of podge on my thighs or my tummy. My breasts are a nice small round shape – a comfortable handful, as Jason once told me.

John and I had been basically out of our scones when we'd started rolling around on the floor of the inn. But it was nice to remember that people could find me attractive without having to have acute psychological trauma first.

I suddenly had the intense sensation of being watched.

I turned my head, and John Lafayette was standing in the doorway. Looking.

I looked back at him, wondering what was going to happen next. It occurred to me to sink down in the tub, below his eyeline. But I wasn't even blushing. After all, it wasn't anything that he hadn't seen before.

What did he want? Was I about to experience a torrent of unleashed Victorian passion? Or was he just doing this to show me he could?

His eyes met mine for a moment. He carefully pulled the curtain back into place. I heard his footsteps receding.

I don't think he knew what he wanted.

Extract ends

Itti-Marduk-balatu sat in the main room of his house, scowling at the opposite wall, trying to eat.

The police had been polite, accepting everything he said – but it was clear they knew about his link with the strangers. They had asked dozens of questions, a scribe jotting everything down on parchment. He had sweated in the morning heat, trying to keep his story straight. Yes, he had met the ruffians' employers. No, he had done no business with them. No, he did not know where they were.

If the police discovered he had warned the strangers – his business partners in a deal that would make him appallingly wealthy – he didn't like to imagine the punishment. Men had died because of his message to the foreigners. What other crimes might he be implicated in?

'Itti-Marduk-balatu,' said a voice.

He looked around, but there was no one there. 'Who is that?' he demanded.

'Over here,' said the voice.

Itti-Marduk-balatu realized there was someone standing in the alley, speaking through the air grille in the wall. He abandoned his breakfast and walked up to it, trying to peer through the holes. But he couldn't see anyone.

'Just listen,' said the voice. 'I'm a friend, a friend. I'm with Wirgaku and Kikitel.'

Itti-Marduk-balatu couldn't help looking around, even though he knew he was alone. 'Who are you?'

'Never mind that,' said the voice. 'They asked me to come here with something for you.'

'What is it?'

'Look behind you.'

Itti-Marduk-balatu turned. There was a container sitting on his desk.

He went up to it – it was glass, very finely made, about as tall as his fist. There was a clear liquid inside. At first he thought it was water, but then he caught a faint smell, like exotic herbs, coming from the fluid.

'What is this?' he said. A sudden coldness gripped him. 'Poison? Do they expect me to die for them?'

'No, no,' said the voice. 'It's a medicine. It's called *forget it*. It would make you forget what you know about them.'

'It would?' said Itti-Marduk-balatu, eyeing the glass suspiciously.

'Yes,' said the voice patiently. 'That way, they'd be safe, and so would you. You can't give yourself away to the police if you can't remember anything incriminating.'

'You were listening during the interview!'

'I was, I was,' said the voice. 'I don't think you're in trouble yet. Your best chance is to drink the *forget it*. You'll even forget talking to me, now.'

Itti-Marduk-balatu swallowed. 'I'll think about it.'

The voice didn't reply. After a few moments, Itti-Marduk-balatu realized that he was alone again.

He looked at the glass of liquid on the table.

Extract from the Memoirs of Bernice Summerfield

I had scrubbed the desert dirt out of my pores and taken off a layer of skin with it. Feeling ready to face anything, I joined Mr Lafayette for breakfast.

He was still wolfing down dates in Ninan's lounge. He smiled at me, but apparently had decided that his indiscretion in the bathroom hadn't happened. Either that, or he didn't want to embarrass me in front of the slaves.

I pulled a chair up to the low table, wondering if I'd give him a heart attack if I tried to play footsies.

The smell of cooking drifted in from the courtyard. There was a pile of fresh-baked bread on the table, flat, crisp discs that smelt like beer. I picked some specks of clay off one of them and ate it. 'God,' I said muffledly, 'what I wouldn't give for a cup of coffee.' John picked up a skewer of cooked locusts and started crunching on the insects. 'You *are* better,' I said.

'Do you know,' he said, 'when I first arrived here, I didn't dare eat or drink. Not even water from the river.'

'That was a good idea,' I said. 'God knows what's living in the Euphrates.'

He swallowed a locust. 'No,' he said, 'it was because of the stories my grandmother used to tell. About people being trapped in fairyland.'

'Oh, of course,' I said. 'Eating fairy food or drink meant you were trapped in the other realm.'

He nodded. 'It was a superstitious thing,' he said. 'But I was quite determined.'

'We don't always do things for logical reasons,' I said, tearing off another piece of bread. There were fine hairs on the backs of his hands, more blond than red. 'Is Ninan back yet?'

John shook his head. 'I asked Miriam, but she would only say that the Lady Ninan had an important duty to perform.'

And I had a pretty good idea what. I decided to keep it to myself, though. It didn't seem like the moment to broach the subject of things that go squish.

John sat back from the table, satiated at last. I continued munching on the crispy bread and wishing for some Irish

Breakfast tea, or a cup of toe-curlingly strong campus coffee, fresh from one of those walking dispenser robots.

He waited until I'd finished before he said, 'Can you tell me now?'

I looked at him. 'Can I tell you what now?'

'The true nature of your mission,' he prompted.

'Oh! Right! Yes!' I looked around, and lowered my voice. 'Yes, I can. Look, if the People can't work out how to shut down the Path, they're going to destroy it. And Babylon with it.'

'Destroy Babylon? Can they do that?'

'Yes, they can.'

John stared at me. I could hear those mental cogs of his grinding.

'It is obscene,' he said. 'How could a people so advanced consider such evil?'

I decided not to mention that Hiroshima was only a few decades ahead of him. 'They're not above brute force when it's convenient,' I said. 'Anyway, only WiRgo!xu and !Ci!citel know how to shut the Path down. Unless a miracle happens, and the People's scientists manage to work out how to do it. I've got one more day before they drop the bomb.' I dunked my hands in the finger bowl. 'Today's the day, John. I'm going to find the renegades again, and confront them today.'

He nodded. 'We must.'

I was about to tell him he ought to stay here where it was safe. And then I remembered how much that particular speech irritates me. 'Right,' I said. 'We must.' I got up. 'Our first stop is Itti-Marduk-balatu's house. And this time, no more Mr Nice Guy.'

Extract ends

Itti-Marduk-balatu looked up from the glass of *forget it*. He still hadn't decided whether to trust the strangers, and take the stuff. If it came from a malevolent magician, it was possible he would be breaking the law. On the other hand, could things get much worse?

His eyes dropped back down to the glass.

A slave coughed to get his attention. 'What is it?' he snapped.

'There are two people here to see you,' said the slave nervously. Itti-Marduk-balatu had bought the lad only yesterday, from a penniless family, and it would take the boy a while to get used to his new duties. 'A man and a woman,' he added. 'I think they're foreigners. The doorman said you'd better see them.'

Itti-Marduk-balatu's heart started to beat faster. 'All right,' he told the slave, 'bring them here.'

'Um, will you want refreshments?'

'No,' said Itti-Marduk-balatu firmly.

A moment later, the slave returned with the visitors. But the man – the man had no injuries at all! 'Hello again,' said Itti-Marduk-balatu.

'Hello,' said the woman, Beni.

'Please, take a seat.' Itti-Marduk-balatu turned to Lafayet. 'I was told you were terribly injured,' he said. 'I'm very glad to see you've quickly recovered.' Had the police been lying, trying to trick him? What was going on?

'I had a very good surgeon,' said the man.

'Which is lucky for the ruffians who almost killed him,' said Bernice. 'They're very frightened. I think they'll do anything to get out of it.'

Itti-Marduk-balatu sat back in his chair, heavily. 'Oh good,' he said. 'Then that will make your investigation much simpler.'

'Well, it's not really our investigation,' she said. She was staring at him, her eyes cool and direct. 'In fact, given that Mr Lafayette hasn't suffered any permanent injury, we're willing to forget the whole matter. All I'm interested in is finding WiRgo!xu and !Ci!ci-tel.'

How easily she pronounced those unpronounceable names. Itti-Marduk-balatu took out a cloth and wiped the sweat from his forehead and neck.

Perhaps he should reach out, take up the glass, swallow the magical fluid. Become innocent again.

But unless there was *forget it* for the hired thugs, it would not save him.

'I believe I can help you,' he said.

'Time for a nap.'

'Indeed.'

'An admirable native tradition.'

WiRgo!xu and !Ci!ci-tel strode down the dirt road, followed by three slaves carrying baskets of shopping. The sun was almost directly overhead.

'Weather control,' said WiRgo!xu. 'They'll all want weather control.'

'One thing at a time,' said !Ci!ci-tel.

'Or nothing all at once,' said WiRgo!xu.

'Here we are,' said !Ci!ci-tel, as the doorman smiled and acted in a generally ingratiating fashion. The thick walls of their house cut off the sun's heat. 'Now for a quick bath and an afternoon nap.'

'Then what? More shopping?'

'More work, I think. We still have some arrangements to take care of. And I want to see how I!qu-!qu-tala got on.'

'Besides,' sighed WiRgo!xu, 'there's Beni to deal with. Maybe we'd better have the helping hands bring her here.'

'Better she stays in the city,' said !Ci!ci-tel.

'Don't you want to find out why she's here?'

'Of course,' said !Ci!ci-tel. 'But in the end, it doesn't matter why she's here.'

They headed for the main room, while their slaves carried their latest acquisitions off to be sorted and stored. Clothing, pottery, jewellery – they'd decided to have one really good binge in the marketplace before they got down to serious work.

Beni was sitting on the table in the main room, wearing darkened spectacles to protect her eyes from the sun. There was a man standing next to her with his arms folded, wearing obviously anachronistic clothes.

WiRgo!xu and !Ci!ci-tel stopped dead, staring at the two of them, like a pair of schoolboys who've been caught out of bounds.

WiRgo!xu was about to shout for the guards when Beni said, 'If you don't listen to me, you'll be dead tomorrow.'

The renegades looked at each other.

!Ci!ci-tel pulled up a chair. He sat down, and said coolly, 'Well, why didn't you say so?'

Extract from the Memoirs of Bernice Summerfield

'We're not armed,' I said. Out of the side of my mouth, I said, 'Are we?'

John shook his head.

'And I don't think you're in any danger from the law. So there's no need to panic.'

'The Babylonians don't worry us,' said !Ci!ci-tel from his chair. 'But you – you're on a mission from God.'

'Yes I am,' I said. 'God's so desperate to keep the Path a secret that it's going to blow it up.'

WiRgo!xu said, 'But they can't do that without the energy spilling out of one of the ends.'

'And guess which end they've chosen,' I said.

'You're joking,' said !Ci!ci-tel. 'That much juice would blow away the city, and a big chunk of the surrounding countryside.'

'Including you,' said the man. 'You will be killed along with all the other people you've endangered.'

'Who is this guy?' said WiRgo!xu. He was almost hopping from foot to foot.

'Sit down before you fall down,' said !Ci!ci-tel. 'I'm telling you, it's a bluff. There's no way God would trash all those innocent bystanders just to get at us.'

'I doubt God gives a flying one about either of you,' I said, bluntly. 'It's the Path it's worried about.' I took off my shades. 'Why didn't you switch the damned thing off?'

'That would defeat the whole purpose,' said WiRgo!xu.

'What is the whole purpose?' I said.

'God knows,' said !Ci!ci-tel. 'It might not have told you, but I have no doubt it's worked it out by now. And no wonder it wants to stop us.'

'Wasn't the last war good enough for you? Didn't you learn anything?'

'No,' said !Ci!ci-tel. 'We didn't. The People didn't learn

181

a thing. We just proved yet again that we're the number-one culture in the galaxy, and that we can do whatever we like.'

WiRgo!xu opened his mouth to say something, but !Ci!ci-tel rushed on. 'Now, these primitives, they don't think they're the centre of creation. They don't even think they're that important. Oh, they're a bit cocky about their conquests and their wealth, but they know the gods could get ticked off at any moment and take it all away.'

'Imagine if we had an attitude like that,' put in WiRgo!xu.

'Don't worry about whether it's true or not,' said !Ci!ci-tel. 'Imagine if we *behaved* as if it was true. Imagine if the People learnt a little bit of humility. There'd never be another war, I guarantee it.'

'The idea is,' said WiRgo!xu, 'we bring groups of People back here to learn from the Babylonians. We provide only essential medical facilities. They *rough it*, to use one of your expressions. They get a taste of what it's like to be helpless – in the face of floods, or invaders.'

'So that's your whole plan,' I said. 'Educational tourism to teach the People humility.'

'God would never have let us go ahead with it,' said !Ci!ci-tel, 'but it's the only way the People can survive. Our own hubris is going to be fatal, sooner or later. We've got hundreds of thousands of years to make mistakes. If not millions. It's going to happen.'

'Yes, and you've just made it happen,' I said, standing up. 'If there's anything you should have learnt from us barbarian humans, it's that you can't cure a war by starting another. Stay back here by all means, but shut down the Path!'

'We went over all of this before we left,' protested WiRgo!xu. 'We went over the simulations. TIG just doesn't have the ability to mess with the Path.'

'I think you underestimate them,' I said. 'And maybe you overestimate your own knowledge of the Path. John is here by accident, after all.'

The renegades looked at him. 'You wanted to know who I am,' John told WiRgo!xu. 'My name is John Lafayette, and I am from the twentieth century. I can see your Path.'

182

'That's impossible,' said !Ci!ci-tel.

'No,' said WiRgo!xu, 'not for someone with the right complement of psi powers.'

'I am here,' said John. 'What more proof do you need? I could see the Path as clearly as a mirror in the desert. I travelled it deliberately. And if I had that power, why not others?'

'A few displaced humans hardly matter,' said !Ci!ci-tel. 'I doubt you're some famous figure from Earth history.'

John looked slightly crestfallen. 'Nonetheless, if you do not switch off the Path, won't others follow me? How much time does the Path cross? How many people might follow it?'

WiRgo!xu looked at !Ci!ci-tel, who said, 'We already agreed to deal with displacees on a case-by-case basis.'

'But psi powers . . .'

'That slightly increases the likelihood of an unintentional journey,' admitted !Ci!ci-tel. 'But once we're established, we'll simply put someone in charge of dealing with it.'

'Hasn't it sunk in?' I said. 'You're not going to get established. You're going to get nuked.'

'Relax,' said !Ci!ci-tel. 'It's not going to happen.'

'The truth is,' WiRgo!xu blurted, 'they can't blow up the Path. That was in our simulations. But we rigged it so that the energy could only spill back into the Worldsphere.'

'Modified the harmonics so there's a unilateral carrier wave,' said !Ci!ci-tel smugly.

I experienced a moment of immense relief, followed by a moment of utter panic. 'But what if they don't realize?' I said. 'What if they try it anyway?'

'Unless we're *over*estimating TIG,' said !Ci!ci-tel dryly, 'that'll have been one of the first things they worked out. They know it's dangerous – they don't want to risk blowing a hole in the sphere.'

'Blowing a hole in the sphere!'

'Trust me,' drawled !Ci!ci-tel, 'they won't be blowing anything up. It's their first lesson in dealing with things outside their control.'

'Should do them some good,' said WiRgo!xu.

'They'll find a way,' I said. 'That's assuming they're not already at war.'

'In which case they won't bother with us, will they?'

'You do realize that you're going to outlive this city,' I said. 'It's at the peak of its power now, but it won't last. Centuries from now this region will still be legendary for its political upheavals.'

I saw John look up in surprise. I!qu-!qu-tala was back. The drone hovered in the doorway, rotating slightly as though it was anxiously looking back and forth between us and the renegades. 'What, what's up?' it said.

'We've just been handed an ultimatum,' said !Ci!ci-tel. 'God's going to blow up the Path.'

'But it can't, it can't,' said the drone. It spun around, suddenly, and again. 'It can't and won't do that.'

'We know that,' said WiRgo!xu. 'Beni, however, isn't convinced.'

'I'm convinced you're all out of your minds,' I said. As ripostes go, it wasn't much. 'You're mucking about with the fates of billions of people. What gives you the right?'

They just looked at me blankly. 'Oh great,' I said. 'That's not a People concept, is it?'

'We have a lot to learn,' said WiRgo!xu. 'That's the point.'

'Yes, you have,' I said. 'You still have to learn that you can't always get what you want. Do you want to know how I learnt that? I was, oh, twenty-three? I was cocky as hell. I reckoned that since I had managed to escape the military and escape the nunnery I could do anything I pleased.'

WiRgo!xu and !Ci!ci-tel were listening with real interest. I wanted to cuff them around the ears until they saw reason, but instead I kept talking before they decided to do something more interesting. 'So I decided to go on a solo dig on Capella 4. Most archaeologists wouldn't risk a lone expedition on an unmapped planet until they had decades of experience under their belts. I brought bug spray, clean knickers, and paperback copies of *Tips for the Solo Archaeologist* and Watkinson's *Glory Under the Mud*. I landed a capsule in a clearing, and went looking for the remains of the

Aurigan civilization. Instead of which, I found a cliff, which I promptly fell off.

'I broke my left femur and my right tibia.' I!qu-!qu-tala made a clicking noise, like a human drawing in breath. 'The cliff had been miles from camp. There was no one else on the whole planet, and my radio was at the top of the cliff.'

John was staring at me in alarm. 'Well, what did you do?' asked WiRgo!xu.

'What would *you* have done?' I said, poking a finger at them.

The renegades looked at each other, and then at the drone. I knew what they were thinking: call God, find a terminal, light a fire until someone saw it, all the things that might have worked on the Worldsphere where help was always readily available.

'It took me nearly a month to crawl back to the camp,' I said. 'I had to splint both legs, and then use my arms to drag myself along, holding on to roots and low branches and rocks. I drank dew in the mornings, sucking it off grass stems. Do you know what I ate?'

They shook their heads. 'I ate night crawlers. Like big spiders. They're attracted to the smell of blood. At first my wounds got their interest, and I'd shove a sharp stick through them. After that I had to cut my own arm open to attract them. Sometimes I cooked them, but most of the time I couldn't manage to get a fire together.' John looked as though he was going to throw up.

'I had intense dreams, for the first two weeks, of being rescued – lights coming through the forest, a capsule landing to take me away. I dreamt that my legs healed and I could walk back to camp. But after two weeks, the dreams stopped. Because I'd realized that no matter what, I couldn't get what I wanted.

'I wouldn't go through that again for all the artefacts in the Braxiatel Collection,' I said. 'But I made myself take the lesson away. I was never so reckless again. I was always prepared to be cut off, to be helpless.'

'That's what we want to learn!' blurted WiRgo!xu. 'How to make do! How not to always get whatever we want!'

I wanted to grab the front of his tunic. 'Then *shut down the Path*. As long as that umbilical cord still connects you with the Worldsphere, you only *think* you're roughing it. But you can always go home. Even when awful things were happening during the War, you were still never far from help. Shut it *down*.'

'Now,' said !Ci!ci-tel, 'what would be the point of that? We need to bring what we learn back to the People.'

'Did you really eat spiders?' said John. Everyone ignored him.

'They can't learn it. Not while they can get back. Not while they can always just take a walk back to Aunty Em. But why didn't you just go to a planet in your own galaxy, your own time? Because –'

I sat down suddenly, because I'd just worked it out.

Extract ends

'I'll make a deal with you,' said God.

It had manifested itself in the form of a giant, seagoing turtle, about one and a half times the size of the island-turtle. Just to make the point. Its voice was a rough boom that carried across the waves, merging with the roar of the ocean itself.

The island-turtle trod water, gazing at the larger version of herself with a mixture of distrust, fear, hope, guilt, regret, and the tearing emotion that doesn't have a name when you wish wish wish something had never happened.

They were in the middle of nowhere, a wilderness stretch of cold ocean free of boats, maintenance and surveillance drones and bots, and curious and intelligent marine life forms. No one could overhear them, no one even knew they were there.

'What do you have in mind?' said the island softly.

'The Solar Mechanics Interest Group are poised to do a full investigation,' said God. 'They want to know who sabotaged the stellar maintenance bot. They'll be working with the friends of the two forensic drones who were blown away in the unauthorized solar flare. Everyone on the Worldsphere is curious about the flare, except the Apathy Interest

Group. And I'm personally very keen on finding out who impersonated me. To make a long story short, an attempted cover-up has backfired appallingly. Whoever's behind it is in for universal attention.'

'Yes, yes,' said the island.

'Now, I have no proof that you were behind it all,' said God. 'But I do know that you planted the bomb on yourself to help !Ci!ci-tel and WiRgo!xu. It doesn't take a hyper-dimensional intelligence to work out why you'd want that kept under wraps.'

'Yes,' said the island. 'But you said you had a deal to make.'

'Tell me everything,' said God. 'And I'll find a way to stop the investigations. I can even convince SMIG that the bot really did malfunction, after copping a burst of radiation through its tiny brain.'

'Are you sure they'll believe that?'

God said, 'People have a tendency to believe what I tell them.'

The island shrugged. Huge waves splashed through the empty sea. 'Oh, there's a lot I can tell you,' she said. 'You must be wondering what they're up to. Why they left the Path switched on.'

'Indeed,' said God. 'I'll bet you know.'

'Yes I do,' said the island-turtle.

It told God. 'Transistors!' swore God.

Extract from the Memoirs of Bernice Summerfield

!Ci!ci-tel seemed to realize what had happened. My huge eyes and dismayed expression were probably a giveaway.

With surprising gentleness, he said, 'The All of Us learnt. When we first met them, they thought they were the most important and powerful people in the universe. Now they know better.'

'You want the Treaty to break down,' I said. 'You want the People to lose a war.'

'As you said,' said !Ci!ci-tel, getting up, 'we have a lot to learn. Now, right at the moment, we need to learn just what

Lafayet did to poor I!qu-!qu-tala on their first encounter.'

John looked astonished. 'I didn't do anything to him. It. I was helpless.'

'When I tried to take that initial tissue sample,' said the drone, '*something* happened. I don't understand what. Some of my internal components failed.'

!Ci!ci-tel said, 'I wonder if it doesn't have something to do with your unusual psi power,' which was just what we were thinking. 'I'd like to take a closer look.'

'I don't think so,' said John. He looked at me, suddenly frightened.

'Just a little genetic workup and a few brain scans,' said !Ci!ci-tel soothingly, which didn't help.

I shook my head. 'Since you two – you three – idiots won't listen, I'm going back up the Path to warn God. There must be some way of sorting this out. And I'm taking John with me. He should return to his own time.'

'I don't think so,' said !Ci!ci-tel.

I!qu-!qu-tala hovered into the room, suddenly looking menacing. And I realized that the renegades were, as usual, going to get their own way.

Extract ends

It didn't take the island-turtle long to tell God everything she knew. 'It's possible even WiRgo!xu and !Ci!ci-tel don't realize just what's going on,' she finished.

'Hmm,' said God, 'that's not likely.'

'I asked them specifically not to tell me what they were up to,' said the island. 'But in fact I already knew. That's the advantage of connections. Or the disadvantage.'

'Why help them?' said God. 'You're in the same boat as the rest of us.'

'No I'm not,' said the island-turtle. 'I haven't been. Not since the War.' She puffed breath through her mighty nostrils, expressing some deep reptilian emotion. 'Maybe I felt like it was time the rest of you understood a little of what we went through.'

'Well,' said God. 'Now it's just a matter of tracking down your connections. You've been very helpful.' A puff of steam erupted from God's back, accompanied by a mechanical ripping noise, as several members of the Weird Locomotive Interest Group started stoking its boilers.

'Now what?' said the island.

'Now nothing,' said God. 'If I can convince the investigators not to investigate. No promises, but I'll do my best. Your life should continue as though nothing had happened.'

'Wouldn't *that* be nice?' said the island.

!Ci!ci-tel had extended a restraint field over the human, just in case. He expected that Lafayet would cooperate as long as they had Bernice, but there was no reason not to take the precaution. He especially didn't want the man panicking when he started work.

I!qu-!qu-tala had produced a miniature medical drone from a hatch in its side. On !Ci!ci-tel's instructions, it took up position over Lafayet's abdomen. 'Spinning jenny,' said the human, incomprehensibly. !Ci!ci-tel assumed it was an expletive, or the name of the man's deity, or both.

The scan took a few seconds. They'd brought only the most basic equipment – I!qu-!qu-tala could handle almost any medical problem, from a scraped knee to heart surgery, so the kit was little more than backup. But it was more than adequate for this task.

The human shrugged in the restraint field, uncomfortable. !Ci!ci-tel pulled up a wooden chair and watched the results of the genetic scan scroll by. The medical drone was projecting a flat screen of data about twenty centimetres high. As he sat back, the screen moved slightly to stay in optimum viewing distance.

It was interesting stuff. There were anomalies buried deep in the man's genetic code – deep enough that it took a detailed scan and sequence to spot them. A casual scan would miss the interesting stuff.

!Ci!ci-tel touched an option on the screen, following a hunch. He was right – the genes in question were adaptive. They had the ability to negotiate with their host's genome, alter themselves, and blend right in. It was like the ability of the People's genome to incorporate the genes of other species, allowing for immense flexibility in breeding.

Interesting. More scans might turn up similar genes in the human population in general. It would be well worth investigating over the next few centuries. Call it a hobby. After all, he and WiRgo!xu would probably eventually want children with someone else than each other.

He glanced at his experimental subject. The man was shaking, just enough that it was noticeable. His jaw was tightly clenched. !Ci!ci-tel realized that he was trying to look as though he wasn't afraid.

'Don't worry,' he told Lafayet, 'I'm not going to do anything horrible to you.'

Extract from the Memoirs of Bernice Summerfield

WiRgo!xu and I were having lunch. That is, WiRgo!xu was having lunch, while I sat there feeling helpless and not even slightly hungry.

WiRgo!xu removed a particularly large bit of grime from his bread and flicked it away. 'It's fascinating,' he said. 'They have no choice but to eat bread like this, because no one knows how to make better bread.'

The drone had extended a small but conspicuous nozzle, which I assumed was some kind of weapon. Even if it was a tea spigot, I was helpless – the drone could catch me in its fields before I could try anything.

I felt a bit silly about the pepper spray.

'When I was a member of the Creative Writing Interest Group,' bubbled WiRgo!xu, 'we had a huge controversy over whether limitations improved or hindered creativity. Oddly enough, it was always the drones who felt limitations sparked their creative juices – including being limited to the written word.'

I wasn't interested. 'Do you have any idea how much damage will be done by the war you're trying to start?'

'Of course we do.'

'You rebuilt the civilizations you destroyed when you were fighting the All of Us. Some of them, anyway. Sometimes there wasn't anything left.'

'We're kind of hoping the People will just surrender,' said WiRgo!xu. 'This wasn't our idea, you know.'

'It wasn't?' Buckets of blood! 'Who put you up to this?'

He wouldn't answer. I sighed and said, 'What's !Ci!ci-tel going to do to John?'

'Just what he said, of course,' said WiRgo!xu. 'What else?'

I didn't want to think what else.

Being captured or imprisoned is a tediously common occurrence in my line of work – whether it's the Zargoids throwing you into their Human Monitoring Chamber, or the local fuzz tossing you in jail because you didn't bribe them enough to keep them out of your excavation. You get used to it, but it never becomes any easier to stand.

There are different kinds of captured – I'm thinking of writing a paper, grading them by ease of escape. The simplest kind is when your captors lock you into a room in a building that was never meant to hold prisoners, and don't leave a guard – it's easy enough to break down a door, climb out of a window or into a ventilation shaft, etc.

WiRgo!xu and !Ci!ci-tel were a bit more cluey than that, having kept me tied and gagged and surrounded by guards. The only chance you have then is outside rescue.

In my current situation, all I could do was negotiate – try to persuade my captors to see reason, let us go, give up their evil scheme.

Yeah, right.

'What about me?' I said.

'Well,' said WiRgo!xu, pushing away his plate and looking at me brightly. 'We have an idea.'

'Wonderful. What is it?'

'Well,' he said, 'you've got so much more experience than we have. At dealing with new situations, new cultures, whole new worlds.'

'Bernice Summerfield: the extraterrestrial tourist,' I said dryly.

WiRgo!xu nodded enthusiastically. 'You can help us integrate. We've already made some gaffes.'

'So I've heard. Listen, I'm no expert on Ancient

191

Mesopotamia. I've got a working knowledge, but that's all.'

'But it doesn't matter where we are, don't you see? You know all the little tricks – how to find what you need, how to work out what's polite and what's outré. You can be our guide. There'll be hundreds, if not thousands of People to help.'

'Forget it,' I said. 'I'm not your slave.'

'You will be,' said WiRgo!xu. 'If we want it.' I looked at him in alarm. 'We could get you tattooed with our names. Sit down, I'm joking! We don't need to go to lengths like that.'

I put my head in my hands. Great, now I'd either be blown up or forced to work as a flight attendant for the renegades' mad scheme.

On the other hand . . . 'Wait a moment,' I said. 'John can help too. He's a linguist – he can translate for you.'

'We'll have translators,' said WiRgo!xu.

'A luxury,' I said quickly. 'If you really want to learn how these people think, you'll have to learn their languages. The drones were right about the written word – and the spoken word.'

'You're right!' he said. 'When !Ci!ci-tel's finished, we'll discuss it.'

There came an almighty, stomach-turning, heart-thumping, horrible scream from the other room.

I!qu-!qu-tala didn't even try to stop me as I bolted out the door.

John was all right, thank God, stuck to a long wooden table by some kind of force field. He was panicking, trying to get up.

!Ci!ci-tel was –

Actually, it's a bit hard to describe what !Ci!ci-tel was.

He was standing a little distance from the table, with his arms flung up, as though he'd jerked back.

At least, I assume it was him. He was a brilliant white outline, with opalescent colours swirling inside it. They might have been real, or they might have been tricks my watering eyes were playing on me.

He was frozen as the colours ran over him. The air was

pulsing with changing temperatures, hot one moment, cold the next, but there was no sound, just this horrible stillness.

The light diminished. For a moment, there was a papery corpse standing there. A mummy face stared up at the ceiling with dried eyes, fingers curling up like the edges of paper in fire.

Then it crumbled, and exploded on the floor, and faded into nothing.

The tiny medical drone shot across the room with a whine of distress, and disappeared back into the hatch in I!qu-!qu-tala's side.

WiRgo!xu just stared. John struggled. 'Shut off the field!' I told WiRgo!xu. He still just stared. 'For God's sake, shut it off!'

He got the relevant widget and pushed a control. John shot up off the table, and I caught him before he fell over. 'He touched me!' he whispered in a high voice. 'I didn't do anything! He touched me, he only touched me!'

Extract ends

11

THE PLAN

> *I will ...*
> *... the world ...*
>
> *What do [they] know*
> *that have not [seen?]*
> *What do they know*
> *that [have not] felt?*
>
> *The flutter of life*
> *beating [against?] the blade*
> *The red steel edge*
> *of silence*
>
> *... write ...*

– Fragment of an Ikkaban poem, *c.* 450 CE (translation
provisional), reproduced with permission from
Summerfield, Bernice S., 2595, *An Eye for Wisdom:
Repetitive poems of the Early Ikkaban Period*, St Oscar's
University Press, Dellah.

Extract from the Memoirs of Bernice Summerfield (continued)

WiRgo!xu picked up some kind of device from the table. I
didn't know what it was, exactly, but from WiRgo!xu's look
of rage and confusion and panic I could guess.

'Hold it!' I shouted, trying to get his attention from John on to me. 'Don't shoot! You don't know what might happen!'

'What did you *do*?' WiRgo!xu shrieked, waving the whatever-it-was about.

'I didn't do anything!' John stammered. 'I didn't do a thing!'

'We have to work this out,' I insisted. 'We have to find out what happened. For all we know, killing John could kill us all.'

'WiRgo!xu,' said a voice solemnly, 'I have a theory.'

We all turned to look at I!qu-!qu-tala, hovering in the doorway. 'The human has somehow stored temporal energy, perhaps because of his access to the Path. When I came into contact with him, a portion of that energy was released. Hence the degradation of my components. My timebase jumped forward two and a half millennia, but I dismissed it as a glitch.'

'Is that what happened to !Ci!ci-tel?' said WiRgo!xu. 'He aged to death?'

'I think, I think, I think so,' said the drone.

WiRgo!xu turned back to John, murder in his eyes.

He stood still, stiff, a look of helpless rage spreading over his face. After a moment, I realized that I!qu-!qu-tala was holding him in its force fields. 'Let go of the bonder,' it said quietly.

A great tremble went through WiRgo!xu's frame, all that rage with nowhere to go. John stared at him in bewildered horror. I tightened my grip on his shoulders.

WiRgo!xu's fingers uncurled from the device. It lifted from his hand. A slot opened in the side of the drone's body, and the bonder disappeared from view.

Carefully, I!qu-!qu-tala relaxed his fields. WiRgo!xu just stood there, as though he was still held.

'It doesn't change anything,' murmured I!qu-!qu-tala. 'We can still go ahead. The land merchants will be here soon, to conclude negotiations. You'll need to be ready.'

WiRgo!xu took a deep, deep breath. His body shook like a guitar string, the vibrations fading to nothing. Even in his human disguise, his eyes were the same disturbing black colour I remembered from the party, a lifetime ago.

'I'll deal with the two of you later,' he promised.

WiRgo!xu didn't have a dungeon to lock us in. Instead, he sent us up to the roof.

I fanned my face with my hat as I!qu-!qu-tala shepherded us away from the ladder. A servant took it away as we walked on to the flat roof.

The farm was one of several I could make out, crisscrossed by irrigation canals, dotted with slaves and hired hands working in loincloths wrapped around them almost like nappies. John said he'd seen workers just like that in his own time; basic irrigation methods hadn't changed in three millennia. The light sparkled on the Euphrates. In the distance, Babylon shot up out of the plain like an enormous brick square.

John and I sat down in the middle of the roof, under the hovering drone. Its face ikon had a downturned mouth. I wondered what machine grief felt like.

'How about a bit of shade?' I asked I!qu-!qu-tala. It obligingly extended one of its fields and turned it opaque. It was like sitting under a giant black umbrella.

John murmured, 'I am afraid I didn't understand the ball's explanation.'

'It's very simple,' said I!qu-!qu-tala loudly. John jumped. 'I should have realized immediately what happened when I came into contact with you. Let me see how I can put this. You have stored a charge of time energy.'

'It must be something to do with your wild talent,' I said.

John nodded slowly. I!qu-!qu-tala went on, 'When you raise an object above the ground, it stores potential energy, which is released when you drop the object. Similarly, you have been "raised" above the "ground" of your own home time. Then, when you came into contact with another time traveller, that energy was discharged.'

'Why wasn't it all discharged when he touched you?' I said.

'I withdrew in haste,' said I-!qu-!qu-tala.

'Wait, wait,' said John. 'I touched Smith, and nothing happened.'

'Smith?'

'A man from my own time. He journeyed to Babylon and back.'

'Naturally – there was no difference in your temporal potential. Smith's potential fell back to normal when he returned to his own time, do you, do you see? A ball fallen to the ground cannot fall further. Since you, since you can walk on the ground without exploding it, the discharge must only occur when you come into contact with another time traveller. Another object with temporal potential. Your ability must interact with it, interact with it.' The drone tilted, as though thinking. 'I couldn't have predicted the effect. I wonder what the equations are.'

'I touched B– Miss Summerfield,' said John, glancing at me. 'And there was no explosion.'

I could have made a dirty joke at that point, but I wasn't in the mood. All this exposition was just an opportunity for me to come up with a brilliant plan.

I!qu-!qu-tala spun slightly, so that its face ikon was pointed towards me. 'Now, that's interesting,' it said.

'Well, you know how much time travelling I've done,' I improvised. 'Maybe I've become bendy.'

'Bendy?'

'Flexible.'

'Temporal flexibility,' said I!qu-!qu-tala. 'Fascinating.'

'It was you, wasn't it?' I said.

I!qu-!qu-tala spun around once. 'What do you mean?'

'You're the time technician. Not WiRgo!xu, and not !Ci!ci-tel. You created the Path.'

I!qu-!qu-tala's face ikon changed, the curve of its sideways smile turning to a flat line. 'We all agreed,' it said. 'It was, it was a cooperative venture.'

'Did they approach you with their plan?' I pressed. 'Did they blackmail you?'

But I!qu-!qu-tala had decided it had said enough. It hovered above us in tense silence.

John looked at me. Tentatively, he reached out a hand.

I took it, and squeezed his fingers gently, and wished I could share the plan I'd just come up with.

Extract ends

Clarence didn't have to stay with the Coping Team, but he did. From time to time, he came up with mad plans to rescue Bernice – activating one of TIG's widgets and running down the Path, battling hordes of barbarians, defeating the renegades and carrying her back snugly in his arms.

He wondered if God had run simulations of him, to see if he was likely to try something. He wondered what the simulations had decided to do.

Most of the time, he watched the work, wishing he still had the brain power to follow the discussions. They had been setting up more machinery around the stub of Path, fiddling with it. Even the machines were surrounded by floating screens now, making the whole site look like a bizarre cubist motion sculpture.

A particular knot of People had formed around !Cin-ta!x. The drones were humming with high-speed dialogue, while the organics struggled to keep up. They were trying to reach some kind of consensus, Clarence reckoned.

Suddenly, the knot broke up. A bunch of People walked across the trampled grass and flowers to the Path, and started shutting down some of the machines that had been set up. Floating screens vanished as the devices powered down.

Clarence got off his perch and wandered over. 'What's up?' he asked !Cin-ta!x.

'Now we know they weren't one of us,' he said cryptically.

'Er,' said the angel.

'Whoever provided the renegades with the information to build the Path. They don't realize quite how ... advanced TIG's researches are. They must have been relying on reports, not on our actual work.'

'Just how advanced are your researches?' asked Clarence, alarmed.

'Advanced enough to discover a booby trap built into the Path,' said !Cin-ta!x. 'It was designed to counter the kind of

198

bomb we designed. It would have shot the energy straight back at us. The Path would have collapsed, but we would have blown a continent-sized hole right through the sphere.'

'They're mad!' said Clarence. 'I can't believe they'd do that!'

!Cin-ta!x raised a finger. 'Oh, I think they intended us to find that, which we did, while preparing the bomb. Hard to miss, actually, once you attack the equations. It was really a sort of warning. No, what they weren't expecting was that we'd find a way around it.'

Clarence's wings drooped. 'You did?'

'We're working on it,' said !Cin-ta!x. 'We already have a promising line of enquiry. We should be able to go ahead with the Path's destruction as scheduled.'

'Great,' said Clarence.

Bernice had suggested they lie down. Despite the miraculous shade provided by the drone – Eye-cuckoo-tala? – the afternoon was heavy with heat.

So they curled in the shadow, facing each other, but not touching. He struggled out of his jacket, and she fanned herself with her white hat.

'What are we going to do?' he said softly.

'Nothing,' she said. She closed her eyes against the glare of the sky. 'There's nothing we can do. I'm going to tell WiRgo!xu to send you home.'

'It would be wrong for me to leave you here.'

'I knew you were going to say that.' She opened her eyes, and smiled gently at him. 'You're sweet, John. But I'll be all right.' She gestured at the drone hovering above them. 'Let's not worry about it any further. Just trust me.'

Lafayette glanced at the hovering machine. Naturally, it was listening to their conversation. Was Bernice holding something back, some important piece of information or cunning?

'I will trust you,' he said.

A few moments passed in silence. They looked at each other. Lafayette remembered the delicate shape of her body, the muscles of her arms, cool water flowing from her skin as she looked at him in surprise. He imagined that shape beneath her mannish clothing, and felt an odd, hot feeling of pride, that it was hidden from everyone but him.

He remembered what she had said about her divorced husband. It had been nagging at the back of his mind for some time. *Former husband and former male prostitute.*

'May I ask a question?' he said awkwardly.

'Go right ahead,' she said.

'What was your husband's name?'

'Jason,' she said.

'Was he . . . was he a procurer?'

'A what?' She frowned for a moment. 'Oh, a pimp. No. I told you, he was a sex worker. I mean prostitute.'

Then he hadn't misunderstood her. But he had never heard of such a thing. 'How did you meet him?'

'Er,' she said. 'I took him hostage in a bar to escape some police.'

Lafayette stared at her. She said, 'Well, we didn't meet properly until later. When he was pretending to be a particularly gormless alien. As it turned out,' she said, with a mixture of fondness and bitterness, 'he was just a particularly gormless human. He saved my life a couple of times, though.'

A few more moments' silence. Lafayette did not want to press her too hard; the memory of her failed marriage seemed too fresh in her mind to be a comfortable topic. 'Is such a thing common in your time?' he said.

'Gormlessness? A human constant.'

'I mean prostitutes who are men.'

'Common? Good question . . . Dellah has a small red-light district, but I've never visited. I know the sex workers' union went on strike last year, though. They got what they wanted, very quickly indeed.' She grinned naughtily, but it faded. 'It was different with Jason. He ran away from home, he was struggling to survive.'

'You were kind to accept him,' Lafayette said.

Benny gave him an annoyed look. 'That had nothing to do with it,' she said. 'You can't eat shame . . .' Her eyes seemed to drift away, into memories.

They lay for a while. Lafayette rolled his jacket into a rough pillow. Benny took a kind of notebook from her pocket, discovered an odd kind of pen in another pocket, and began to write. He had seen her jotting down notes in the book before. 'Your archaeological notes?' he asked.

'My diary,' she said. 'Here, I'll show you.'

He rolled over. The book was disorganized, with many additional pieces of paper slipped between the pages. It was crammed with her experiences, with her impressions and memories of many worlds. She had devoted several pages to Babylon, writing in odd moments.

The last page was particularly interesting. Lafayette's eyebrows rose as he read the last few sentences.

'I would like to add something to your diary,' he said. 'Something to remember me by, perhaps.'

She handed him the unusual pen. He thought for a moment, and started to slowly write.

I!qu-!qu-tala contracted its fields and powered down its nonessential systems, some of which were still busy repairing the damage from the temporal discharge. Maintenance subroutines kicked in with gusto, restoring and replacing damaged microcomponents, reinstalling software. A millisecond later, the drone had a full repair report: no damage had been done that its onboard systems couldn't deal with.

Which was a good thing, because the nearest repair facility was a lot of years in the wrong direction.

It was so *quiet*. On the Sphere, there had been millions of similar minds to talk to, compare notes with, gossip, ask questions, swap recipes. Here, I!qu-!qu-tala was unique. The silence made its receptors ring, missing the input.

The humans talked for a while, in low voices, even though they knew he was listening. They talked about Lafayet's interests, about Beni's travels. At one point she took out her diary, scribbling in it. After a while she asked him to say something in the diary as well, and he jotted words in some other human language.

WiRgo!xu's flash of homicidal rage had been frightening, but brief. I!qu-!qu-tala consulted the personality profile it had constructed. There was a high probability that the worst was over, if it fitted the usual pattern of the outbursts: an abrupt spike of emotion, cut short by external intervention, followed by a resolution phase of extensive sulking.

I!qu-!qu-tala had always found it curious that !Ci!ci-tel was the one who had faced direct combat, and yet showed fewer psychological aberrations than WiRgo!xu, who had never been directly engaged in the War. He had always stayed on a Ship, running his tactical simulations over and over, never killing anyone or seeing anyone die. Whole planets would have been destroyed, and he would have seen nothing more than the inside of the operations room.

On the other hand, perhaps it wasn't that curious.

I!qu-!qu-tala thought about the time he met !Ci!ci-tel. The drone had been providing ground support during a nasty little engagement, one of the rare instances of hand-to-hand fighting in the War. It was far easier to just locate and destroy an enemy base, even an enemy planet, than to send in troops. It was also far more boring, which I!qu-!qu-tala suspected was the reason that as many as five per cent of engagements had seen some troop involvement.

The People's agents had based themselves in a giant warren, a maze of stale and dusty tunnels left by some giant burrowing mammal. It had amused them, as they installed sonic showers and scanner-scrambling devices, to think that from the outside their entire camp looked like an empty pile of dirt and rubble. Besides, the All of Us were used to flashy, frightening People appearances, arrogant vehicles and giant bubble houses sprouting from nothing on their planets, like mushrooms coming up overnight.

The insects had a tactical base on the side of a mountain, with a linear accelerator for launching spy missions and small fighters. The series of metallic hoops ran right up the side of the mountain, jutting out on long metal stems. While the People watched, more of the miniature ships were forced up through the accelerator and tore into space, leaving smoking orange trails through the atmosphere.

That was the insects' way – send a million expendable ships instead of one unconquerable one. It reflected their own cavalier attitude to reproduction: if you have enough children, some of them are bound to survive. Their civiliza-. tion was similar – scattered like spores across hundreds of conquered worlds, a little of Us here, a little there. The People were centralized – how can you need more living space than a Dyson Sphere?

It made the All of Us harder to kill, of course. They could evacuate easily, pop up unexpectedly, seed a dozen new worlds with people and technology while you weren't looking. Kill one of their bases, and six more would turn up.

I!qu-!qu-tala wondered if the human race would be like that, one day.

Of course, the All of Us never got anywhere near the Dyson Sphere. Naturally, they'd known where it was for centuries; you couldn't hide the infrared signature of something that size. But they hadn't known exactly what they were looking at. The religious and culture shock that resulted when they found out played a major part in starting the War.

And then there were People like !Ci!ci-tel, who were psychologically normal but nonetheless got a thrill from risking their lives. For real. With no safety nets. Except the medical drones, the emergency teleportation systems, and the ever-present Ships.

Only one Person had been injured on that mission; I!qu-!qu-tala had reattached the man's severed limb without difficulty, and had to talk him out of continuing with the assault on the accelerator. To the best of their knowledge, only four of the All of Us died, three of them when the accelerator exploded.

The other one !Ci!ci-tel killed with a hand-made projectile weapon. It fitted into his palm and threw flattened triangles of steel-hard plastic. The killing took only a moment; an insect unexpectedly encountered the party while performing repairs on the accelerator's base.

!Ci!ci-tel had just thrown up his hand, almost in panic, and the projectiles had cut through the barbarian's carapace in eight places. It died instantly, without even speaking. The projectiles embedded themselves in the mountainside or ricocheted from the metal supports of the array.

!Ci!ci-tel had been unwell after that, and I!qu-!qu-tala's job had been to return him to the Ship and keep him under surveillance while a new psychological profile could be worked up. In the end the drone decided it was just first-time jitters and pronounced !Ci!ci-tel ready for further field duty, if he wanted it.

WiRgo!xu never displayed acute symptoms. There was never a breakdown, never a period of impaired functioning. Not until he returned to the Worldsphere, when the sudden outbursts of violence began.

The first time, it had just been someone's work of art, smashed in a moment of fury during an argument about surfing. The second time, he had ordered a nonsentient house to destroy itself. At least, they hoped it was a nonsentient house.

I!qu-!qu-tala had stayed in contact with !Ci!ci-tel at his request. The drone had 'adopted' WiRgo!xu some months later, after helping with the house incident. Both of them had gone on with their lives; they kept in touch, traded stories with other veterans, pursued their interests, and were politely avoided by everyone.

In I!qu-!qu-tala's opinion, that was when the real damage had been done.

When the opportunity had come along, when the drone's long researches had come to fruition, it could hardly leave the two of them behind.

!Ci!ci-tel had been bright, and manipulative, easily bored, but easily entertained. I!qu-!qu-tala spent a few microseconds playing back its memories of him. There wasn't enough information to create a personality simulation. There wasn't anything left of him at all, now.

All the more reason, concluded the drone, to continue.

Extract from the Memoirs of Bernice Summerfield

John and I ended up dozing on the rough roof, hand in hand, under the shadow of I!qu-!qu-tala's darkened field. The air gradually lost its fierce heat, until it was almost comfortable. I don't know how long we lay there, both of us frightened and exhausted.

I had a little knot of angry hope in my chest. The Plan.

A voice woke us. At first I thought it was I!qu-!qu-tala, but when I looked up the drone was gone. The darkness we had been sleeping under was the night sky. Blackness from horizon to horizon, a dull hint of light from the great city, a soft red glow from somewhere inside WiRgo!xu's house, but blackness, blackness. And overhead, the sky gone crazy with stars, sharp enough in the clear air that you could see their colours clearly, and hanging above the horizon, Venus, Ishtar's eight-pointed star, like a beacon.

A servant's head had appeared above the edge of the roof, lit from below. He spoke again. 'Come on, wake up! My master has need of you,' he said. 'Beni, you must come down this ladder at once. Lafayet must stay where he is. The guards are watching to make sure he doesn't jump from the roof.'

'Right,' I said. 'I'm coming.' I stretched the cramps out of my limbs, feeling hot and sticky. 'Stay here,' I told John gently. 'Everything's going to be fine.'

He watched as I climbed down the ladder. There were torches lit in the courtyard, servants cooking and filling jugs with water from the reservoirs.

I followed the servant inside, where WiRgo!xu was sitting on an elaborately carved wooden chair, a barber trimming his beard into a regally square shape.

'Listen,' I said, before WiRgo!xu could get a word in. 'I've decided. I'll stay with you.'

'You will!' he said. Whatever he had been going to say, he forgot it. 'I mean, you will?'

'I'm not going to say I agree with your plan,' I said. 'But it's too late to stop it. You're going to teach the People a lesson. You need my help to make the best of the sorry situation.'

'What about your friend?' said WiRgo!xu.

'The safest thing to do is send him home,' I said. 'Get I!qu to do the calculations. He can probably just walk home.'

WiRgo!xu nodded. 'Yes, let's get him out of here.' He clapped his hands. 'I have some more business to conclude tonight. I'll want you there as an adviser, Beni.'

'What about John?'

'We'll take him to the Path tomorrow,' said WiRgo!xu. 'For now, I want him up on the roof.'

'Another visitor, my lord,' announced a slave.

WiRgo!xu had been discussing Babylonian cuisine with me for over an hour. I was doing my best to be entertaining, coming up with interesting trivia, cracking jokes. I was trying to look resigned, relaxed, toying with my hat in my lap. Keeping his mind off John.

WiRgo!xu put down his bowl of beer and waved at the servant. 'Send him in.' He looked as smug as a kid winning a board game. 'This is the last of them. Once these deals are struck, we'll have three farms, plus six houses in the city. More than enough room for the first set of visitors, as well as providing an economic base. It's going to be exciting.'

'Yes,' I agreed, 'it is.'

'I just wish !Ci!ci-tel was here to see it . . .' WiRgo!xu's cheer slumped into a mope. 'Hey, who are you?'

I turned in my seat. The Lady Ninan was standing in the doorway.

'I am Ninan-ashtammu, priestess of Marduk,' she announced. There were two servants and two guards with her, crowding the hallway. 'I wish to speak with you.'

WiRgo!xu looked at me, suspiciously, but I shrugged my shoulders. 'I don't know how she found us,' I said. 'I really don't.'

'It's not difficult for me to find things out,' Ninan said. 'I have lived in Babylon all my life. A thousand mouths might speak the words I need to hear.'

She strode into the room, followed by her retinue. A servant scurried to offer her a chair, but she waved him away. 'I want you to release Beni and Lafayet.'

'You're a bit late,' said WiRgo!xu.

'I'm staying of my own accord,' I told Ninan. 'Just as Ishtar stayed in the underworld of her own accord.'

Ninan looked at me, at WiRgo!xu, and back to me. 'Then there is nothing I can say to change your mind?' she asked carefully.

206

'I'm afraid not,' I said. 'But we'll be sending Lafayette home tomorrow.'

'Perhaps I can assist,' said Ninan. 'I own a boat. I'd be happy to make it available.'

'We don't need it,' said WiRgo!xu.

'Thank you for your gracious offer,' I told Ninan. 'John won't be travelling on the Euphrates. It's all arranged. Listen, I'd like you to have this.'

I handed her my hat. She turned it over in her hands, curious. 'It's an original from Groenewegen's Millinery,' I said. 'It had to be specially made. They don't normally make this kind of hat in white. Look, you can tell from the tag.' I turned the fedora over. 'All the way from Neo-Sydney,' I said. Ninan examined the tag intently. 'It's perfect for keeping the sun off,' I finished weakly.

'Thank you, Beni.' Ninan reached out and took my hand. 'I do not understand how you can settle as easily as you have travelled,' she said. 'How you accept change so readily.'

I remembered those long nights in the Aurigan jungle, after a lip-smacking meal of night crawler, trying to keep myself from going mad. It would always take forever to go to sleep, listening to the jungle noises, having horrible visions of night-crawler vengeance or being trapped in a sudden flood or bushfire or . . . If I could get the fire lit, I would read Edward Watkinson. 'The archaeologist is prepared for anything, because the past, like the future, may contain anything.'

If I didn't, I would talk to myself, encouraging words, badly constructed limericks, sometimes a wavering song. I told myself my life story. I made up the bits I couldn't remember or didn't like. After that, I started keeping a diary. And still made up the bits I couldn't remember or didn't like.

'I suppose,' I said, 'I always take me with me.'

Extract ends

A few hours before detonation, God arrived to supervise proceedings. It turned up in its favourite form, an easily recognizable, yellow, spherical drone. There had been a brief trend among the drones of copying God's design, but after several embarrassing social *faux pas* the joke had gone out of fashion.

Clarence watched as God hovered about the site, taking its own readings from the Path, digesting TIG's equations, chatting with the People. The work had slowed, now they were confident of what they were about. Even the constant drizzle had stopped, beyond the edges of the solidigram.

Finally God hovered up to Clarence, perched despondently atop one of the bubble houses. The remote drone raised itself until it was face to face with the angel. 'Well,' it said.

'Well,' said Clarence. 'All ready for a little mass murder?'

'You're here because of Beni,' said God. 'You know as well as I do we don't have any choice.'

Clarence looked at the Path. He'd been staring at it for hours, hoping to see her appear from nothing and step along its length and on to the grass. 'Do you think she'll make it?'

'I'm surprised we haven't seen her already,' said God. 'On the other hand, maybe WiRgo!xu and !Ci!ci-tel are fanatical enough to go through with this, even if it kills them . . .'

'Were they like that during the War?'

'You don't remember that either.' Clarence shrugged. God lowered its voice and said, 'They want another war. They want us to lose.'

'God!' said Clarence.

'That was my reaction,' said God. 'They might get half of their wish. My agents report a great deal of activity on the part of you-know-who. I think they're aware that something fishy is up, and they're dying to know just what. They're probably reading the fine print of the Treaty right now, wondering how much they can get away with . . .'

'We would lose, too,' said Clarence. 'Wouldn't we?'

God said, 'XR(N)IG, of course, will insist a pre-emptive strike is our best chance for survival.'

'Bugger XR(N)IG,' said Clarence. 'They got us into the last war. Our only hope this time is not to have a war at all.'

'So,' said God, 'you see how important it is to destroy the Path – before our side finds out about it, let alone the other side. Whatever the collateral.'

A few moments' silence.

Clarence said, 'Maybe she'll make it back in time.'

Extract from the Memoirs of Bernice Summerfield

Even WiRgo!xu had to sleep, after a while. A slave led me to a spare room, and two others dragged a bed in. I asked where John was, but they didn't answer. I think he was still up on the roof.

Between the long afternoon nap and worrying about the Plan, I couldn't sleep. It wasn't much of a plan. I needed a Plan B. There was little chance John and I could escape, not with I!qu-!qu-tala ready to grab us with a force field. It might be possible to flatter or trick WiRgo!xu, but not to force him.

But then, WiRgo!xu wasn't really the problem, was he?

About an hour later, I!qu-!qu-tala came floating in through my window. The drone was twitching, nervously, its face ikon jigging from side to side.

'I'm awake,' I said.

'I know,' said the drone.

'Thanks for saving John,' I said. 'I thought WiRgo!xu had lost his mind for a moment there.'

'Perhaps, perhaps he had,' said the drone. It settled on to the end of the bed.

I sat up, resting an elbow on my knees. 'His psychological profile said he was quite sane.'

'Do you, do you think it's sane,' said the drone, 'to be starting a war?'

'I suppose it depends on why you're doing it,' I said. 'At least invading someone to grab their land makes a kind of sense.'

'Greed makes sense?' said I!qu-!qu-tala. 'Wanting to help the People doesn't?'

'You mean wanting to help the survivors,' I said. 'If there are any.'

'We need suffering!' said the drone. 'How can we grow, change, evolve, survive without it? Just think how much is being learnt here in Babylon!'

'I'm sure it's a lot easier to believe that when it's not you doing the suffering,' I said. 'Why don't you ask the slaves what they think of it? Or go and find yourself someone who lost an arm or a leg in battle. Or a child who sleeps in the rubbish and begs for a living. Why don't you see what they have to say about suffering?'

'That's why I'm here!' said I!qu-!qu-tala. 'When the war begins, the Path will become a route for evacuation. The People will, will, they won't have any choice but to come here. And learn.'

'They won't have any choice?'

'No,' whispered the drone.

'I thought *forced* wasn't a People concept.'

'Have you heard of the Apathy Interest Group?' said I!qu-!qu-tala.

'Yes,' I said. 'But I thought they were a joke.'

'I founded the group,' said I!qu-!qu-tala. 'Everyone thinks we're a joke. That's the point. But do you know why we really don't care?' I shook my head. 'We're the ones who think the People's way of life is *wrong*. We get everything we want. That's how we got into the War.'

'Oh bleargh,' I said. 'My big speech was a total waste.'

'That's what we want,' insisted I!qu-!qu-tala. 'Not to get what we want. We opposed the War, of course. But we oppose everything. We're always trying to get the People to think twice about what they do. Now they'll have to.'

'Why are you telling me all this?'

'You're on our side now,' said I!qu-!qu-tala. 'You need to know.'

'Right,' I said. 'Tell me, did you come up with the idea before you discovered the Path? Or did the Path suggest it?'

'A little bit of each,' said I!qu-!qu-tala. 'I read a lot of Ke Chedani research when I was working in intelligence. It was obvious they would develop time travel, sometime in the next thousand years. I just put two and two together.'

'Why bring WiRgo!xu and !Ci!ci-tel? You could have engineered all this on your own.'

'They're my responsibility,' said the drone. Its face ikon turned glum again. 'Medical drones and personnel volunteered to "adopt" fellow veterans who needed monitoring and help. I couldn't leave them behind. Anyway, they thought it was a great idea.'

I was suddenly realizing how fragile the People's utopia really was, how delicately balanced its tensions were. One well-placed lunatic could bring it all down in a heap.

'What do you think the war will be like?' I asked.

Extract ends

12

RAIN AND SNOW

> As Inanna was about to leave, the judges of the underworld seized her. 'No one escapes the land of the dead unmarked!' they told her. 'If Inanna wants to leave the underworld, she'll have to provide someone to take her place here.'
>
> – The Descent of Inanna

The progress of the war will be easy to track. You simply take a radio telescope, point it at the patch of sky that contains the Worldsphere, and check to see if the People's homeworld is still there.

Sometimes it is, sometimes it isn't. Very occasionally you might see its ruins – the sudden appearance of the star like the yolk inside a broken egg, chunks of its shell larger than gas giants floating loose, obscuring the yellow disc. Sometimes it will be half finished and abandoned, a skeleton of crisscrossing ringworlds like a cage around the star.

But most of the time, it simply won't be there at all. Far easier than raising an army, or building great battle Ships: stop the People's history before the Sphere can be built, their power in the galaxy consolidated. Reach out through history with a time loop, and trap their original homeworlds before space travel can be invented, or before they can develop stellar engineering, or before they can develop the technology needed to create the Worldsphere.

This won't be a crude war, like the cat-and-mouse game with the insects. Ships chasing one another, comparing the size of their guns, antimatter bombs, remote forced quantum singularities, none of it. This will be a much simpler, more elegant war. You stop us from having existed, we stop you from stopping us. Free agents, allies and spies protected by temporal bubbles will survive each disappearance of the Worldsphere, find the time-loop generator responsible, and destroy it – after learning how to build their own.

Of course, the People's opponents won't dare give away their own location by operating from their own planet. They'll establish bases in the People's own galaxy. From time to time, an X-ray source will suddenly move and then vanish, as a black hole is captured as a natural well of energy for their weapons. One or two fat, ripe stars will conveniently collapse, adding to the stockpile.

More stars will abruptly flare or burst as the People turn to brute force. Any star exhibiting certain characteristic behaviour, suggesting enemy activity, will become a target.

Of course, both sides will avoid destroying the suns that shine on innocent bystanders. At first. As the double bluff becomes a tactical advantage, both sides will hide their bases on or near inhabited worlds. Daring their opponents to genocide.

Those worlds, and the living worlds cooked in the radiation from the numerous novae and supernovae, will be counted as collateral damage, to be dealt with after the war's conclusion.

As the war presses on, the People's forces will find ways to reach their enemy's home galaxy, the same spiral as contains the Earth. The pattern of the war will remain unchanged as the People search for and strike towards the homeworld of their opponents.

Meanwhile, their enemies will attack again and again at the People's most vulnerable point, their most important asset. God will die, and never have existed, and exist once more, and be lobotomized, and live, and die, over and over.

Seen from a great enough distance, over a long enough period of time, both galaxies will flare like a box of firecrackers. Some impossibly distant, alien astronomers may even realize that they are seeing a war, a war that took place millions of years ago. Perhaps they will wonder if and when the war will reach their own galaxy – if ten million years, a thousand million years, a million million years is long enough for the conflict to jump across the void and infect them.

All of which assumes that the cumulative damage to space-time doesn't cause the entire cosmos to collapse in on itself in a premature Big Crunch.

Both sides would agree that that was the ultimate technical achievement.

Extract from the Memoirs of Bernice Summerfield (continued)

'That's what the war will be like,' said I!qu-!qu-tala. 'According to our simulations.'

'Well,' I said.

Extract ends

It was after midnight when the doorman admitted a visitor to the Lady Ninan's house. She met him in the main room, attended by servants. There were also three of the temple guard present, swords at their sides, faces solemn in the lamplight.

'Nabu-zuqup-kemu,' she said, without formality, 'I'm glad to see you. I need your help urgently.'

'Always a pleasure, my lady,' said the scribe. A slave pulled up a chair for him. 'Is there an urgent message that must be sent?'

Ninan exchanged glances with Miriam, who was holding Beni's hat. 'The message is certainly urgent, but it needs to be read.'

The slave woman brought the hat around to Nabu-zuqup-kemu, and another slave carried a lamp around. An astonished expression slowly crossed the scribe's face as Miriam presented him with the hat.

Then he saw the writing inside the rim. He grabbed the hat and held it close to his face. The servant with the lamp brought the light closer, carefully.

'It's Aramaic,' he said. 'Who wrote it? It's terrible.'

'Presumably Lafayet,' said Ninan. 'Can you understand it?'

'I think so,' said the scribe. 'First I'll want a copy on proper parchment.' He reached for his supplies.

'You have to be philosophical about it,' said God.

'That's easy for you to say,' said Clarence.

They were watching TIG put the last touches on the detonator. There had been a huge cluster of junk at the Path's terminus, all sorts of devices in different shapes and sizes and colours. One by one, the scientists had taken them away, leaving just a single white cube, its surface marked with warning messages in livid orange writing.

'No, seriously,' said God. 'You'll never even know if Beni was killed, or if she got out of the city before the Path was detonated. And since you'll never know, it won't really matter, will it?'

'I'll never see her again in either case,' said Clarence.

'Exactly,' said God.

'Thanks. That makes me feel much better.'

'Go on, then,' said God impatiently.

'Go on what?'

'Go and rescue her. Fly down the Path, seek her out, bring her back here.'

Clarence spread his wings, hopping down from the roof of the bubble house. 'You're sure?'

'You'll scare heck out of the locals,' said God. 'But if you're quick, you can find and rescue her before the Path is destroyed, and the pair of you with it.'

Clarence dithered.

'You see?' said God. 'You have to be philosophical about it. Your life span is so much greater than hers, you'll meet so many people and make so many friends in your life . . . is it worth risking all that time for one person?'

'Sometimes,' murmured Clarence.

'It's not the sort of question the People have to ask themselves,' admitted God. 'Normally.'

* * *

Nabu-zuqup-kemu put down the parchment. 'That's all it says,' he said. 'The grammar is poor, but the meaning is clear.'

Ninan nodded. 'Thank you.' She turned to the soldiers. 'I think we should change our plans.'

The eldest of the three stroked his short beard. 'If we want to take them,' he said, 'now would be the best time. Darkness and sleep will be on our side.'

'Though not surprise,' another soldier pointed out. 'We can't rely on it.'

'That's true,' said the eldest. 'Lady, the final decision is yours.'

Ninan drummed her fingers on the wooden table. 'I don't wish to risk their lives through hasty action,' she said. 'These criminals have proven themselves to be more than willing to turn to violence. No, we must wait until the right moment.'

'My lady,' said the old soldier, 'do you know what the quarrel is between these people?'

'I do not,' said Ninan. 'But I do know that Lafayet and Beni are being held by those willing to kill for their purposes, and that I promised them my protection.' She slapped the table, decision made. 'Prepare your men,' she said. 'We will confront them in the morning.'

Extract from the Memoirs of Bernice Summerfield

This bit is from my diary. I wanted to reproduce it just as I wrote it, because it captures my feelings at the time so perfectly.

It'll be dawn soon. The sky is deep, dark blue – just enough light to see the colour, not enough to obscure the stars. You can feel the heat coming, creeping up on the horizon with the sun.

Here in this desert, I find myself thinking about rain and snow.

It rains all the time on Dellah. Not all the time, but much of the time. It was already rather damp where they built St Oscar's, but the needle of the spaceport disrupted some local meteorological thingumajig, bringing the rain down in buckets. The bricks of the university buildings are rainproofed, immune to the constant drizzle.

Sometimes it's the pleasant kind of rain, the sort where you're indoors with some good books and a cuppa and your cat, maybe a real trad jazz 78 playing on a real wind-up record player, watching the rain come down and knowing you're inside and warm and safe.

Sometimes it's the kind of persistent dampening drizzle that got into everything from your socks to your heart, making everyone and everything seem miserable and wet, inside and out. Very occasionally it's a tree-limb-tossing, rain-going-sideways downpour.

I won't see rain like that again. Not of any kind, really, except the tiny shower or two you can expect in the Mesopotamian year. Even the twin rivers aren't fed by rain, but by melting snow from the high mountains.

I never thought I'd feel homesick for rain.

I hope bloody Mark Mbangi does a decent job of the rest of Mesoamerican Literature and Music. My students deserve it. Poor Anne-Marie – I've got a mental picture of her going to Dr Follett with my letter in hand, face solemn, eyes wide, rather hoping that it's all a joke and knowing in her heart that it isn't.

Maybe my tragic and mysterious disappearance will galvanize them all to greater academic efforts. Maybe they'll establish the B.S. Summerfield Memorial Trust Fund and Sculpture Garden in my honour, solemnly keep a seat empty for me at official faculty functions.

Maybe they'll wait almost a month before throwing out my junk and my cat and installing some fresh-faced archaeological upstart in my rooms.

Wolsey. I'm never going to see Wolsey again.

I'll never see Jason again either, which is not entirely without its positive side. It does rather step on the small, squeaky part of my mind that's hoping that someday we'll have some kind of miraculous happy reunion. (That's the part that enjoys watching the rain come down on the windowpane, brown paper packages tied up with string, etc.)

I'll never see snow again.

When I left Olundrun VII, I remember thinking that I never wanted to see snow again in my life. After I crash-landed there, and the monks locked me out of their monastery, I used to live on the snow. A few tins of food, a few loaves of bread stuffed into my sleeping bag to try to stop them from icing up, and the morning ritual of relighting the fire, struggling with the damp wood and the matches, and then melting fistfuls of snow over the pale green flame. The day's water for drinking, for lightning-fast washes, shivering on the lee side of the tent with my boots on.

Nowadays I'd know better than to take the monks at their word. They said they wouldn't let me in, that I must decide what it was I wanted. Standard practice – if you're really desperate for enlightenment, you won't take no for an answer, you'll sit outside those gates until you're in danger of starving and they have to take you in.

They used to pop out and check on me, leave more food. One persistent and hopeful monk taught me a few meditations, the pair of us crammed into the tent while the wind whipped the snowflakes against the thin cloth.

After all those weeks of snow, I knew I didn't want to be a nun. Inside the walls of the monastery it would be warm and dry, but there would still be a daily ritual, still the absolute sameness. No more travel, no more walking. Snow for ever.

Babylon for ever.

Ha. My poor publishers. Waiting for a book that's never going to be finished. All those monographs and papers left half written . . . Oh well, they can always publish Summerfield: the Unfinished Works or What Happened to Bernice Summerfield?

It's a shame I don't have my puter. There's still so much we don't know about the Babylonians, even in the twenty-sixth century; I could find out the answers

*to all sorts of interesting questions, especially the ones
about sex. I could expand the Babylonian section of*
Repetitive Poems, *do some on-the-spot research on the
influence of Ikkaban culture on the locals. Now, that
would make my publishers happy, a guaranteed
bestseller:* Benny Summerfield's World Tour of
Ancient Mesopotamia.

*Yes, it's a shame I don't have my puter, assuming the
floptical disks would survive the next three millennia.*

*I might get lucky. Sometime in his long lifetime,
WiRgo!xu might get bored enough to go and visit
somewhere that it rains, somewhere that it snows.*

You never know.

That's enough of the diary. No doubt you're dying to know
what happened next.

Hours after I handed Ninan the message, it occurred to me I
might have blown it. If she decided to attack the house,
WiRgo!xu would just summon up his secret weapon. The
drone would repel any sortie with ease, probably taking
prisoners rather than killing anyone, but putting them out of
the way. That might mean there was no one left for the
morning.

I should have tried to give her some kind of warning. But
then, there's only so much room inside my hat.

John had translated the short message in my diary, and
then painstakingly inscribed it in my hat in biro. If I!qu-!qu-
tala had wondered what we were doing, it didn't ask. I think
it might have been in some kind of shutdown mode – after a
while, its face ikon blinked out. Maybe it was taking the
drone equivalent of a nap.

I had a few panicky moments, wondering if it was all a
ruse, and I!qu-!qu-tala was perfectly capable of reading
Aramaic. Surely it would have said something, done something? Or was it bluffing?

Numerous dirty digs have cured me of the habit of chewing my nails. Or so I had thought.

* * *

We left at dawn. WiRgo!xu's clothes and hair were in disarray; I don't think he'd slept, either. He gave John a look of pure poison. John stared back, defiant, which I wished he wouldn't do.

I hoped John wouldn't end up hating me for the Plan. It's a lot easier to justify suffering when it's not you suffering.

I wanted a bath, but WiRgo!xu wasn't having any of it. He and I!qu-!qu-tala shepherded us out of the house. It was already baking hot and miserable, waves of heat rising from the cracked mud of the plain. The slaves were hard at work in the fields, clearing muck out of an irrigation canal, up before dawn. I wondered how they could stand it.

Servants and slaves brought us horses, burly, rough-coated animals, snorting, flicking away the flies with heavy tails. I wanted my hat, squinting into the brightness. I put on my dark glasses, smeared my face and neck with sunscreen, and tossed the little bottle of ointment to John. He caught it, easily. Used to the saddle. So was I, though I wished I actually had a saddle – my trousers were chafing me as we headed off across the plains.

It was like a funeral procession. I!qu-!qu-tala led us – as I watched, the drone's external fields blurred and rippled, and it became close to invisible. Not quite invisible. There was an obvious shimmer, if you knew where to look.

WiRgo!xu followed, riding his horse with difficulty. Then John and I, a little less awkward.

For a nasty moment, I hoped WiRgo!xu would never get used to horses. That the sun would always be too bright and the gravity would always be slightly wrong, that he would hate looking just like a human and hate the way we smell and the way we make love, everything. I hoped, for that moment of utter vengefulness, that he'd created his own hell.

After a couple of hours' ride, we came to the patch of land where the Path had let me and John off. The landscape was dotted with palm trees, more of them towards the river. I could see sails moving down there. Behind them, Babylon's walls rose up out of the plain.

John and I hadn't spoken during the ride. Once, he reached

for my hand again, and we rode for a little while side by side.

We dismounted while I!qu-!qu-tala buzzed about, a circular smear in the shimmering air, taking readings.

'Can you see it?' I asked John softly.

He nodded. 'The drone is passing back and forth above it.'

'Does it look . . . any different?'

'No. Just as I first saw it.'

'Listen,' I said. 'I'm not quite sure what's going to happen next. The Path should let you off where you got on, back in your own time. But it's possible you'll end up on the Worldsphere.'

'The Worldsphere?'

'WiRgo!xu's homeworld, at the other end of the Path. The People there will take care of you, don't worry. Tell them everything you can remember, and don't be afraid.'

He nodded again. He didn't look at me, his mouth a straight, angry line. Some of it was anger with me, I know, anger because I wasn't coming with him. Like the anger a little girl feels when her parents die, resenting their betrayal – what did she do to deserve that?

I!qu-!qu-tala did something. There was a hot, metallic sound, and suddenly the Path appeared.

We both looked up. The Path stretched away to the horizon, an illusion of a mirrored road crossing the landscape, diminishing to an impossibly distant point.

'All right,' said WiRgo!xu. 'Get going.'

'Just a minute,' said I!qu-!qu-tala. 'I'm checking, checking the Path's calibrations. We don't want any surprises.'

'There's nothing to worry about,' insisted WiRgo!xu. 'We set it all up.'

'We don't want any surprises,' repeated the drone.

WiRgo!xu fidgeted in the heat while I!qu-!qu-tala hovered, doing whatever it was doing.

I reached out to John, and hugged him. His whole body stiffened up as I touched him, but after a few moments he relaxed into the embrace, letting me hold him. 'Everything's going to be fine,' I murmured. 'Take your shoes off.'

'Take my shoes off?'

'For luck,' I said. 'Ancient Babylonian custom.' He glanced at me, and reached down and started tugging off his shoes. 'Socks too,' I said.

'Right,' said I!qu-!qu-tala. 'Let's get Lafayet on his way before the natives spot us and we start a new religion.'

I was looking around, hopefully, but we were quite alone. John gave me a restrained smile, shoes in hand, and turned and stepped up to the Path.

For a moment he just looked down its distance, and gave himself a little hug. I could tell from where I was standing that every hair on his body was standing on end, reacting to the unnatural vibes of the space-time rift.

He turned back, and gave me a long, last look, right out of a bad romance film. I gave him a little encouraging wave.

He took his first step on to the Path.

At this point, my Plan went completely bung.

Extract ends

They evacuated most of TIG. God's remote drone hung around with an air that was a mixture of cheerful smugness and polite sobriety. If the remote got wiped out in the Path's destruction, it had a million more like it – literally.

Clarence hung around because, despite the deceptive vulnerability of his naked body, he could withstand most shit that got thrown at him. !Cin-ta!x had assured the nervous angel that the total energy the Path could release would be far less than a direct hit from an artificially aimed solar flare.

'But still enough to drill a hole through the sphere,' said Clarence.

'Only if the booby trap fired,' said !Cin-ta!x, 'and we've disarmed it. The only danger now is an unpredicted backspill of energy on detonation. And I'm sure that's not going to happen.'

'How sure are you?' said Clarence.

'How close to the Path am I standing?' said !Cin-ta!x.

'Her time's up,' said God quietly.

Clarence wrapped his wings around himself. !Cin-ta!x took a remote from his sleeve, and pressed his thumb into the little cube of plastic. The cube next to the Path began to hum.

'It'll take just a moment for the harmonics to synchronize,' he said.

Extract from the Memoirs of Bernice Summerfield

John stepped on to the Path, and nothing happened.

I had been counting on *something* happening. I had in fact been counting on his touching the Path and shorting it out, just as he'd shorted out poor !Ci!ci-tel. I'd even made him take off his shoes to ensure proper contact.

I'd expected the Path to collapse out from under him in a flash, sending John sprawling in the desert dust and trapping the lot of us here. No Path, no war, no destruction of Babylon, no worries.

Blast. Sod. *Knickers*!

I looked around again. Still nothing.

I folded my arms and watched as John slowly trudged along the Path. Shortly I!qu-!qu-tala would shut off its device, and he would be lost to view. Either he'd make it home, or God would look after him. He was safe, at least, for the moment.

'Could I have your attention, please,' rang out a voice.

I swivelled. Ninan was standing at the top of a rise.

She had what appeared to be a small army with her, but was probably actually the temple guard. In her hands, she held my white hat.

'Rock and sodding *roll*!' I burst out.

WiRgo!xu's face went several interesting colours. 'What the hell is this?' he said.

'A bust,' I said.

'Yeah, sure,' said WiRgo!xu. 'What are they going to do – destroy the Path by hitting it with clubs?'

'We are going to arrest you,' said Ninan, 'because of the part you played in Beni's kidnapping.'

'I can't believe you're doing this!' WiRgo!xu turned on me. I glanced at John, but he was well up the Path, disappearing into its illusory vanishing point. I suspected that what seemed like a journey of hours to him was taking only a few seconds in objective time.

223

'Believe it,' I said. 'You wanted to learn about not getting your own way.'

'You can't arrest us,' WiRgo!xu told Ninan. 'I!qu-!qu-tala, show yourself.'

The drone blinked into visibility. Ninan's miniature army held their ground, but you could see their uncertainty, the shuffling and glances. 'Stay back,' said the drone, keeping moving, tracing lazy patterns in the air. 'Don't offer, don't offer us any violence. Or we will defend ourselves.'

'What is that?' said Ninan.

'Think of it as a kind of friendly demon,' I said. 'It won't hurt you if you don't try to attack.'

'Impasse,' smirked WiRgo!xu. 'It doesn't matter, anyway. We've already got rid of Lafayet, and Beni has agreed to help us. Everything's settled.'

'Whoever you are,' said Ninan, 'you arrived secretly in our city, but now every eye will be on you. We know of the business deals you have struck – we know you are planning to bring more of your countrymen into the city. If this is the beginning of a secret invasion, it has failed.'

'It's not an invasion!' said WiRgo!xu. 'If we wanted to, we could take over your city in about four minutes.' He spread his hands, walking towards her. 'We just want a chance to learn from you,' he said. 'We need a chance to start again.'

'He's not telling the full story,' I said. 'This ... magic gateway you can see links Babylon with his ... home city. He has broken the law by building it. That means war between his People and their rivals – and thousands of refugees coming through the gateway and seeking shelter in Babylon.'

'Is this true?' said Ninan. 'If you needed our help, why did you not just ask?'

I looked at WiRgo!xu. 'It never occurred to you,' I said. 'Did it? Babylon was just here for the taking. Was that how you thought about the All of Us? Just an opportunity for some fun and games, a chance to show off your superiority?'

He was looking definitely wobbly. Suddenly, I had my Plan B. I pressed the attack. 'You even thought of John as an experimental subject. You wanted to learn from him, so you just tied him to a table. You always get whatever you want. So you thought.' Home stretch, Benny. 'And now !Ci!ci-tel's dead, because you just had to have what you wanted.'

WiRgo!xu snapped. It was like a switch clicked into place in his head. He screamed and jumped at me.

He looked very puzzled as I!qu-!qu-tala caught him in a field, holding him up in an awkward position. WiRgo!xu howled in anger, struggling in the field, hating everything.

He had never got to kill anyone.

I!qu-!qu-tala hovered down next to me. 'He needs looking after,' I told the drone.

'None of this is his fault,' said I!qu-!qu-tala. 'It was all my idea, my idea. I couldn't leave them behind, leave them behind, they agreed with me and wanted to help and I needed to keep them close. And now !Ci!ci-tel's dead, !Ci!ci-tel's dead and look at poor WiRgo!xu, poor WiRgo!xu.'

Yes! 'Then put things right,' I told the drone. 'Shut down the Path!'

'Where will we go?' wailed the drone, spinning. 'What will we do?'

'I have an offer,' said Ninan.

The drone turned towards her. She started at the sketch face staring at her, but she held her ground.

'I will protect you,' she said. 'If you are powerful, you will protect me. I wish to travel.'

'Travel?' said the drone. 'Travel?'

'I wish to leave the city,' said the priestess. 'I wish to see the world. You are travellers. You will be safe far from Babylon – safe from the crimes you have committed here, safe from your own people. Will you accompany me?'

WiRgo!xu just struggled and fought inside the field. I was worried he was going to hurt himself, but he could barely move, his arms and head fighting through the thickened air in slow motion.

I!qu-!qu-tala said, 'Look what I've done. Look what I've done. I can't take him home, and he needs help.'

'Won't the People take WiRgo!xu back?' I said. 'If he wasn't responsible for his actions –'

'He was responsible,' said I!qu-!qu-tala. 'I know that, I'm his medical drone. He needs my help.'

'Then give up your plan,' I said. The drone dithered. 'Send a message back to the People, make sure they know what you've done, and why. Give them something to think about.'

'Hold everything!' said I!qu-!qu-tala, in a hugely amplified voice. 'There's something the matter with the Path!'

'What!' yelled WiRgo!xu breathlessly.

'The harmonics have changed,' said the drone. It hovered close to the Path, the lights on its surface flashing and blinking, its face ikon frowning. 'I think we could be in trouble here.'

'The harmonics?' said WiRgo!xu. 'But isn't that –'

'Bloody TIG,' said I!qu-!qu-tala. 'They've just disabled the booby trap.' The drone hovered up to WiRgo!xu. 'If we don't shut down the Path, right now, we're going to find ourselves standing at ground zero.'

'I think your decision has just been made for you,' I said.

'No,' said WiRgo!xu. 'Let them do it. Let them change history, they'll still be violating the Treaty, there'll still be war –'

'Hush, hush,' said I!qu-!qu-tala. He did something to the field, and WiRgo!xu's head nodded forward. 'Don't worry. I'm going to take care of you.' The sleeping Person drifted softly to the ground.

The drone hovered up to Ninan. 'We accept your offer,' he said. 'Beni, by my calculations, you can still get back before I shut the Path down – go now! Go right now!'

'Just a moment.' I rummaged in my jacket, and found the handful of silver. 'Ninan, this is for Miriam – for her freedom. Is it enough?'

The priestess took the handful of money. 'It is enough,' she said. She handed me my hat. 'Go, quickly!'

'Have a nice trip!'

She grinned at me. I returned the smile, hopped on to the Path, and legged it.

I don't think I've ever run as fast in my life, and I've done a *lot* of running. The silvery trail felt slippery, spongy, starting to come apart at the seams.

I glanced back once, and I saw the Path crumbling, some-where behind me. Silver pieces flaking off, the damage gathering speed, catching up with me as I watched.

I actually overtook John, who was jogging along the rippling silver, losing his balance as it disintegrated out from under us. I grabbed his arm, pulled him up, and we ran hand in hand towards the far end of the dying Path.

Extract ends

13

WALKING ON HOME

Is there an ear, an eye for wisdom
that may perceive
across the depths
across the dark
across the spiralling cycles of the stars?

Etched in the flesh of this world
will my words still speak
though I be dust and silence?

Will these stones still sing
praising
naming
explaining
when we again are gone
across the depths
across the dark?

Is there an ear, an eye for wisdom
that will perceive
across the spiralling cycles
the soul of what I needs must say?

(Yemayan poem, c. 1450 BCE. This uncharacteristically
introspective poem was found on the back of a stone

stela, the face of which had remnants of a formal relief worn to illegibility.)

– Reproduced with permission from Summerfield, Bernice S., *An Eye for Wisdom: Repetitive Poems of the Early Ikkaban Period*, St Oscar's University Press, 2595.

Extract from the Memoirs of Bernice Summerfield

We didn't think about where we were going. We didn't think about anything. We just ran like the devil. We didn't even stop when we were suddenly running on grass, stumbling over rocks and bumps in the ground.

John and I fell, rolling, with me shrieking, 'Don't do it! Don't do it! They shut it down!'

'It's all right,' someone said. 'We know.'

I pushed myself up on to my hands and knees, looking back. Behind us, the Path shortened, and shattered, hexagonal shards dancing in the air. Then there was a sort of sucking *pop* and a *splitch*, and it was gone.

I stared at the place it had been. I was vaguely aware of John, looking around.

We were at the centre of a collection of huts, like big white bubbles with doors and windows. The ground was slightly damp. We had left a trail of crushed grass and wild flowers as we'd run and tumbled.

I was still staring, my palms pressed against the ground. There were People moving all around us. John was picking something up.

'Beni?' said a voice.

I turned my head slightly. It was Clarence, his dark hair in disarray, reaching a hesitant wing around me.

'This,' I said, 'is not MD 20879.'

John had finished picking up the contents of my exploded satchel. He pushed my diary into place and closed the buckle. 'Bernice,' he said, 'where are we?'

'It's called the Worldsphere,' I said. My voice sounded as though someone else was using it. 'Um, don't look up.'

John looked up.

The first thing he saw was Clarence, standing over me. An angel, right out of a Bible illustration, naked as a jaybird and with a ten-foot wingspan.

The next thing he saw was that the world went away for ever and curled to the sides and up over his head, past the sun and the smiling planet that circled it.

A yellow-coloured drone floated up. 'Hi,' it said. 'I'm God.'

I expected John to faint. Instead, he said, 'Bernice, are you feeling all right?'

I would have answered, but I decided to fall over in the grass and have a little sleep instead.

I woke up in someone's House, listening to a distant roaring noise.

I could see my clothes moving around the room, being cleaned and folded by miniature energy fields. As I watched, my battered, filthy trousers were squeezed in an invisible ball, the dust forced out in an explosive puff. A tear in my shirt sleeve was being magically mended, the edges of the fabric rejoining until the damage had disappeared.

I was lying in a bed, a very conventional bed, spring mattress, sheets, pillows. Given the weird variety of ways in which the People slept, I appreciated the touch. Maybe John had described it to them.

Heck. John! Where was he? How was he dealing with all of this?

I got out of bed. I was wearing the People's approximation of pyjamas – men's pyjamas, with long stripes. Now I was sure John had described what I needed. I doubted he'd have much idea of what a nightdress looked like.

The room was square and white, very minimal – there was only the bed and a tall rectangular prism with a red and blue knob inside. I'd seen one of them before, a People shower.

John. I had trapped him, just as effectively as if the Path had been destroyed while we were in Babylon. Either he would have to stay here on the Worldsphere, or he would have to come back to Dellah with me.

He had a choice between a banged-up archaeologist with an unremarkable salary, and paradise.

I took a moment to look out of the square window. The view was breathtaking. The House was perched halfway up a mountain, and I was looking down the slope, over the tops of trees and rocks, past a pounding waterfall sending out a great cloud of grey droplets. I thought I could see houses in the valley, partly hidden by the spray. Oh, yes – there was a gigantic red kite, hovering above the geometric shapes.

I wondered what would happen if you brought in machinery and started digging away the mountain rock. Would you find a skeleton, a hollow structure over which the fake mountains had been draped? Or did the People simply peel off chunks of surface from other worlds, and glue them to the inside of the Sphere?

The landscape stretched away, to an imagined horizon and beyond. You could see a hell of a long way from this high up – my view took in more mountains, more valleys, some kind of floating city, a desert, an ocean glittering with huge metallic vessels . . . until the distance was hidden by clouds and the imperceptible curve of the sphere.

All this might have been destroyed.

Other than the waterfall, there was absolute silence. For a panicky moment, I wondered if I had been left here ·by myself, isolated for some reason.

I'm a danger to the People. Did they want to contain me?

Jumping to conclusions, especially when it came to the People, was always a bad idea. My clothes had migrated to a neat pile on the bed. I'd grab a quick shower, then go and see where everyone was.

I pulled off my pyjamas and got into the shower cubicle. The glass door slid silently shut behind me. I hadn't actually seen one in operation before, but the single control was a bit of a giveaway.

I tried pushing, pulling and twisting the knob before I hit on tilting it from side to side. Immediately, water started to gush into the shower cubicle. I worked out how to adjust the temperature before I could freeze to death.

The only thing was, I couldn't make the water stop. It was already up to my knees, pleasantly warm and faintly scented, creeping up my body inch after inch. I tugged the knob back and forth, without success.

Up to my stomach. I didn't want to make a mess in the bedroom, but I didn't have a lot of choice. I grabbed at the door.

It wouldn't open.

Oh shit. Ignorant barbarian has tragic accident in perfectly ordinary shower. No further details in treaty-violation mystery.

I kicked at the glass, but it wouldn't break. The water was up to my chest. I shoved my full weight against the side of the cubicle, but it must have been fixed to the floor. It wouldn't budge.

At this point, sensibly, I allowed utter panic to take over. I started pounding at the glass with my fists and yelling my head off.

After a moment, the water stopped, just below shoulder level.

'Do you want a bath, or don't you?' said the House, grouchily.

I found John having breakfast in the garden with one of the People. It was a very functional garden, geometric rows of vegetables and herbs, smelling like freshly turned soil and unripe tomatoes. The sky was pale grey, and a cool breeze was blowing.

They were sitting in the centre of a square patch of perfect grass. I felt slightly naughty to be walking on it, even in freshly repaired and cleaned boots. The seats were white cubes with wire backs, the table a single tall cube.

'Hello, Bernice,' said John. 'I trust you're feeling better?'

'Lots,' I said. 'Despite a little dispute with the plumbing. Hi.'

The blue-haired Person nodded at me. 'I'm !Cin-ta!x,' he said. 'Formerly of the Temporal Interest Group. I was part of the Coping Team dealing with the Path.' Another chair rose up out of the garden, right in front of me, the grass and soil parting perfectly around it. 'Please join us.' I sat down. The chair shifted to accommodate my shape.

'How are you holding up?' I asked John. His clothes had been cleaned and repaired just as mine had; he looked curiously perfect for the setting in his early Edwardian suit.

'This place,' he said, 'this vast place – it is awesome.' He looked up at the impossibly distant ceiling of the sphere. 'On our journey here, we passed over endless continents and oceans. Kintak tells me that we travelled further than if we had gone around the Earth five times.'

'But you're all right? Not, you know . . .' Hell, how to say this without sounding patronizing? 'You seem to be coping,' I finished.

'Perhaps,' said John, 'after a certain amount of the astonishing, a little more makes no difference.'

'Maybe you're right,' I said. Though I suspected that we'd been sent to an isolated, rather low-tech spot to make us (and John in particular) feel a bit more at home. Which was rather the opposite of my initial paranoid assumption.

Our host was smiling, the pupils of his cat's-eyes dilated. His hair was pulled back and twisted into a sky-coloured braid. 'You must be hungry,' he said.

'Just ask the table what you want,' John informed me. 'You have to describe it, though.' He indicated his plate. I was pretty sure those were cucumber sandwiches.

'Right,' I said. 'I'll have a single scoop of chocolate ice cream, with a spoonful of peanut butter on the side.'

After a moment, the table opened up and my order – or the People's closest approximation of it – emerged from the white plastic. The plate and spoon were made out of the same glassy stuff. I took a spoonful of the ice cream and picked up just a little of the peanut butter in the tip.

Perfection. I sighed happily, sitting back in the chair. 'All right,' I said. 'You can start with the questions now.'

!Cin-ta!x laughed. 'Actually, I!qu-!qu-tala's message explained pretty much everything we needed to know.'

'So what has the reaction been like?' I asked, taking another spoonful. 'What are the People saying about it?'

'Only I and God have read the message,' said !Cin-ta!x. 'It won't be made public.'

I wanted to say, 'What?' or 'How dare you!' or something, but instead I just gripped my spoon and closed my eyes.

Of course they weren't going to make the message public. It would only take one more lunatic with the right information to start the whole problem all over again – to build another Path, or find some other way of provoking the People's enemies.

I opened my eyes. 'You need a better treaty,' I said.

'You could be right,' said !Cin-ta!x. He poured another glass of whatever it was he was drinking. 'You must have questions of your own.'

'John's ability to see and reach the Path,' I said. 'Can you explain it?'

!Cin-ta!x shook his head. 'We discussed this a little, earlier, while you were sleeping,' he said. 'My assumption is that it's some kind of psi power, but that's not really my field of expertise . . . The temporal discharge, though, that's easily predicted by the equations.'

He tapped the table, and a small control panel appeared, flush with the surface. He put his fingertips on the controls, and a computer screen appeared in the air. He turned it so I could see it. 'The tendency to accumulate a temporal charge diminishes with repeated temporal displacement,' he said. 'Just as I!qu-!qu-tala surmised.'

'So the more I travel in time, the less charge I build up?' I said. 'But I've never had that short-circuiting thing happen.'

'The charge is characteristic of time-travel methods such as the Path,' said !Cin-ta!x. 'It is essentially a primitive technology.'

'Temporally flexible,' I said. 'Oh, of course. John couldn't destroy the Path by touching it. It's in constant motion through time.'

!Cin-ta!x nodded enthusiastically. 'Its charge diminished to zero within microseconds of its establishment. There was no differential. If I!qu-!qu-tala had understood the technology properly, it would have realized the potential danger.'

'I did wonder why you asked me to remove my shoes,' said John.

'I'm sorry. I didn't get a chance to tell you what I had in mind,' I said. 'I reckoned that since you weren't hurt either time, you could safely collapse the Path. That's a point – why wasn't John hurt? Why didn't the short-circuiting thing affect him as well?'

!Cin-ta!x had to shrug. 'Presumably it has something to do with his wild talent,' he said. 'Few of the People have psi powers. We don't understand them very well.'

'With your technology, you don't need to.' It suddenly struck me. 'Is God monitoring our conversation?'

'No,' said !Cin-ta!x. 'Officially, God doesn't know anything about any of this. I'll make a final report to him before I leave.'

'Where are you going?'

'I'm leaving the Worldsphere,' said !Cin-ta!x simply. 'I know too much.'

'That's not fair,' I said.

'I've always known rather too much,' sighed the man. 'I made sure the other members of the Coping Team never had more than a small part of the overall picture. But I know it all. I could construct a working Path just from the equations in here.' He tapped his head. 'TIG know far more than even God realizes. We're a vital resource, and a terrible hazard. So I'm packing up my House and heading for a nice, quiet world somewhere.'

'Will you have visitors?' John asked.

'Perhaps,' said !Cin-ta!x.

'You could come back with me,' I said suddenly. 'We could find you a spot on Dellah. You'd fit right in, no one would even notice you.'

'I wish I could take you up on that,' he said. 'But my visiting the Milky Way would only put the People in even more danger.'

He was right, of course. 'It's so unfair,' I said. 'So much of it is unfair.'

'It is the lesson that I!qu-!qu-tala learnt,' sighed !Cin-ta!x. 'You can't always get what you want.'

Sometimes I feel like the snake in the People's garden.

It's not fair to blame myself for I!qu-!qu-tala's plan. It was all worked out well in advance of my visit. Maybe they planned to use me to suggest a destination, get a time and a place and a few details. Maybe I just precipitated the whole thing.

I suppose !Cin-ta!x knows, and God, too, and maybe even the nameless island-turtle. But the rest of the People, all two trillion of them, will never even know any of this happened. And neither will the People's enemies.

!Cin-ta!x asked us to stay for a few days, ostensibly in case there was anything that God needs to clarify as the investigation was wrapped up. There's no trace of the Path's terminus left, I'm told; they even force-grew the plants back over the area.

I have to say this for the People: they know that dead men tell no tales, but they haven't made it their policy. In many societies – including a lot of human ones – I'd expect there to be a lot of corpses, including mine, to make sure the secret stays a secret.

But !Cin-ta!x's exile is completely voluntary, and the island-turtle has been blackmailed into silence. According to !Cin-ta!x, they're pretty sure it was I!qu-!qu-tala who reprogrammed the killer solar maintenance drone – leaving a little piece of its own mind inside the bot, obsessed with protecting WiRgo!xu and !Ci!ci-tel.

But as I sit here in my room at !Cin-ta!x's house, watching the clouds below, I can't help but wonder if this is a paradise that would only work if it had no outside. Imagine if it was just the inside of the Sphere, no space, no barbarians, no enemies . . . Still, I suppose that a civilization with a probable life span of billions of years is inevitably going to run into trouble, without outside help. There'll be a plague, or the sun will develop problems, or one group of citizens will try to conquer the rest. God knows. And it probably does, running endless simulations of the future.

I wonder how much of this whole incident it predicted. I wonder if it knew someone would try to break the Treaty to bring on a war. I wonder if it even ran that bloody high-level simulation of me that it's got to see if I'd be willing to help prevent it.

That's the problem with dealing with beings a million times as intelligent as you are.

Just got a message. From Sara!qava! Haven't seen her, er, it's him now, since Jason and I got married. He wants me and John over for dinner. Great! I wonder why he didn't come and say hello during my quick visit, though . . . busy? We'll see.

!Cin-ta!x has been giving John tours of the House and gardens. Right now they're out on a mountain trail. I was worried there'd be another breakdown, another outburst.[1] But I think John was right – once he had accepted the extraordinary once, he was ready to accept it again and again.

John. What am I going to do about John? What is John going to do about John?

Extract ends

The House was enumerating endless lists of stuff they'd need to pack when God called on the phone.

!Cin-ta!x was looking through his cookbooks, fat bundles of handmade paper filled with his careful handwriting. He didn't look up when God's voice floated through the kitchen. 'Well?'

'The House will upload the results of the scan for you,' said !Cin-ta!x.

'Did you take a look at it?'

'Of course I did,' said !Cin-ta!x. 'I don't know much about genetics. But the House tells me this is a new one on its databases.'

God read the report while !Cin-ta!x turned the page of his cookbook. 'Temporal awareness via psi powers,' said God. 'Via genetically engineered psi powers.'

'Or worse,' said !Cin-ta!x. 'Natural powers that someone's trying to spread around.'

'It could evolve into a defence,' said God. 'A distant early warning system spread throughout the species of the Milky Way.'

'Of course, right now, it's probably nothing more than a

---

[1] And possibly another round of entirely unmotivated but excellent sex.

tiny number of rogue genes in a tiny number of species.' God didn't answer. 'Just because the time sensitivity gene isn't compatible with our genome,' insisted !Cin-ta!x, 'doesn't indicate conspiracy.'

'You're right,' said God. 'Right now, it's nothing to worry about.'

'So you'll be contacting the Tiny But Interesting Interest Group?'

'Already done,' said God. 'Bye for now.'

'God's such a worry wart,' said the House.

'Look who's talking,' said !Cin-ta!x.

Extract from the Memoirs of Bernice Summerfield

John and I took a transit capsule to Sara!qava's house. He's still living in the coastal town of iSanti Jeni, in the same house – the one that smells wonderfully of cooking bread. He's also started a new hobby – making a Worldsphere equivalent of pesto. He's given me a few jars to take back. I wonder if I'll be able to get it through customs.

!Cin-ta!x wouldn't come. Worried about contaminating other People with the taint of his forbidden knowledge, I expect.

John and I sat in silence in the transit capsule. The grey ball could seat six, but we were the only passengers, reclining in fluffy chairs while pleasant music played. After a while, by tacit agreement, we switched off the music, and sat with our own thoughts.

The People tend to live in small groups, communities of a few thousand like iSanti Jeni, rich with small-town gossip. But the transit capsules and the communications networks and the Interest Groups mean that gossip is smeared over 2.77×10^{17} square kilometres. Here, everyone really does know what everyone else is doing.

Or they would do, if the People weren't experts at keeping secrets. No one here technically has any power over anybody else. But having a secret is power, knowing someone else's secret is power, threatening to reveal it, that's power. Sara!qava had lived with a secret like that for much of her life.

Until I earned a genuine professorship, I lived in the constant fear that someone would pop the balloon of my forged credentials. I don't mean I spent the whole time chewing my fingernails up to the shoulder, but that I was always aware that the carpet could suddenly be pulled out from underneath my life.

Sometimes I still find myself in some academic waiting room, gnawing my lip, wondering if some snooping administrator has found an anomaly in some ancient personnel record. That they'd decide that the Edward Watkinson Chair of Archaeology should go to someone with a more proper record. That my real experience and credentials and hard work wouldn't count as much as the bloody rules.

Which brings me back, of course, to the Babylonians. Their gods were never as interested in morals and ethics as they were in getting their breakfast. And even if you made the right sacrifices and said the right prayers, they could still get ticked off for some reason and abandon you.

How many People were waiting for the unmistakable feeling of sliding carpet?

And yet that threat still came from inside, from other People. Even the uncertainty that the War had brought – uncertainty about just what the People were capable of – came from inside.

Even the uncertainty that I!qu-!qu-tala had wanted to introduce had come from inside, from People sabotage. Ultimately, the drone had no lesson to teach them at all.

After all, when you were that powerful, there weren't a lot of threats that *can* come from the outside.

I still remembered just where Sara!qava's house was, in one of the narrow streets that ran off the esplanade. He'd told me his house had become sentient, but I was still startled when it said hello. 'Beni and Lafayet!' exclaimed the front door, as I raised my hand to knock. It had a warm, girlish voice. 'Fabulous to see you! Everyone's here, come right on in.'

The door swung open, and a couple of drinks floated up to us in wide, cylindrical glasses. I caught mine while John stared at the beverage hovering in front of him, waggling impatiently. 'Go on,' said the House. 'I've been talking to !Cin-ta!x's House. We think we've got the recipe nearly right.'

I took a careful mouthful. 'It's beer!' I said.

'Is it good?' asked the House.

'It's not quite what I'm used to,' I said. 'But it's a pretty good effort.'

I made little nodding and glass-waving motions at John. He took the hint, carefully plucked his glass out of the air, and tried it. His eyebrows skittered up. 'It is perfect,' he said.

'Come to think of it,' I said, 'Crimson Star Lager does have some alien additives you wouldn't be familiar with in 1901.'

John took another mouthful. 'I wonder what the Babylonians would have made of this,' he said.

'It might taste different,' I said, 'but I'll bet they'd know what it was.' We clinked glasses, and the House led us upstairs to the room with the ocean view.

It was a very small party, especially by People standards. The flock of children I remembered were staying with a relative for the evening. Sara!qava was wearing a grey jumpsuit that matched the silvery sheen of his dark-blue hair. He was slim, with pale skin dusted with yellow, and huge brown eyes. 'Hello, Beni,' he said. 'Still digging things up?'

'Here and there.' My eyes slid sideways to John. 'You'd be amazed what you can find.'

Clarence was draped in a long white robe with hemmed slits in the back for his wings, looking like a biblical illustration. I suspected his unusual modesty was for John's benefit.

There was a huge, low, circular, wooden table, covered in tiny bowls of sauce and huge bowls of pasta. The suspicious yellow dip was conspicuous by its absence. 'Didn't you invite God?' I asked Sara!qava, and John and I settled into seats, huge green chunks of some kind of foam.

'Not this time,' he said. He tapped his fingers on the edge of the table, showing us how to turn it to reach whatever we wanted. 'As much fun as God can be, sometimes you just feel like a break from the nosy old bugger. Pesto? So are you two a couple, or what's going on there?'

John turned an extraordinary shade of purple-red. I sighed. This was going to be a long party.

And it was. Mercifully, it was gatecrashed by Sara!qava's daughter Dep and a bunch of her friends. For a while, it was quite pleasant to be in a room with three men who were desperately in love with me,[2] but even a sex goddess like me needs a break eventually.

The arrival of all the extra People gave us a chance to break up into smaller groups. Dep's daughter, iKrissi, looked about eight years old, with a big smile and a loud giggle. John seemed enchanted by her, and Dep's friends good-naturedly let him join in with their games of chasing iKrissi about, playing with model Ships, etc.

Sara!qava got me alone in the kitchen. 'Offer's still open,' he said.

I did a sort of double-take-hesitate-awkward-silence. Sara!qava said, 'I didn't mean to make you uncomfortable. Any more uncomfortable. I don't think you're sure what the situation is with this Jonlafayet person, either.'

I sagged against the counter. 'You've probably deduced by now that his culture is very, er, what I mean to say is that he –'

'He's totally screwed up about sex,' said Sara!qava. 'I could introduce him to some members of the Celibacy Interest Group, if you like.'

'There's a Celibacy Interest Group?' I said, astonished.

'Of course. They spend all their time finding people who are celibate. They're *terribly* interested in them.' Sara!qava grinned. 'Talk to him about it, if you can get him away from iKrissi's admirers. Ask House to show you to the red room upstairs, if need be. Look, this isn't actually what I wanted to talk to you about.'

I just nodded, taking another swig of the House's beer.

---

[2] I exaggerate for comic effect.

'I'm sorry I didn't come to God's party,' he said. 'The one on the turtle's back.'

'I didn't even know you'd been invited,' I said.

'Of course God invited me – he knows we're old friends.' Sara!qava started taking fresh jars of homemade pasta sauce from some kind of storage device, reaching through a blue field that stretched around his fingers.

'It was the veterans, wasn't it?'

Sara!qava gave a little nod. 'They make me nervous,' he said. 'Especially the ones God had at his party.' He looked at me, deep brown eyes troubled. 'Nobody knows what mission God sent you on, or where this other barbarian came from. But everybody knows it had something to do with that night, with the vets. So I wanted to make it up to you. Throw you a party before you went home.'

I put a hand on Sara!qava's arm. 'If you really want to make it up to me,' I said, 'throw some of them a party. There's stuff you need to talk about. I mean, the vets, and the rest of the People. There's things they need to tell you.'

'Rumour has it,' said Sara!qava, 'that God keeps bringing you here because there's something it wants us to learn from you, and we keep missing the point.'

I shook my head. 'Your problems come from inside,' I said. 'And that's where the solutions are going to come from.'

I was following iKrissi's laughter, looking for John, bumping into clusters of adolescents on the stairs and closing certain doors with embarrassed speed.

I ended up on the roof. There was a fabulous sea breeze, a clean, salty smell, taking me right back to the Vandorian beach of those childhood holidays. The lighthouse's pale beam passed overhead in a steady, sweeping rhythm. I was startled to see stars, until I realized they were the lights of cities, glittering through layers of atmosphere. But – there! Real stars, through the six-sided gap of the spaceport.

Clarence arrived in a soft rush of feathers. I suppose he used some of his sensors to find me, which was cheating. Or perhaps he just asked the House.

He didn't come close, perching at the edge of the roof. 'I could have tried to help you,' he said, in a very quiet voice.

A guilty angel. That was a new one. 'It's not your planet,' I said. 'It was my responsibility, not yours.'

'Yeah, but it was my lot who caused the trouble in the first place,' he said. 'Anyway, you're a friend. I should have come after you.'

I put a hand on Clarence's cheek. He looked very fetching, moping guiltily like that. As if on cue, it started to drizzle, tiny droplets, slightly warm.

'It was a job for an expert,' I said. 'It needed someone who could blend in. Someone who's done this sort of thing a lot. Come on, that's not you, neither as a Ship nor as an angel.'

'But that wasn't why I didn't go,' said Clarence. He looked at me, tiny droplets glistening in his hair. 'I didn't go because you're going to die anyway.'

'Clarence,' I said, a little awed, 'are you immortal?'

'Course not,' he said.

That was a relief. Eternal life gives me the creeps. 'Then you're going to die anyway too,' I said. 'So we're even.'

' 'Spose so,' said Clarence. I gave him a hug, and he enfolded me in his wings, gently. 'Still want a ride home tomorrow?'

'Yes, please,' I said.

'How many passengers?' said Clarence.

We both looked up at some small sound. John Lafayette was standing in the doorway to the roof, staring up at Whynot and getting drizzled on.

'Let me get back to you on that one,' I said.

Clarence had enough tact to leave John and me standing alone on the roof in the gentle rain. I was starting to wonder if maybe God *was* listening in, and had orchestrated the rain just for us.

John came over to the railing where I was standing. The odd flash of gentle lightning lit up the ocean, glass in windows, the beach. Couples and families were walking down there in the pleasant rain, carrying waterproof paper lanterns and laughing.

'I have been invited to stay,' said John. 'On the World-sphere.'

'I thought you might have been,' I said, crestfallen.

'Anything is possible here,' he said. 'I would live a long and enjoyable life, without fear of illness or war.' It was true; the war with the All of Us had never come near the World-sphere. 'It is a utopia.'

'You're right, of course,' I said. 'You'd be crazy not to take them up on it. You'll have a wonderful time, John. I'll even be able to visit you, occasionally.'

He shook his head. His hair and shoulders were damp with the drifting rain. 'I do not wish to stay here,' he said.

I reached out and touched his shoulder. 'You want to come with me?' I said. 'Are you sure?'

'What I want,' he said, 'is to continue the important work of translating inscriptions and tablets from Mesopotamia.'

'You what?'

'Certain negotiations have been taking place,' he said. 'Certain accommodations have been reached.'

He nodded at something, down on the beach. I squinted into the darkness. After a few moments there was a great flash of lightning, and I saw Clarence standing on the sand, talking to someone.

'It's one of them, isn't it?' I said.

John nodded. 'The People's rivals. They are satisfied that everything has been put back the way it was. Except for one thing. When the party is finished, I will be returned to my own time.'

'Did you have a choice?' I said.

John gave one of his small smiles. 'They are convinced, apparently, that I represent no threat to the balance of the universe. They left the decision with me.'

I was going to tell him he was out of his mind, but the question asked itself before he could ask it. Why didn't *I* stay?

Because there were digs to dig and kids to teach. Back home, I had a role to play, a job to do. Here, any old drone could do the same work a thousand times better. On Dellah, I mattered.

'Oh God,' I said. 'If you're going back to 1901, I'll never see you again.'

'Given your effect on my morals,' he said, with a small but very wicked smile, 'that may be for the best.'

I couldn't laugh. I gripped the rail. 'You know,' I said, 'we have an opportunity here. We might be able to make something more of this.' I couldn't look at him. 'Any chance at love is a *chance*.'

'Bernice,' he said. He put his hand on my shoulder. 'I admire you. I am a little in awe of you. But I do not think I am in love with you.'

'Imagine what you could learn . . .' I trailed off, but I knew I was talking nonsense.

In 1901, he *mattered*.

He took my hand, kissed my wrist.

And that was it. We stood there for a bit more, and any urge I had to grab him and shag him wildly in the rain was dampened into nothing by the sure knowledge that he didn't want me, didn't want any of Wonderland. He just wanted to go home.

And God, so did I.

When I got out of the shuttle on Dellah I stood in the rain for ten minutes. Not the desert, not the automated Worldsphere weather, just honest-to-God, normal, wet, random rain.

That was my first priority taken care of.

Wolsey met me at the door of my rooms, meowing. He rubbed himself all over my legs as I tried to make it to the study and my puter. I picked him up and put down my satchel in the same awkward movement, and carried him purring into the other room.

I brought up all my files on the Neo-Babylonian period and read them, and then read them again.

Nothing had changed. Nothing major enough to have affected history. Babylon still got conquered and reconquered and finally abandoned as the trade routes shifted. Western civilization still ran along the same lines. Dellah wasn't inhabited by a species of archaeologist-eating purple mutants.

I couldn't find anything about the priestess Ninan-ash-tammu, and there was no sign of WiRgo!xu or I!qu-!qu-tala. I want to know if they got to go travelling, where they visited, how they got on, but they've quietly disappeared from history. That's probably for the best, I think.

'We managed not to screw anything up,' I told Wolsey, scratching him between the ears. He purred and rubbed himself against my chin.

I guess that's the only medal I'm going to get.

Against my better judgment, I then did a data search on John Lafayette.

I found a reference to him in one genealogical database, and a miniature biography in Watkinson's classic *Translate This, You Invading Bastard*. He did get married, eventually, and had a couple of children. He did a lot of grunt work, translating thousands of tablets. Good work, mostly business letters and the odd poem. He never stumbled across another *Epic of Gilgamesh* or *Enuma Elish*.

He never wrote a book, and never went on another expedition. He stayed at home in Cambridge, reading transliterations in dimly lit library rooms. There was no record of his journey through time. No indication that anything out of the ordinary ever happened to him again.

I hope that means he was happy. I hope that it was all he wanted.

I think it probably was, actually.

These memoirs are based on my diary entries. Seventeen of my diaries have survived. I've lost count of the ones that were destroyed or left behind somewhere – it's at least six, sometimes with only a few pages scribbled on, sometimes quite full.

Most of my shelves are pretty messy, but the diaries are arranged in chronological order. They're an odd mixture of notebooks, bought on different worlds and in different time periods. Most are stuffed with Post-it notes, brochures, restaurant menus and other souvenirs, bookmarks, even a few pressed flowers.

That's a lot of tourism.

I'll buy a new notebook tomorrow. Once I put this diary away, it's time to get back to work. I'm going to finish *An Eye for Wisdom* this week, if it kills me. There's a pile of mail and marking to deal with, but it'll have to wait until the book is completed.

Such is the life of the academic. You can only spend so much time messing about on field trips, rummaging about in the ruins and collecting data, before you have to sit down and actually do something with what you've found.

In between saving the world, of course.

Acknowledgments

Many thanks to:

Jon Blum, who will be my husband by the time you read this

Jennifer Tifft for numerous suggestions, and for kind permission to use her poems 'The Pomegranate Lament', 'Leap like Lightning', a fragment of 'I Will Write my Will in Warrior's Blood', 'An Eye for Wisdom', 'The Wanderer's Dedication', and for writing Appendix I

Arturo Magidin for Hebrew translation and advice

Rebecca J. Anderson, for answering far too many questions!

Appendix I: Ikkaban Poetry

Reproduced with permission from Summerfield, Bernice S., 2595, *An Eye for Wisdom: Repetitive poems of the Early Ikkaban Period*, St Oscar's University Press, Dellah.

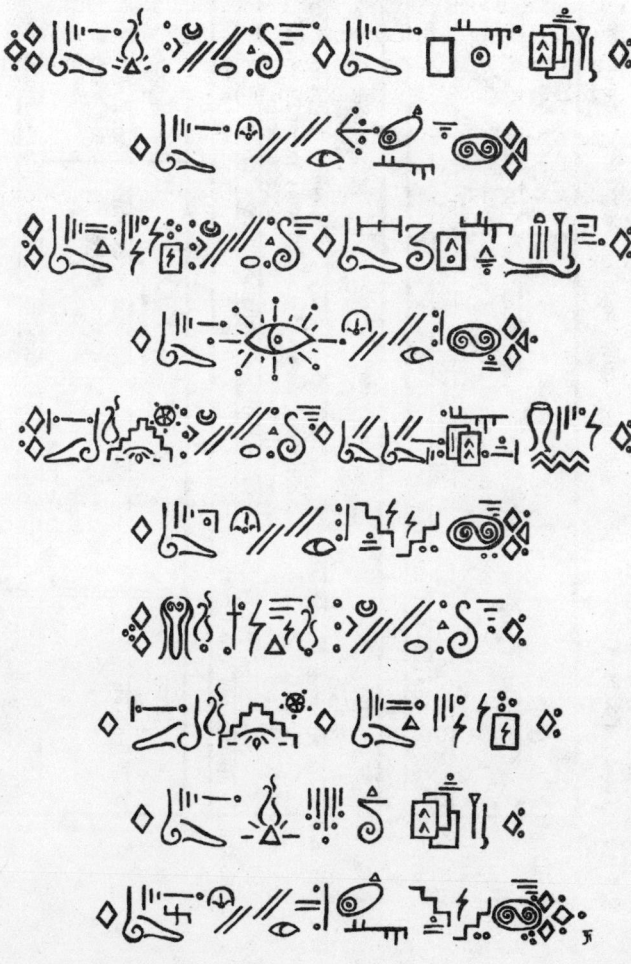

Appendix 1: The Wanderer's Dedication
Table 1: Ikkaban Glyphs, Glyph Definitions, English Transliteration, Poetic Translation

(glyph)	(glyph)	(glyph)
Walk, go forward [imperative]	Temple-fire, need-fire, dedication	One without ties to place/time, poet, traveller, walker of hidden paths
Go forward [into] [the] fire, [vocative] One who wanders/travels		
Walk into the fire, O Wanderer		

(glyph)	(glyph)	(glyph)
Walk, go forward [imperative]	Time-place not yet seen/experienced, uncarved stone, potential	[Holding, with] record tablets, actual/potential words/records/poems
Go forward [into] [the] future time-place [holding] communication/words		
Walk into the future with your words		

(glyph)	(glyph)	(glyph)	(glyph)
Walk, go forward	Experiencing/travelling the unknown, time-place above/beyond beautiful/terrible	The stars, the cosmos [implied future]	Among/inside/within [of a person]
Go forward experiencing the beautiful unknown among the stars [you are/will be] within/among			
Walk wondering among the stars			

Table 1

(glyph)	(glyph)
Go forward with intent [imperative]	[Wanderer]
	Chaos/uncertainty, bad weather, potential for destruction & rebirth
Go forward [strongly into] bad weather/chaos [vocative] One who wanders/travels	
Step into the storm, O Wanderer	

Table 2

(glyph)	(glyph)
Walk to measure/mark, make official record [imperative]	Time-place here & now, actual, mundane
	Holding chisel/writing tool, ready [already] to record/write
Walk to measure the present time-place prepared to write/writing	
Pace the present, chisel-pen in hand	

Table 3

(glyph)	(glyph)	(glyph)	(glyph)
Walk, go forward [imperative]	Open-eyed, alert, aware, taking in everything [adj]	The unknown, time-place above/beyond/ outside, beauty/terror	Among/inside/within [of a person]
Go forward [strongly] with eyes open/aware the beautiful/terrible unknown [you are/will be] within			
Walk open-eyed amidst wonder			

Symbol	Meaning
	[Wanderer]
	The [Queen/Turtle] Temple, place of dedication & sacrifice
	Walk away, reject, contrary intent

Walk away [from] the Queen's Temple [vocative] One who wanders/travels

Turn from the Temple, O Wanderer

Symbol	Meaning
	Spill/pour with intent, open/lay out
	Time-place experienced, distant, behind, long ago
	Direction of travel, road to walk, map [object]

[As] a road to walk, past time-place [you are/will] pour with intent

Pour out the past as a path

Symbol	Meaning
	Among/inside/within [of an object]
	Broken temple/forbidden place [past], chaos-touched, not always silent, stones-now-dust [obj]
	The unknown, time-place above/beyond/outside, beauty/terror [subj]
	Walk, go forward [indicative]

Walks beautiful/terrible unknown [things] the stones-now-dust among

Wonders walk within the dusty stones

(glyph)	(glyph)	(glyph)
Hold, be held by, commit to [imperative]	Change-by-fire, inspiration, unusual sacrifice, (the 'storm glyph'), lightning	[Wanderer]
Hold and be held by lightning/inspiration [vocative]		One who wanders/travels
Embrace the lightning, O Wanderer		

(glyph)	(glyph)	(glyph)	(glyph)
Walk away, reject, contrary intent [imperative]	The [Queen/Turtle] Temple, place of dedication & sacrifice	Go forward with intent [imperative]	Chaos/uncertainty, bad weather, potential for destruction & rebirth
Walk away [from] the Queen's Temple		Go forward [strongly into] bad weather/chaos	
Turn from the Temple		**Step into the storm**	

(glyph)	(glyph)	(glyph)	(glyph)
Walk, go forward [imperative]	Temple-fire, need-fire, dedication	Precipitating, as from a wound, bleeding	Record tablets, actual/potential words/records/poems
Go forward [into] [the] fire, bleeding actual/potential poems			
Walk into the fire, bleeding words			

⟋⫽⟍	⊘⫽⫽⊘	◔	⌁⌁	◉
Walk, go forward [present imperative]	Experiencing/ travelling the unknown, time-place above/ beyond beautiful/ terrible	The stars, the cosmos [implied future]	Broken temple/ forbidden place [past], chaos-touched, not always silent, stones	Among/inside/ within [of a person]
Go forward [strongly, right now] experiencing the beautiful/terrible unknown the stars/future [and] stones/past [you are/will be/have been] within/among				
In wonder walk among the stars and stones				

❖	◇	◈	⸭
[Begin poem/thought]	[line-break]	[New grouping begins]	[End]

Notes on the structure of Ikkaban poem PsSpt7-ii, known commonly as 'The Wanderer's Dedication':

This inscription is one of the most formal in structure of all the early repetitive Ikkaban poems yet located. It seems to be a dedication: that is, the writer is committing themself to the action/work described. This is apparent in the unusual form of the 'wanderer' glyph: the strongly marked 'S' curve and the changes in the last element. This strong self-identification is seen elsewhere only in the fragmentary (and very early) EpSco2-v (no common name), and at the end of Ach4-iv ('The Pomegranate Lament'). This does not come across particularly well in English.

It is thought that this is a formal dedication also because of the strong structure and scansion present. The repetitions are patterned, not only in the glyphs/concepts, but in the structure. Close examination of the original carving shows this clearly.

Various orthographic and stylistic idiosyncracies point to the author of this piece also being the author of ZAq4-i ('The Wanderer's Lament'), ElN4-iii ('An Eye for Wisdom') and possibly ElN6-vi ('The Gravity Well') and the aforementioned Ach4-iv.

Index of poems included in the current study:

Catalogue Name	Common Name	Other Info
ZAq4-i	'The Wanderer's Lament'	
PsSpt7-ii	'The Wanderer's Dedication'	
ElN4-iii	'An Eye for Wisdom'	
Ach4-iv	'The Pomegranate Lament'	
CrSt5-ii	'The Path of the Glory Rose'	
EpSco2-v		Very fragmentary
ElN6-vi	'The Gravity Well'	
Yem4-i	'In The Queen's Temple'	
Yem4-iii	'You, Traveller'	
EpSco2-viii	'Eater of All Flesh'	

Catalogue names for Ikkaban inscriptions are generated out of the astronomical abbreviation for the star, followed by the planet number, followed by the inscription number (in order by discovery in each location).

Appendix II: Bibliography

Summerfield, Bernice S., *Devil Gate Drive*: *The Influence of* The Descent of Inanna *on Twentieth-Century Popular Culture*, J XX Pop. Cul., 23(5), pp. 216–220, 2594.

Summerfield, Bernice S., *Down Among the Dead Men* (Revised Edition), St Oscar's University Press, Dellah, 2593.

Summerfield, Bernice S., *An Eye for Wisdom: Repetitive poems of the Early Ikkaban Period*, St Oscar's University Press, Dellah, 2595.

Summerfield, Bernice S., *S for Surprise: Memoirs of an Unorthodox Archaeologist* (unpublished).

Watkinson, Edward, *Glory Under the Mud*, St Oscar's University Press, Dellah, 2524.

Watkinson, Edward, *Translate This, You Invading Bastard: Intersections Between Language and Archaeology*, Youkali Press, Youkali, 2503.

ALSO AVAILABLE
IN
THE NEW ADVENTURES

OH NO IT ISN'T
by Paul Cornell
ISBN: 0 426 20507 3

Bernice Surprise Summerfield is just settling into her new job as Professor of Archaeology at St Oscar's University on the cosmopolitan planet of Dellah. She's using this prestigious centre of learning to put her past, especially her failed marriage, behind her. But when a routine exploration of the planet Perfecton goes awry, she needs all her old ingenuity and cunning as she faces a menace that can only be described as – panto.

DRAGONS' WRATH
by Justin Richards
ISBN: 0 426 20508 1

The Knights of Jeneve, a legendary chivalric order famed for their jewel-encrusted dragon emblem, were destroyed at the battle of Bocaro. But when a gifted forger is murdered on his way to meet her old friend Irving Braxiatel, and she comes into possession of a rather ornate dragon statue, Benny can't help thinking they're involved. So, suddenly embroiled in art fraud, murder and derring-do, she must discover the secret behind the dragon, and thwart the machinations of those seeking to control the sector.

BEYOND THE SUN
by Matthew Jones
ISBN: 0 426 20511 1

Benny has drawn the short straw – she's forced to take two overlooked freshers on their very first dig. Just when she thinks things can't get any worse, her no-good ex-husband Jason turns up and promptly gets himself kidnapped. As no one else is going to rescue him, Benny resigns herself to the task. But her only clue is a dusty artefact Jason implausibly claimed was part of an ancient and powerful weapon – a weapon rumoured to have powers beyond the sun.

SHIP OF FOOLS
by Dave Stone
ISBN: 0 426 20510 3

No hard-up archaeologist could resist the perks of working for the fabulously wealthy Krytell. Benny is given an unlimited expense account, an entire new wardrobe and all the jewels and pearls she could ever need. Also, her job, unofficial and shady though it is, requires her presence on the famed space cruise-liner, the *Titanian Queen*. But, as usual, there is a catch: those on board are being systematically bumped off, and the great detective, Emil Dupont, hasn't got a clue what's going on.

DOWN
by Lawrence Miles
ISBN: 0 426 20512 X

If the authorities on Tyler's Folly didn't expect to drag an off-world professor out of the ocean in a forbidden 'quake zone, they certainly weren't ready for her story. According to Benny the planet is hollow, its interior inhabited by warring tribes, rubber-clad Nazis and unconvincing prehistoric monsters. Has something stolen Benny's reason? Or is the planet the sole exception to the more mundane laws of physics? And what is the involvement of the utterly amoral alien known only as !X.

DEADFALL
by Gary Russell
ISBN: 0 426 20513 8

Jason Kane has stolen the location of the legendary planet of Ardethe from his ex-wife Bernice, and, as usual, it's all gone terribly wrong. In no time at all, he finds himself trapped on an isolated rock, pursued by brain-consuming aliens, and at the mercy of a shipload of female convicts. Unsurprisingly, he calls for help. However, when his old friend Christopher Cwej turns up, he can't even remember his own name.

GHOST DEVICES
by Simon Bucher-Jones
ISBN: 0 426 20514 6

Benny travels to Canopus IV, a world where the primitive locals worship the Spire – a massive structure that bends time – and talk of gods who saw the future. Unfortunately, she soon discovers the planet is on the brink of collapse, and that the whole sector is threatened by holy war. So, to prevent a jihad, Benny must journey to the dead world of Vol'ach Prime, and face a culture dedicated to the destruction of all life.

MEAN STREETS
by Terrance Dicks
ISBN: 0 426 20519 7

The Project: a criminal scheme so grand in its scale that it casts a shadow across a hundred worlds. Roz Forrester heard of this elaborate undertaking, and asked her squire to return with her to sprawling and violent Megacity – the scene of her discovery. Roz may be dead, but Chris Cwej is not a man to forget a promise, and Bernice is soon the other half of a noble crime-fighting duo.

TEMPEST
by Christopher Bulis
ISBN: 0 426 20523 5

On the wild and inhospitable planet of Tempest, a train is in trouble. And Bernice, returning home on the luxurious Polar Express, is right in the thick of it. Murder and an inexplicable theft mean that there's a criminal on board; the police are unable to reach them; and so the frightened staff and passengers turn to a hung-over, and rather bad-tempered, archaeologist for much-needed assistance.

If you wish to order any of these titles, or other Virgin books, please write to the address below for mail-order information:

Fiction Department
Virgin Publishing Ltd.
332 Ladbroke Grove
London W10 5AH

COMING SOON

OBLIVION
by Dave Stone
0 426 20522 7
Published: 19 March 1998

A man called Deed is threatening the fabric of the universe and tearing realities apart. At the heart of the disruption, three adventurers, Nathan li Shoa, Leetha and Kiru, are trapped. Their friend Sgloomi Po must save them before they are obliterated – in his desperation he looks up some old friends. And so Bernice joins her feckless ex-husband Jason and her old friend Chris on the rescue mission; but then Sgloomi picks up someone who should really be dead.

THE MEDUSA EFFECT
by Justin Richards
ISBN: 0 426 20524 3
Published: 16 April 1998

Medusa, an experimental ship missing for twenty years, is coming home. When one of the investigation team dies mysteriously, Bernice is assigned to help discover what went wrong. But to do so she must solve a riddle. Somehow the original crew are linked to the team put on board – their ghosts still haunt the ship. And the past is catching up with them all in more ways than one.

DRY PILGRIMAGE
by Paul Leonard and Nick Walters
ISBN: 0 426 20525 1
Published: 21 May 1998

Thinking she has been offered a blissful pleasure cruise on Dellah's southern ocean, Benny gladly accepts. After all, she has some time on her hands. But trapped on a yacht with an alien religious sect who forbid alcohol, she soon discovers that all is not well. And, as the ship heads towards a fateful rendezvous, she must unmask a traitor or risk the system being torn apart by war.